UNCOMMON COUNSEL

A novel by

Art Smith

UNCOMMON COUNSEL

Copyright © 2018 by Art Smith.

All rights reserved. Printed in the United States of America. No part of this book may be used or reproduced in any manner whatsoever without written permission except in the case of brief quotations embodied in critical articles or reviews.

This book is a work of fiction. Names, characters, businesses, organizations, places, events and incidents either are the product of the author's imagination or are used fictitiously. Any resemblance to actual persons, living or dead, events, or locales is entirely coincidental.

For information contact:
ArtSmithWriter@gmail.com
http://www.artsmithwriter.com

Cover artwork by Kait Moon Arts
Published by Obumbravit Press, Fulton, MO USA

ISBN: 978-1-7321733-0-9

First Edition: May 2018

10 9 8 7 6 5 4 3 2 1

UNCOMMON COUNSEL

Acknowledgements

This book was born as part of NaNoWriMo (National Novel Writing Month, http://www.NaNoWriMo.org) in November of 2017. NaNoWrimo is a fantastic exercise in writing for authors at all levels. This was my seventh year participating and the first that resulted in a story (hopefully) worthy of publication. I highly recommend NaNoWriMo to all authors or would-be authors. As with any skill, practice breeds perfection, and nothing helps you get the words out of your head like the challenge of writing 50,000 of them in thirty days.

This novel, like everything in my life, is only possible with the loving support and encouragement of my wife Amanda. She not only puts up with my peculiar sort of madness but seems to thrive on it, and for that I am eternally grateful.

Special thanks to Sir Dandelion for personal insights into schizophrenia. If my portrayal of a schizophrenic mind is authentic, it is largely because of their guidance; if it is not, it is because of my shortcomings as a writer. Their contributions throughout the process of writing and editing this work were invaluable.

Thanks also to Meredith Julian for consultations on the clinical therapy of schizophrenia, as well as discussions and comments through all stages of development. You are a gem!

A thank you, too, to Denny and Ed for brief but essential consultations on legal ethics.

Finally, thanks to all the readers at every step along the way, including you—yes, you! Thank you so much, I hope you enjoy the ride.

Saturday, June 3

No place is safe! I'm followed everywhere. You'd think I'd be used to it by now, but how do you ever get used to this?

This morning I woke at 6:40, as usual. There were two pair of eyes on the wall opposite my bed. They were studying me with a menacing glare. I want to fill the wall with artwork, or even a busy wallpaper—something to remove any blank spot for the eyes—but they won't let me do that. If I block them from here, they'll come after me elsewhere and they won't be happy. Not that they ever are.

The muttering voices were already active, of course. They never go away, but at least I'm mostly used to them. Still, it's disconcerting to come to consciousness knowing you are the subject of a conversation you can't quite make out.

The eyes on my shower wall had a mouth today. That happens sometimes. It was silently shouting at me the whole time I was there. No words, but I didn't need words to tell it was upset with me.

Coffee and toast standing in the kitchen was better—just the mutterers and their never-ending wordless commentary like some sort of personal Greek chorus. I put some Verdi on the sound system to drown them out, but they cut through. They always do.

I had to run into the office and pick up some papers for the Stafford case. I don't like to work on the weekends, but with the case already at trial I don't have the luxury of time. Mara and Kala didn't give me the crucial information to clear Stafford until the day before the trial started, so I've been scrambling to subpoena the new witnesses and build my defense. We'll win, I'm sure, but not without effort.

As I left the apartment to get in the car, I could see a hawk circling. It was too high to identify—probably a red tail or a Cooper's hawk—but it was watching. They ride the morning thermals up to where they can see everything. Hunting their prey.

Hunting me. It, or another like it, was at the office when I got there, too.

The office was empty—typical for a Saturday morning, especially in the summer—but that just left more opportunities for eyes and mouths, and a silence for the mutterers to fill. Fill it they did, murmuring their imprecations and chastisements that I can't quite make out, but know nonetheless. Scolding me for my inadequacies. I grabbed the papers I needed and left right away. I couldn't work there.

Once I got home, I took the papers out into the back garden. I'm just about the only person in the building who uses that little space, and I've pretty much laid claim to the wrought iron lounge and the little matching table as my outside workspace. The overgrown privacy fence means that there are no blank surfaces for the eyes where I can see them. There's the back wall of the apartment building, of course, and they watch me from there, but that's behind me. I can sense them watching me, making the hair on the back of my neck stand up, but at least I don't have to see their angry glare.

It was dry and not too breezy, so I could spread my papers out on the table. The birds in the nearby trees and the feeders I stock were singing merrily, so I knew there weren't any raptors too close. The buzzing of the hummingbirds at their feeder added a little percussive flavor to the droning chant of the mutterers.

I was hoping that Mara and Kala would show up and help me with more information, but they didn't make an appearance. I don't usually see them in the mornings; they tend to come by in the early evening when the sun is just settling behind the mountains. The shadows kill the thermals, discouraging the day hawks. There's a golden hour before the owls and other night predators come out, and that's when Mara and Kala like to visit. There was another Steller's jay that was scolding me from the trees, but it was just an ordinary jay, shrieking like any other bird.

I got maybe an hour of work done before I noticed the birds had gone silent. Looking up, I could see why. There was a sharp-shinned hawk circling low overhead. It had clearly spotted some-thing and was waiting for the best opportunity to strike. Just because it had found a target didn't mean it would ignore other opportunities, though. The birds know this, so they quiet them-selves, and hide in the foliage. I know it, too. A hawk couldn't eat me, of course, but that doesn't mean I'm not prey.

I went back inside to escape the hawk's attention, trading one set of eyes for others. *La Traviata* helped mask the mutterings, but the walls hosted several sets of eyes and mouths. They watched me, judging me and wordlessly scolding me while I tried to pull things together for the case.

I thought about taking a hike in the afternoon, but decided against it. It had stormed the last two days and looked like it could blow up another storm this afternoon. Getting caught up in the hills in a thunderstorm can be dangerous and is always uncomfortable.

I wish I could have gone, though. Hiking in the foothills off Highway 15 is a good escape. Headphones help to quiet the mut-terers, but they also leave me deaf to the warnings of the passerines or the hunting cries of the raptors, so I usually don't bother. At least the broken terrain leaves no place for the eyes and I can escape their judgment for a few hours.

I worked until the Metropolitan Opera broadcast—a repeat performance. I listened to it with my eyes closed. I knew I was being watched. I could feel the accusing stares, but at least I didn't have to see them. It was nearly an escape—as close as I ever come.

After the opera I went outside again, hoping to see Mara and Kala, but they haven't shown up. I worked a little more on the Stafford case, but there's not much more I can do until Monday. So now I'm writing here in my journal, killing time until it grows dark.

I'll go in and fix my supper soon and maybe try to figure out a plan for Monday. I'll have court in the morning; that's the easy part. That afternoon, though, I have my first appointment with the new psychiatrist, Dr. JoAnne Filtner. I know nothing about her, other than that Dr. Weber recommended her.

I wish Weber hadn't retired. He wasn't great, but at least he didn't push for too much change. We'd settled into a routine. Appointments followed a conventional script, one that kept my medications stable and kept me out of the hospital. It was rare I was with him more than fifteen minutes. I don't hold out much hope that that pattern will continue with the new shrink, though. I'll have to fight for my stability again.

The birds went silent again. Maybe they're just off to their nests for the evening, but it could be an early appearance of an owl. In any case, it's too threatening to stay outside. Even the garden is unsafe.

Psychiatric Intake Report

Patient Name: William "Rip" Taylor

Date: June 5, 2017

Diagnoses:
Schizophrenia (Paranoid) *F20.0*
Tardive Dyskinesia (subacute, drug-induced) *G24.01*

Medication List:
Risperidone 4 mg PO SID (QHS)

Physical Findings and Mental Status:
Physical Description: 42-year old white male in apparent good health, 178 cm tall (5'10"), 88 kg (195 lbs), displaying pronounced and frequent grimaces and eye-blinks, lip-smacking, chewing and tongue motion, and some random limb motion characteristic of tardive dyskinesia.
Vitals: Unremarkable (P 72, BP 134/82, T 36.9°C (98.4°F)).
Mental Status: Alert and oriented to person, place, and time.
Comportment: Well-groomed, alert posture, unremarkable.
Mood and affect: Cooperative and situationally appropriate.
Ability to concentrate: Unremarkable.
Tone and rate of speech: Appropriate and unhurried.
Danger to self/others: None.

History and Presentation:
Mr. Taylor has a history of schizophrenia, first diagnosed in October 1997 (age 24) following a psychotic break that resulted in an overnight involuntary hospitalization. Onset of schizophrenia was likely in early 1993 (age 20). Initial history post-diagnosis included a year of intermittent inpatient stays, mostly voluntary, as medication was titrated. Mr. Taylor has been under continuous psychiatric care (primarily outpatient) since the diagnosis. Most recent hospitalization for psychosis: April 2002 (age 29).

Mr. Taylor is prescribed 4 mg Risperidone, taken in the evening before bed (4 mg PO SID (QHS)). This dose has been stable for approximately three years. He states that he takes no other prescription medications, psychotropic or otherwise. Mr. Taylor denies recreational drug use beyond moderate consumption of alcohol (non-daily consumption, rarely exceeding 2 drinks per day). He denies current or past use of cannabis or tobacco in any form.

Mr. Taylor states his present medication provides general relief of the positive symptoms of schizophrenia (hallucinations and delusions) with some manageable breakthroughs (details to follow below). Negative symptoms (apathy, blunted emotional response, reduction of speech, anhedonia, and sexual dysfunction) and cognitive symptoms (disorganized or slowed thinking, difficulties in attention, concentration, memory or comprehension, and difficulty expressing or integrating thoughts) are reported as present but tolerable. Side effects reported include drowsiness for the first 8-12 hours after taking medication and cumulative tardive dyskinesia. TD symptoms include lip smacking, tongue jutting and tic-like blinking and grimacing as noted above. Mr. Taylor reports TD causes some distress at this point due to interference with his work as a criminal defense attorney.

Mr. Taylor's affect is generally positive. He is affable and loquacious without indication of word pressure or hurried speech. Emotional response and affect are appropriate to topic. Physical mannerisms are within normal limits other than the previously noted tardive dyskinesia. His physique appears good, though he is moderately overweight, perhaps partly due to the medication. He states that he hikes occasionally, but does little else for exercise due to limited leisure time.

Blood was drawn for a complete blood count and metabolic panel (results to follow). Vitals were unremarkable. Mr. Taylor states no known allergies to any medications and no known food allergies. His health is generally good. His most recent doctor's visit, other than routine check-ups, was for influenza three years ago. This passed with an unremarkable course. No recent non-psychiatric hospitalizations.

Mr. Taylor is single and lives alone in an apartment in southern Colorado Springs. He reports no close family and no romantic partners of either sex. He denies significant social interaction beyond his work environment, though this does not appear to distress him. His work as a defense attorney consumes the bulk of his time. Leisure activities are limited, primarily listening to opera (recorded and occasional live performances) and solo outdoor activities such as hiking. Mr. Taylor has an intense fascination with birds, but denies being a "birder." His history indicates he is intensely aware of the presence of raptors (birds of prey), which he fears at a level approaching phobia. Asking about birds of prey evoked moderate distress, confirming this issue remains. No basis for this fear is noted in the history, and it does not appear to have been a focus of treatment to date.

Mr. Taylor feeds other birds at home and during breaks at work. His history notes a preoccupation with a pair of Steller's jays that have apparently learned his habits and attend him regularly to get food. Upon inquiry, he reports that he has named them ("Mara" and "Kala") and treats them as pets, though they remain wild birds. He indicated that they visit him both at his home and his work, though given the separation (roughly eight miles) it seems more likely there are two sets of birds that he conflates. It is possible these jays are hallucinations, though that seems unlikely given their simultaneous visual and auditory nature. Also, Mr. Taylor denies that the jays are symptomatic, unlike the "mutterers" and "eyes" and "mouths" (see below) which he acknowledges stem from the schizophrenia. He claims that both neighbors and coworkers are aware of the birds. He suggested that the jays will find him here if he keeps coming, though that is most likely a delusion secondary to his fantasy of their attentiveness to him.

Positive symptoms, as noted above, are mostly auditory hallucinations now reduced to "muttering" rather than distinct speech. He is often aware of them and is sensitive to their tone if not actual words. Without medication or under stress they may become distinct voices that cause him greater distress. He is aware that these voices are part of his illness, though he states they are "real." He is aware that others do not perceive these voices but denies that makes them unreal. Additional auditory hallucinations that appear at times of stress have distinct recurring personalities, but Mr. Taylor states these breakthroughs are now rare. Additionally, there are visual hallucinations of disembodied human eyes and mouths on walls and other smooth blank surfaces. These are perceived as expressing emotion, frequently judging or accusing. The eyes and mouths come and go during the course of the day and multiply with stress. Again, Mr. Taylor acknowledges that they are a product of the schizophrenia and acknowledges that others do not see them, but he maintains their reality nonetheless.

When questioned, Mr. Taylor denied any visual or auditory hallucinations at the present time, though he did look around the room furtively when asked, and continued to glance at the blank wall to my left throughout the interview, indicating he may be untruthful.

Mr. Taylor appears to be functional at the present time, maintaining a respectable, even notable, legal practice as a senior partner in a well-respected criminal defense law firm. He lives relatively frugally for his income level and does not report any financial stress. He rents a one-bedroom apartment where he spends most of his non-work time, unless he is outside hiking or feeding birds.

He denies any recent sexual contact (going back "several years") claiming a lack of interest, though he states he has had previous sexual experiences, exclusively heterosexual. There is no evidence of tension when discussing these matters, though he seems a bit vague. Whether that is due to genuine disinterest or evasiveness is not yet clear.

Mr. Taylor complains of the negative/cognitive effects of the disease, claiming these are amplified rather than reduced by the medication. He claims to have been exceptionally bright prior to the onset of symptoms, and while he continues to be high-functioning, he states that his mental abilities are much diminished by the combination of cognitive symptoms and neuroleptic side effects of his medication.

Current Symptoms:

Mr. Taylor reports occasional mild to moderate positive symptoms of schizophrenia as noted above, including frequent auditory hallucinations of multiple unintelligible and undifferentiated voices and occasional visual hallucinations of disembodied facial elements (eyes and mouths). He denies further positive symptoms at this time, though he acknowledges a history of distinct voices.

Mr. Taylor reports ongoing mild to moderate negative/cognitive symptoms of schizophrenia including decreased ability to concentrate, slowed mental functioning, and somnolence, especially in the hours following his medication. He believes these symptoms are primarily effects of the medication rather than schizophrenia.

Mr. Taylor reports mild anxiety/phobia related to raptors. He denies that this interferes with his daily life.

Mr. Taylor reports moderate to severe symptoms of tardive dyskinesia as observed above, resulting from cumulative antipyramidal side effects of psychotropic medication.

Interventions:

Exploration of mental state and specific symptoms. No challenges made to delusions at this initial visit.

Patient Response to Interventions:

Generally unremarkable. Non-verbal clues indicate that positive symptomology may be more acute than he admits. This judgment is based on defensive body language, attention to nonexistent stimuli, and fearful/furtive facial expressions.

Clinical Impressions:

Mr. Taylor appears to be high functioning despite ongoing schizophrenia that is moderately undermanaged by current medications.

Tardive dyskinesia caused by years of antipsychotic medications is readily apparent and causes him significant distress.

Mr. Taylor does not appear to be a threat to himself or others at the present time.

Plan:

An increased dosage and/or change to newer antipsychotics would seem to be indicated by the residual positive symptoms and unwanted side effects, but the tardive dyskinesia and "mental fog" (his words) argue against increasing dosage. Mr. Taylor's medical records show several other antipsychotics have previously been tried, both second and third generation, before settling on Risperidone approximately eight years ago. Previous notes indicate Risperidone has provided the best tolerated balance of symptom reduction and side effects. Many new antipsychotics have become available since that time and may need to be explored. I will maintain the current medication and dosing for the present, at least until a baseline is established.

Mr. Taylor may be a candidate for Ingrezza, a new medication recently approved to treat tardive dyskinesia. I will need to investigate this and further familiarize myself with the indications and contraindications of this medication. Mr. Taylor responded positively to the possibility of this treatment.

Next appointment in two weeks.

Rx:

Risperidone 4 mg PO SID (QHS), Q 30

Signed:

JoAnne Filtner, M.D., Ph.D.

Tuesday, June 6

Yesterday I had the intake meeting with the new psychiatrist. Dr. JoAnne Filtner will be my shrink now that Dr. Weber has retired. She seems competent, I guess. The usual tests and questions—how many times have I gone through this now? Too many. At least she seems to understand and accept that I've tried most of the newer antipsychotics and good old Risperidone is the only one that makes life tolerable. Either the other meds do nothing to quiet the angry voices, or they make everything go away, including my ability to understand Mara and Kala.

I didn't mention understanding Mara and Kala, of course. I've learned that lesson! I tried to explain my need for balance between too much and too little medication, but I'm pretty sure she is going to want to increase my meds. It seems I'll have to be very circumspect about what I reveal if I want to continue functioning. Why is that always the case?

She had some exciting news about the tics: apparently there's a brand new drug that just hit the market that specifically treats tardive dyskinesia—the first ever. She's going to see if I can get approved for it—apparently it's still somewhat limited. It sounds like she's only just learned of it herself. At least my insurance should cover it, I think. I'll give Mike credit; he looks after us well that way. Recently the tics have gotten severe enough to interfere with court appearances. Stopping the Risperidone for a couple days helps a little, I think, but then the voices start to return.

Dr. Filtner didn't seem too fazed when I discussed Mara and Kala as birds, though I could tell she didn't quite believe that they follow me between home and work. Of course, I couldn't tell her that I knew they were the same birds because we would continue conversations. I tried to explain that I could tell the difference based on their looks and behavior, but I could tell she was dubious. It would maybe help if they could visit me during a session with her, though I don't know how I could prove that they were the same birds since she can't understand them. I can't even admit I am expecting them if they *do* say they'll be there (which they haven't yet).

Dammit, I wish I could be honest about them! But I learned that lesson too many times. No one believes that they talk to me; people think it's another delusion and won't even consider that it could be true. They just up the dose on the meds until they turn me into a zombie that can't do anything more than drool in the corner. The hell with that! This is a special ability, given only to me, and if the price of that ability is secrecy, well, that's nothing new to me. My entire career as a defense lawyer has been built around keeping other people's secrets. I can certainly keep my own.

It's better this way, anyway. They are too valuable to risk. This Stafford case might never have broken if it weren't for their help. They see so much. Even if they can't tell me anything I can use as evidence, they give me confidence in my clients' innocence and lead me to pursue avenues others would ignore. It's better than when I was a prosecutor, too—then I had to prove things beyond a reasonable doubt, and without admissible evidence, that can be hard. Now I just have to show that reasonable doubt exists, and most of the time the truth is reasonable (ah, but not always, not always!).

Waiting on their input has given me a reputation about being slow to decide whether or not to accept cases. Mike has scolded me plenty of times that I need to be faster. But he listens to results, and I only take cases I can win—and I win the cases I take, mostly thanks to the unusual and inadmissible counsel that my jays give me. If they say someone didn't do something, they didn't, and vice versa. Their facts are always right. They refuse to understand the *law*, but they know what happened. That's to be expected, I guess. That's my job in this odd partnership. They identify truth, and I translate that into jurisprudence.

If only I knew they would always be there. If I were sure of their safety. Every time I hear a hawk scream or find a bunch of blue and black feathers, I worry that they've been attacked or killed. They've told me not to worry, but I've seen the threat and it's real. Bigger birds than they are have been snatched out of the air or stricken on the ground while feeding. Just because they are wise to the ways of humans isn't going to protect them, no matter what they say. Smart and conversant or not, they are still just Steller's jays, aren't they? They say they are.

Today was a good day. The mutterers were pretty low key, and only a couple of eyes watched me in the courtroom. Closing arguments will be tomorrow, and I expect the jury to return a not guilty verdict pretty quickly.

With the Stafford case wrapping up now, I'll be interviewing new potential clients soon. I wish there were a way to have Mara and Kala in the office then. They do see everyone who comes in and goes out, it seems, but they don't know who needs investigating and who doesn't. How could they? And they can't travel back in time to see what happened when the crime was committed. At least, I think they can't. They *say* they can't. But then they come back a couple days later with specific information as if they'd been there.

I know they have an army of informants—all the corvids (and many other birds) watch everything—but how do Mara and Kala know who to contact about which people? Is there a human information clearinghouse for all the observant birds? That sounds crazy, but how else do you explain it? And what about nighttime activities? Do they have owls as allies? Bats? They never tell their sources—they speak as if they saw everything themselves, even though that must be impossible. They're not magic, right?

I need to stop at the store on the way home and pick up some more cashews for them, as well as feed for the other birds—both the sunflower seeds and the millet are low. I swear they eat more and better than I do. I should go soon, too—it's later than I realized. This summertime sun is deceptive, but it's sinking behind the front range now. I was hoping Mara and Kala would stop by before I left, but I guess they are busy observing. The hawks hunt later now in the longer days, too, so they must be careful. I would think the raptors would be done by now, though, even that nasty peregrine I've seen here lately. Where are you, Mara and Kala? What secrets are you learning? Ah well, I'll probably see them tomorrow.

Wednesday, June 7

Closing arguments today, as expected, and now the Stafford case is to the jury. They didn't get it until almost 4:30, and they didn't return an immediate verdict, so they'll have to consider again tomorrow, but I doubt they'll be long. Even the prosecutor knows that ship has sailed and it's going our direction. They couldn't possibly convict on any of the major charges—the only serious deliberation should be on resisting arrest, and I think even that will go our way.

Stafford honestly didn't understand what the police were asking. The resisting charge only makes sense if you assume knowledge from guilt. The officer's own testimony indicates his instructions were unclear to someone unaware of the crime. I expect a verdict before noon tomorrow and fully anticipate acquittal on all charges.

It's a pity Mara and Kala couldn't (wouldn't?) tell me who *did* commit the assault—there's no better defense than a positive identification of the real guilty parties—but throwing out all the circumstantial evidence piece by piece is sufficient when there is nothing but circumstantial evidence.

Frankly it's hard to believe the prosecutor even took this case. Yes, Stafford was their only suspect, but he wasn't a strong one. They had to know their case was weak. Sometimes I think they press charges just to look like they're doing something, with no thought to whose lives they destroy along the way. Was it that bad when I worked for them?

How different this might have turned out if Stafford had had a less capable attorney, say someone like myself without the aid of Mara and Kala. Max was quick to point this out, of course. He laid into me while we were waiting to see if the jury would come back today.

"Well, shithead, I guess you feel pretty proud of yourself," he said.

I didn't respond.

"Of course, you didn't have much to do with it. The damn jays handed you the case all tied up with a bow, just like always. Have you ever thought what you'd do without them?"

I had, of course. Max knew that, too, and didn't wait for me to not respond.

"Face it, shithead, you're a sorry excuse for a lawyer on your own. Mike should list the birds as senior partners with you clerking for them. Though of course, he doesn't know about them, does he? Your precious little secret. One of these days they're not going to be around, and you'll have to face up to your incompetence. That should be entertaining!"

There was more, of course. And, as always, I can remember every word. Hyperthymesia, my crazy memory for conversations, can be a blessing in my profession, but is a definite curse where Max is concerned. Max can carry on for hours on the matter of my inadequacy, a subject about which he is an uncontested expert. Fortunately, he wasn't given hours this time.

I decided to walk back to the office to let Max wind down. He quieted abruptly, however, when Mara and Kala met me as I came out of the courthouse. He doesn't care for them. They don't share his jaundiced view of my competence, and while neither he nor they is ever wrong in the facts, the dissonance of their approaches makes agreement impossible. The physical nature of Mara and Kala's existence almost always wins out, and they quickly banish him from audibility. If only I could learn that trick myself.

They took turns eating cashews from my hand and carrying on the whole way, to the delight of everyone around us. That made it hard to talk with them, of course, but I got a few words in. It went like this:

Mara: You're still defending Stafford?

Me: Yes. Nearly finished now.

Kala: But we told you he didn't do it!

Mara: We told you that weeks ago.

Kala: We didn't see who did do it...

Mara: ...but we saw him when it happened...

Kala: ...and he wasn't there.

Mara: No, he wasn't there at all. Somewhere else.

Kala: Somewhere else entirely. All alone.

Mara: Reading a newspaper.

Kala: Sitting in the park.

Mara: Not paying attention to us at all.

Kala: But we paid attention to him.

Mara: The whole afternoon.

Kala: Well, not the whole afternoon. But while he was there.

Mara: True, he wasn't there that long, you're right.

Kala: But he was there for an hour.

Mara: Or two.

Kala: Long enough.

Mara: And we told you.

Kala: Days and days ago!

Mara: So why are you still defending him?

Me: Things happen slowly with us. It's almost done.

Kala: Tomorrow? Tomorrow you'll know?

Mara: One more night?

Me: I hope so, yes.

Kala: And then you'll be working with someone else.

Mara: And we'll help you.

Kala: Who will it be?

Me: I don't know yet. I haven't even started interviewing.

Mara: Can't start one until the last one's done.

Kala: That's what you told us.

Mara: A silly rule.

Kala: All your rules are silly.

Mara: No wonder you're slow.

Kala: Indeed! Deliberate.

Mara: Plodding.

Kala: Laborious.

Mara: Boring!

Kala: Most boring! Not fun!

Mara: How do you stand it?

Me: It's our way. We can't always determine truth so easily as you, so we have rules about how to find it. Rules to make sure everything stays fair.

Kala: What's fair or not fair about truth?

Mara: Truth is truth...

Kala: ...is truth!

Me: But we don't always know the truth. The law has to work even when truth isn't known. The goal is justice, but jurisprudence must serve when justice is not clear.

Mara: But it is clear!

Kala: Black and white!

Mara: We told you.

Me: Yes, I know. But I can't tell the judge and jury something is so, just because you say it is.

Kala: Why not?

Mara: We never lie.

Kala: Rarely, anyway. And never about this.

Me: I believe you. But the judge won't. The jury won't. They can't understand you, for one thing.

Mara: Yes, we talk, but they don't listen.

Kala: Nobody listens.

Mara: Nobody but you.

Kala: And even you don't hear us sometimes.

Mara: Which makes us sad.

Kala: But we keep talking.

Mara: And then you understand us later.

Kala: Which makes us happy again.

Mara: But that hasn't happened for a long time.

Kala: Not understanding us.

Mara: Years and years.

Kala: You always understand us now.

Mara: But at least you feed us even when you don't understand us.

Kala: Lots of humans do that, though. And they never understand us.

Mara: Not lots, Kala.

Kala: Not lots. But some. Not just you.
Mara: Some throw things at us, or try and catch us.
Kala: We stay away from them, though.
Mara: Unless we need to watch them.
Kala: Even then we stay away—just not far away.
Mara: And we hide.
Kala: And stay quiet.
Mara: Which is ever so hard.
Kala: Yes. Sometimes we have to stay quiet for a whole hour.
Mara: Or longer!
Kala: And that is so hard.
Mara: Unbearable!
Kala: But we do it when we have to.
Mara: Because we understand duty.
Kala: And truth.
Mara: Even if you silly humans don't.
Kala: Even if you are slow.
Mara: And take forever to decide anything.
Kala: Even though we've told you.

By this time, I was back at the office. I fed them each one last cashew and went inside. As the door was closing behind me, I heard a hawk scream, but it sounded far away. Stay safe, my feathery counsels.

I'll be sorting and filing for just a few minutes more; then I'll be out of here. An early start to the morning tomorrow—the jury resumes deliberations at 8:30 and could decide quickly, so I'll need to be at the courthouse. A quick dinner tonight, listen to some *Traviata* to relax, and then early meds and off to bed.

Thursday, June 8

As expected, the jury in the Stafford case returned a verdict quickly this morning. They announced they were ready at 9:10, and by 9:30 the judge had banged the gavel: not guilty on all counts.

Even though I was confident that would be the result, it's always a relief to hear the foreman state the verdict. I was back in the office by ten. Mike had kind words for the win, which was nice, and encouraged me to have the next major case lined up by next Tuesday, which was less so.

I spent the rest of the morning collecting all the bits and pieces of this case and putting the file to rest. The busy work helped me ignore the eyes, which were multiplying alarmingly on my office walls. How do they always know when I'm under pressure to find a new case? They just love to torment me then. Fortunately, Max left me alone. I wonder where he goes when he's not harassing me?

After I got things put away, I enjoyed a lunch in the park. I listened to Act 2 of *Madama Butterfly* and fed the motley assortment of sparrows and starlings, at least until the pigeons figured out what was going on and drove the others away. Goddamn rats with wings! I kept expecting the peregrine to dive bomb them, but he apparently was hunting somewhere else, so they and I were both spared that trauma.

Mara and Kala showed up unexpectedly towards the end of the hour, just at the conclusion of the humming chorus. After such a beautiful moment of calm, they were a jarring return to reality.

Kala: Are you finally done?

Me: Yes. Not guilty, all counts.

Mara: We knew that.

Kala: We told you so.

Me: But now it's not only true, it's settled.

Mara: It was settled before.

Kala: How could it not be? It's in the past.

Mara: Not the future.

Kala: Not even the present.

Mara: Done.

Kala: Settled.

Me: Yes, I know. We're slow, and things don't always settle as you would expect.

Mara: You are slow.

Kala: It's true.

Mara: But we still like you.

Kala: And not just because you feed us.

Mara: But that's part of it.

Kala: And a tasty part, too.

Me: I'll be needing to start a new case soon. I hope you can help me.

Mara: Don't we always?

Kala: We tell you the truth.

Mara: And you convince the other people.

Kala: They should just believe you.

Mara: Like you believe us.

Kala: Instead of making you argue.

Mara: And track down all sorts of silly details.

Kala: That don't matter because you know the truth.

Mara: But you are slow.

Kala: So we help.

Me, laughing: I appreciate it. I'll be interviewing potential clients starting this afternoon. I've got two coming into the office this afternoon, and tomorrow I'll see at least two more at the jail. I'll want your help in deciding which case to take.

Mara: You want to know who did the bad things.

Kala: The bad things others say they did.

Mara: Right. You all do bad things.

Kala: Even you.

Mara: Though you feed us.

Kala: Which is a good thing.

Mara: So we'll help you.

Me: How do you know the answers? How do you even know who I meet with?

Kala: We watch people come and go.

Mara: We look in your office window.

Kala: We know lots of things.

Mara: And what we don't know we find out.

Kala: And then we know.

Mara: And tell you.

Kala: So you know too.

Me: But what about when I meet with prisoners at the jail? How do you know who I meet.

Mara: That's easy! You tell us.

Kala: You do. You tell us their names.

Me: How do you even know their names?

Mara: We know lots of things.

Kala: Big things.

Mara: Little things.

Kala: Things like names.

Mara: We watch.

Kala: We listen.

Mara: We know.

Me: I still don't get it, but that's OK. Pay attention these next two days. I'll be reviewing the clients' files on Monday and will need to decide by Tuesday. My boss is riding my tail to decide quickly.

Kala: You don't have a tail.

Mara: Or do you tuck it into your pants?

Kala: Such a silly thing, pants.

Mara: And why hide a tail?

Kala: If you even have one. I don't think you do.

Mara: Certainly not enough to ride.

Kala: But he's right, you're slow.

Mara: But so is he.

Kala: All humans are slow.

Mara: Not like us.

Kala: We're fast.

Mara: And we see many things.
Kala: Hear many things.
Mara: Know lots of things.
Kala: Even secret things.
Mara: Monday evening, we will help you decide.
Kala: Look for us then.
Mara: Look for us before then, too.
Kala: And feed us!
Mara: But we'll be there then.
Kala: With answers.

So once again, I'll be basing my client selection on the advice of two jays, the real brains in this uncommon arrangement.

The eyes continued to watch me this afternoon as I reviewed possible new cases. Their obvious disapproval made it hard to concentrate. There were a few mouths, too, voicing their silent displeasure with me.

I often wonder if other people truly don't see the eyes, or if they have simply learned to tune them out. Put them in their blind spot. They do see Mara and Kala, even if they don't understand them (or don't admit to understanding them). Why don't they see the eyes and mouths? How can they just edit them out of their reality? They say I have the "sick" mind because I am different: "neurodivergent" as they are "neurotypical." But is it healthy to be so blind and deaf? Which of us is disabled?

Sometimes I envy the neurotypical masses. I'd love to be able to just not see the eyes, not hear the mutterings, be happily oblivious. The only time that happens, though, is when they bash my brain with the blunt tool of medication. Medication that in small careful doses allows me to function, but that too easily renders me not only insensate like them, but insensible, too. Just a small change in medications can take away my ability to understand Mara and Kala, and as Max loves to observe, without them I wouldn't be half as successful in the courtroom. I envy the neurotypicals, but I also feel sorry for them. I may be slow, but at least I'm aware of what's around me.

Monday, June 12

The eyes have been multiplying all day. Watching, waiting. Eager to see me make the wrong choice, to see me fail. They always watch when I have to pick a case, more eyes than mouths typically. And the mutterers keep swelling. They come and go, but each time they come back, they're more strident. Building inexorably, like a tide coming in.

Inevitably, the tide will crest when I make my decision and then recede—at least until the court date looms, when it will grow again. I know that rhythm. The tide comes in, and the tide goes out. It will get better. If I keep writing that, maybe I'll even believe it.

Who am I trying to kid? The eyes are watching because they know I am incompetent. The mouths are predicting my failure. They know I'm nothing on my own. They know that without help I couldn't possibly make the right decision. I am worthless without Mara and Kala. The eyes and mouths know. The mutterers repeat it over and over. They are predators, the same as if they were hawks. And like all predators, they know when their prey—me—is most vulnerable.

I've interviewed five potential clients under their watch, and they're all good cases. Almost definitely, someone in the firm will take each of them, but as a senior counsel, I'll have first pick of the one I will personally represent, the others being covered by junior counsels with some guidance or support from me as needed.

For the most part, the other attorneys don't want anything to do with me, and I'm OK with that. I'm not sure whether they resent me taking cases that can be "easily" won (if they only knew!), or if it's the tardive dyskinesia that puts them off. Or maybe I'm just scary. Whatever it is, they do their job and I do mine. It works.

I'm leaning towards the Patterson case, a domestic assault charge. I don't think he did it, but that's more a gut response than anything certain. Hopefully, I'll know more when Mara and Kala arrive soon. At least that won't be seen as taking an easy case. There's never anything easy about domestics.

There are two cases that should be a simple matter of hiring the appropriate expert witness, and another that is a pretty weak case of he-said, she-said. Any of our counselors should be able to win those, as long as nothing too unexpected comes up in discovery. There may be some detective work needed, but they can all handle that. The last one, I don't know. I think he did it. That doesn't mean he doesn't deserve a competent defense—that's the American way, after all—but I don't want any part of it.

It's a hollow victory to get a guilty man acquitted, though some defense lawyers really get off on that. I'm more interested in seeing real justice served, which is why I'm so picky about my cases. And so thankful for Mara and Kala! Max is right; I'm nothing without them.

I told Mike I'd have my choice tomorrow morning. I'm counting on Mara and Kala to show up as promised. I'm a little concerned that they're not here yet, but there's still time. If they don't show up, I guess I'll take Patterson and hope my gut is right. The eyes should love that.

* * *

Update: Just as I wrote that last sentence Mara and Kala landed on the sill and tapped at my window. Here's what ensued:

Me: You're here! I was beginning to worry.

Mara: We said we'd be here.

Kala: Monday. This is Monday.

Mara: And here we are.

Me: Yes. And you know the five cases I've looked at last week and today?

Kala: We do.

Mara: We know all about them.

Kala: Well, not all.

Mara: But enough.

Kala: Don't defend Schmidt.

Mara: No, he is bad.

Kala: He's lying.

Mara: He did it.

Me: I thought as much. Someone will still have to defend him.

Kala: Why? He did it.

Mara: Truth is truth.

Me: But justice is something different, and jurisprudence is something else entirely. We've had this discussion.

Kala: But we don't understand it.

Mara: We hear the words.

Kala: But they don't make sense.

Mara: Truth is truth.

Kala: Justice is justice.

Mara: The same thing.

Kala: And jurisprudence is stupid.

Me (laughing): It probably is, but it's the system we have.

Mara: You need a better system.

Kala: Like us!

Me: Some other time. I won't defend Schmidt, though someone will. The others are all innocent?

Mara: Innocent?

Kala: No one is innocent.

Mara: Not past the age of two, anyway.

Kala: But they didn't do what the others say they did.

Mara: They may not be good.

Kala: But they didn't do *these* bad things.

Me: I'm thinking about the Patterson case. Can you help me with that one?

Mara: We can.

Kala: He's not a good man.

Mara: But he's not that bad.

Kala: He didn't assault his wife.

Mara: She assaulted him.

Kala: But that's not how she got hurt.

Mara: He barely defended himself.

Kala: He left the house...

Mara: ...rather than fight with her.

Me: That's what he said. He told me she'd come at him swinging, and he walked out before anything more could happen. He said he didn't want to fight.

Kala: It's true.

Me: So how did she get hurt? Somebody obviously bashed her good. If it wasn't Patterson, then who was it?

Mara: Her lover did it.

Kala: Not her husband.

Mara: She has both.

Kala: And she had him do it.

Mara: The lover.

Kala: She told him to hit her.

Mara: She knew her husband would be charged.

Kala: And she figured she'd win the case.

Mara: A big settlement.

Kala: A divorce.

Mara: And then she marries the lover.

Kala: They had it all worked out.

Me: You're saying she let that happen? She voluntarily got her head bashed in?

Mara: Yes, she's bad.

Kala: And her lover is worse.

Mara: She took pills so it wouldn't hurt as much.

Kala: But it still hurt.

Mara: Especially when he used the bat.

Kala: He thought he'd killed her when he swung it.

Mara: But he didn't kill her.

Kala: He broke her jaw.

Mara: She fell right over.

Kala: And didn't get up.

Me: So the bat was used? The cops found the bat at the scene. It had blood on it, but the shape of the bat didn't match the trauma, and the only fingerprints were the husband's. That's the prime evidence.

Mara: The lover used it.

Kala: He used it backwards.

Mara: Held it by the fat end...
Kala: ...and swung the skinny end at her.
Mara: Then he used a rag.
Kala: He smeared the blood...
Mara:...around the end he had held.
Kala: The fat end.
Mara: Then he dropped the bat.
Kala: And he left her there.
Mara: Unconscious.
Kala: Maybe dead—he didn't know.
Mara: But she wasn't dead.
Kala: No. She woke up.
Mara: And called the police.
Kala: Just like they planned.
Mara: Only they didn't plan her being unconscious.
Me: Did they take blood when she was at the hospital?
Kala: They always take blood.
Mara: What do they do with all the blood?
Kala: They stick it in machines.
Mara: Silly humans.
Me: If they kept some of the sample we can do a drug test and maybe show the painkillers were in her system prior to being treated at the hospital. And the bat is in evidence so we can check the wide end for fingerprints and check the narrow end for a match to the injury. Yes, this will all support the case. Where did Patterson go when he went out.
Kala: He walked.
Mara: Walked and walked.
Kala: He walked for three hours.
Mara: He was walking home when the police found him.
Kala: But he was still far from home.
Me: He was walking *toward* the house?
Mara: Yes.
Kala: Definitely.
Me: The police report should show that, I hope. And he was walking, not running?

Mara: He only walked.

Kala: Didn't run at all.

Me: OK, thanks. You've given me a lot to work with. I'll take this case.

Mara: You'll tell the truth.

Kala: And get justice.

Mara: Same thing.

Kala: We don't know about jurisprudence.

Mara: You'll win the case.

Kala: So you can buy us more cashews.

I laughed and sent them on their way. The eyes have thinned out and the mutterers are less agitated now. The tide has gone out at last. It seems I've made the right choice again, thanks to Mara and Kala. At least the eyes think so, and they're usually right.

I'll put a note on Mike's desk before I leave so he sees it first thing tomorrow. I'll tell him I'm taking the Patterson case. That should make him happy, anyway. This should be an interesting case.

Psychiatric Progress Notes

Patient Name: William "Rip" Taylor

Date: June 19, 2017

Diagnoses:
Schizophrenia (Paranoid) *F20.0*
Tardive Dyskinesia (subacute, drug-induced) *G24.01*

Medication List:
Risperidone 4 mg PO SID (QHS)

Physical Findings and Mental Status:
Vitals: Unremarkable.
Mental Status: Alert and oriented to person, place, and time.
Comportment: Well-groomed, alert posture, unremarkable.
Mood and affect: Cooperative and situationally appropriate.
Ability to concentrate: Unremarkable.
Tone and rate of speech: Appropriate and unhurried.
Danger to self/others: None.

Symptoms:

Mr. Taylor reports no change in symptoms since intake. He reports frequent auditory hallucinations of unintelligible voices ("muttering"), and occasional visual hallucinations of disembodied eyes and mouths on blank surfaces consistent with earlier. He considers these "manageable." He denies other hallucinations or delusional thinking. Negative and cognitive symptoms continue as before and are also reported as "manageable." His anxiety due to the raptor phobia is reported as "mild."

Mr. Taylor again reports that tardive dyskinesia is his chief complaint. He states it is especially troublesome when he is required to appear in court.

Interventions:

I challenged Mr. Taylor's acceptance of any level of positive symptoms as "normal" or "manageable." I also challenged his perception of the admitted hallucinations as "real."

We discussed adding Ingrezza to his daily medications. This is a new medication that gained FDA approval just this year for the treatment of symptoms of tardive dyskinesia. I have reviewed the studies of this medication and believe that Mr. Taylor would be an excellent candidate. Ingrezza is very expensive, however, and as a new medication it has no generic equivalent and is not covered by most insurance. I will nevertheless pursue this with Mr. Taylor's insurance company on his behalf.

Patient Response to Interventions:

Mr. Taylor reacted quite negatively to the challenge of eliminating all positive symptoms. He replied that previous treatment to extinction of positive symptoms left him feeling overmedicated and "stupid." He expressed strong concern that any increase in dose would increase the extrapyramidal effects and worsen the tardive dyskinesia.

Mr. Taylor was excited to hear about Ingrezza and assured me that his insurance would cover it.

Clinical Impressions:

Mr. Taylor's schizophrenia appears superficially stable at this time, though significantly under-managed through medication. Hallucinations and delusional thinking persist unchallenged. While Mr. Taylor appears to be functioning well under these circumstances, there is obvious room for improvement. I am still establishing a baseline for treatment, but an increase in antipsychotic medication is clearly warranted.

Plan:

No change to medications at this time. Continue monitoring for baseline.

Next appointment in two weeks.

Rx:

None.

Signed:

JoAnne Filtner, M.D., Ph.D.

Monday, June 19

Did I say this would be an interesting case? Maybe in the sense of the apocryphal Chinese curse: "May you live in interesting times."

Patterson is turning out to be a mighty unsavory character. He didn't beat his wife, at least not this time, but I can understand why she'd want to be rid of him. Defending him is one of those distasteful tasks that comes with the profession. He cheats on his wife, runs scams, and preys on the more vulnerable parts of society (primarily the elderly and destitute). He's controlling, vain, and completely unapologetic. But he didn't beat his wife that night. And while he does many despicable things, he mostly stays on the right side of the law—just the wrong side of decency.

So I'm defending him, just as vigorously as I can. It will be a fight this time, as his reprehensible nature is widely known and will doubtless be brought out during the trial. The jury will want to believe that he did it, and I can't blame them. But this isn't about good or bad, decent or nasty. It's about justice, and the just thing to do is to win him acquittal.

The mutterers don't approve, of course. They are a judgmental lot, and they have lately been mumbling their displeasure more or less constantly. The eyes and mouths are angry, too, and multiplying. At least that helps me keep my eyes on Patterson when we meet, even though I'd like to look away. Any other place I might look is covered with disapproval. His is the least unpleasant visage in the room, which is a dismal state of affairs.

Max has been talking to me, too. He's derisive as always, of course, but he's also supportive of my decisions this time. At least I guess that's how I'd have to characterize it. He says things like "Well, shithead, you have a real test of character this time. So far you haven't fucked it up like I thought you would, but I have faith you'll find a way yet." From Max, that's high praise. I think I liked him more when he was uniformly negative. This is just weird.

Mike seems pleasantly surprised I'm staying on the case, given my historical selectivity. Admittedly, this is the sort of case I'd normally refuse, but I know something Mike doesn't. I know Patterson is innocent. Well, maybe not innocent, but not guilty of this particular crime, anyway. Granted I can't prove that yet, not in any way a court would accept, but I know it just the same. Mara and Kala have never been wrong before, and I'm not about to doubt them now.

At my request the crime lab is checking the bat again for fingerprints—checking all over now, not just the grip. They really should have done that the first time! They know that, too, which is the only reason they're checking again.

The medical examiner has confirmed that the grip of the bat is consistent with whatever weapon broke the wife's jaw, unlike the meat of the bat. But if there aren't any fingerprints to be found, that's no help. Even if there are fingerprints, there probably won't be a match. The boyfriend has no record and likely has never been fingerprinted, and so isn't in the system. I can't compel him to be fingerprinted without grounds for suspicion, and I don't have any valid legal grounds. Just the truth.

I've asked Mara and Kala for any help they can provide. I'm hopeful there is something they know that I can use, I just have to ask the right questions. That's always the challenge, finding the right questions to ask. I do wish they had an understanding of rules of evidence and the whole legal process. I swear they are being deliberately ignorant sometimes.

So far they've told me that Patterson didn't meet anyone while he was walking, so there's no easy witness to confirm he wasn't at home. I've asked them for the route he walked, but their understanding of geography is... well, it's birdlike. I know what types and sizes of trees he walked by, and any other perches like ledges, banners, and signs. Not what's *on* the banners and signs, mind you, but exactly how easy they are to perch on, how high they are, and what cover they offer. I'll have to do some walking on my own and see if I can match a path to their description.

Maybe there will be surveillance cameras somewhere that can pin down his presence at a specific time.

In better news, Dr. Filtner told me more about a new drug at my appointment today. Ingrezza has been approved to treat tardive dyskinesia. According to the studies it not only stops its progression but actually may reduce the tics. She's working with my insurance to get coverage for it—which *should* go through. Thank heavens for the good insurance Mike provides.

I'm actually looking forward to my next appointment so I can start on the Ingrezza. According to Dr. Filtner, I'll have two weeks at a half-dose and then I should go up to the maintenance dose. The Independence Day holiday will delay things, unfortunately, but I'm scheduled for the 6th as long as court dates don't interfere. I'm not sure if we'll be to trial then or not; it'll be close.

Unfortunately, I think Dr. Filtner is going to want to increase the Risperidone soon, too. She's already indicated as much. And with Max and the mutterers growing in intensity, maybe it makes sense. God knows I could do with less from Max! But stepping up the dose makes me slower. Mornings are hard enough without adding more brain fog. And the last time I was on a higher dose, it interfered with understanding Mara and Kala, too. They still came around, and I think they were still talking to me, but all I heard were the squawks of a Steller's jay, the same as everyone else. It seems that too much Risperidone blocks all of my special perception indiscriminately.

I can't afford to be without Mara and Kala. Not now, and not ever. As Max has told me countless times, I'm worthless without their help. And much as I hate to admit it, Max is never wrong.

All of which calls into question—again—the meaning of "hallucinations." Dr. Filtner and all the other shrinks would tell me that they are the product of a damaged mind and nothing else. No one will acknowledge the reality of my perception. Their idea of a "cure" is to completely eliminate these "derangements." "Total extinguishment," that's their byword. Nothing less than that will satisfy them.

The truth is much more subtle and important. It's all real. The "hallucinations" exist independent of me. That others can't see them is a measure only of their blindness, not the unreality of the voices, eyes, mouths, etc. Schizophrenia makes me particularly sensitive, uniquely perceptive, that is all.

I take their medications because I can't function when I see and hear too clearly. I need to temper my hyper-perception a bit, like putting on sunglasses on a bright sunny day. I don't want to be blind; I just want to be able to see clearly without distraction. Unfortunately, the shrinks are like everyone else: they have unconsciously masked their own perception to the point that they've forgotten they ever could see. They think blindness is normal and desirable. They would handle an over-bright day by permanently locking a blindfold on my head.

I've tried to explain this so many times. Everyone I've talked to who didn't share my sensitivity—this "disease" they call schizophrenia—is threatened by this revelation. They argue so convincingly for their collective blindness that they believe *us* to be crazy. So, no more. Dr. Filtner will not hear this argument. None of this will be in the "clean" journal I show her. I won't let her damage me more; I will just use her to give me the balanced control I need to remain functional while still aware.

If only there were a doctor who understood....

Wednesday, June 21

I found it!

It took hours, but I was able to take Mara and Kala's distinctly avian description of Patterson's walk and figure out where he went. He walked past two different shops with outside security cameras that I should be able to get the tapes for, and one of them looks over where he was picked up by the police. With luck it should show him walking towards the spot, heading towards his home, not away from it. This isn't proof positive, of course, but it definitely helps support his story. We're making progress.

Also, when they picked him up, they processed his hands to look for traces of blood that would tie him to his wife's injuries. Obviously they didn't find any blood, but he'd had to fill his printer with ink at work that day, and he still had ink on his hands from that. I have a copy of the police report with that information on it, which demonstrates that he didn't do the sort of thorough cleaning that would be needed to remove all traces of blood.

With both of those bits of evidence secured, I think I have the beginnings of a defense. I hope so, anyway. I'm still looking for more proof. No report back yet on the second search for prints on the bat. It shouldn't take that long to determine if there *are* prints or not, so I'm hoping this means they found prints and they are waiting on the results of searching the AFIS database for a match. I'll check again tomorrow. Assuming they do find prints and they are not in the database, I'll need to come up with some reasonable suspicion to pull in the wife's boyfriend (which relationship is not common knowledge, of course).

Patterson is trying to be helpful, but he's so slimy that his idea of help is introducing all sorts of unsavory character references and coming up with easily penetrated schemes to give him an alibi. I wish he'd just sit back and let me do my job. Or, to be honest, to let Mara and Kala do my job. I just hope I can get him to keep his mouth shut on the stand. He's definitely the sort to be his own worst enemy, no matter how well he's coached.

Trial is set to start on July 10, which is pretty quick for some reason. The prosecutor may be trying to cut my time short so I can't put too many things together, but I can probably get a continuance if I need it, as long as I can offer some legitimate reason. Hopefully I can get all my ducks in a row by then anyway and I won't need it. I could sure use one more piece of solid evidence.

Mara and Kala haven't been around for a while—I'm not sure what to make of that. Hopefully nothing has happened to either of them. I last saw them on Sunday. It's not uncommon for them to be gone for a day or two, but this is beginning to be worrisome. The hawks have been out every day, and I fear the worst.

Fortunately, this case has kept me busy enough that I haven't had much time to worry about them. The mutterers know something, I think. Whenever I hear a hawk scream they get very quiet for a few seconds. And they seem to be talking amongst themselves more—talking to each other rather than at me. The eyes aren't looking at me, either, and the mouths are grim. At least Max hasn't made himself known this week. I'm seriously considering skipping my meds tonight just to make me a little more aware. I'm worried that I'm missing something because of how the Risperidone blunts my perception.

I still have to deal with the shops' security teams to get access to the camera tapes. That could get awkward if I cut back the meds, but I think it will work out OK. One missed day doesn't usually bring much effect... as long as I don't go crazy and forget the next day, too.

I'm going to stop by Chinatown on my way home and pick up some take-out. I don't feel like dealing with cooking or cleaning tonight. Take-out and Puccini and maybe a bath. Hopefully that will let me sleep, even if I don't take the Risperidone.

Thursday, June 22

Mara and Kala have come through again!

They showed up this afternoon, earlier than normal for them, but fortunately I was alone. I figured something was up because the mutterers had been particularly agitated all day. The jays tapped on my window as usual, but I couldn't talk to them in the office in case anyone came in. I pointed out the window to Antlers Park and they flew off in that direction. My heart was pounding by the time I ran there.

Me: Where have you been? I've been worried about you.

Mara: We've been busy.

Kala: Helpful even.

Mara: We knew you needed the boyfriend picked up.

Kala: By the police.

Mara: Need them to do something.

Kala: Something with his fingers

Mara: Yes. Take his fingers.

Kala: Though what they do with them we don't understand.

Mara: He still has his fingers.

Kala: But the police have them, too?

Mara: I don't think they take his fingers, Kala.

Me: Never mind, I know what you're talking about. They took his fingerprints. Why was he picked up? What did you do?

Mara: He's been edgy.

Kala: Jumpy.

Mara: Quick to anger.

Kala: Very nervous.

Mara: So we made him a little crazy.

Kala: It was easy.

Mara: Fun, even!

Kala: We kept tapping on his window.

Mara: And dropping little rocks on him when he went outside.

Kala: And making lots of noise wherever he was.

Mara: Dive bombing him.

Kala: We got other jays to join in.
Mara: They thought it was fun, too.
Kala: A good game.
Mara: So we kept it up all day.
Kala: And we even had a screech owl help.
Mara: They don't normally help.
Kala: But this one thought it was fun, too.
Mara: Three times a night he'd screech.
Kala: Right beside the boyfriend's window.
Mara: He finally lost it.
Kala: The boyfriend.
Mara: Not the owl.
Kala: He came out with his shotgun.
Mara: We weren't there.
Kala: But we heard about it.
Mara: We warned them all he'd do that.
Kala: The other jays.
Mara: So they were ready and knew to hide in the tree.
Kala: But keep making noise..
Mara: He shot off his gun.
Kala: So loud!
Mara: That's what we were told.
Kala: Nobody got hit.
Mara: But the neighbors complained.
Kala: And the police came.
Mara: We know you can't shoot guns in the city.
Kala: And this was in the city.
Mara: So the police came.
Kala: And they took him away.
Mara: He came home again after a few hours.
Kala: But they took his fingers.
Mara: And gave them back?
Kala: He has them anyway.
Mara: We saw them.
I could hardly stop laughing long enough to chide them.
Me: You could have been shot. You can't take that kind of risk!

Mara: We weren't even there.
Kala: But others were.
Mara: And they didn't get shot.
Kala: They know how to avoid it.
Mara: We like baiting humans.
Kala: It's a fun game.
Mara: And if you do it long enough...
Kala: ...and hard enough...
Mara: ...they usually do something stupid.
Kala: Almost always.
Mara: And we knew you needed this.
Kala: He's a bad man.
Mara: Worse than Patterson.
Kala: Much worse.
Mara: So it was good to make the police find him.
Kala: And now they have his fingers.
Mara: Except they gave them back.
Kala: Because he still has them.
Mara: All ten.
Kala: We counted to be sure.

So now I just have to hope that the police *did* find prints on the bat, and that they'll match one Randy Balk, the boyfriend. And then my reputation as the luckiest defense attorney in the state of Colorado will remain intact. I can take my meds again tonight!

Monday, June 26

I received word today that the prosecution has dropped the charges against Patterson. The judge dismissed the case this morning. They *did* find fingerprints on the upper end of the bat: prints that did not match either Patterson or his wife, but that did match the boyfriend that they had just brought in after he fired his gun at the birds. The prints were in the blood on the bat, so they definitely were applied during or after the injury.

The police picked up Balk this weekend and got a confession out of him by promising not to prosecute him on assault charges (which were weak anyway, since the "attack" was more or less consensual). They still have him and the wife both on fraud and conspiracy charges. They picked her up early this morning. I met Patterson at the jail and explained what had transpired and that he was a free man. He's working on his divorce proceedings now.

So another case won, this one without even going to court. Everyone thinks I did tremendous detective work and then got incredibly lucky with the boyfriend being picked up. Of course I owe it all to Mara and Kala, but I'll just keep that to myself, thank you. I've seen what happens when I talk about things like this.

I'm going to spend the rest of the day putting the case to bed: filing all the paperwork, writing up the notes, making sure all the billing gets done, that sort of thing. After that, I'm going to take the rest of the week off as well as next Monday. Tuesday is the Independence Day holiday, so I'll have a full week off. Mike is fine with that—he actually said I'd earned it with this win. I'm not going to argue!

I think I might drive out to Santa Fe and take in some live opera. It's a week too early for Central City Opera, which would be closer and easier, but the Santa Fe Opera is putting on *Lucia di Lammermoor*. If I can get tickets, I'm going to go. It's a pretty drive and Santa Fe is a lovely town so I might just make a proper vacation of it.

I'll have to interview prospective clients for the next case when I get back, but until then I'm going to relax. The mutterers have mostly gone quiet, and the few eyes and mouths that are on the walls are almost smiling. It's not all roses, of course. It never is. Max made an appearance this weekend.

Late Saturday night I was just getting ready for bed. The upstairs neighbors had been running relay races from the sound of it, and someone in the building was having a party. It had finally quieted down, and then Max spoke up.

"So, shithead, it looks like the birds won another case for you. You'd be nothing without them—probably living on the street. What are you going to do when they go away? They've been here too long anyway—jays only live about ten years, you know? You've been talking to them for nearly twice that. They'll go away. Then what will you do? Everyone will know you've cheated."

He's right, of course. There was more like that, but it faded away after I took my meds. I know the meds don't act that fast, but apparently Max doesn't. His message got through, in any case.

I've wondered about that myself. Mara and Kala first showed up when I came to Denver for law school—not at UC Boulder like I'd dreamed, but at Sturm College, respectable enough. They first made their appearance right before I had the break that led to my diagnosis, which was back in '97. The next year was pretty spotty with all the meds and being in and out of the hospital, so I don't remember that they were there much, but certainly they've been steadily advising me since 1999.

Max is right, Steller's jays do only live about ten years—so how is that possible? It's definitely the same jays; there's been no discontinuity. I could ask them, I suppose, but I'm not sure I want to know the answer. I'm just thankful they keep coming back. But even if they are oddly immune to old age, there is always the raptor threat, to say nothing of provoked humans with guns. And Max is right: without them, I wouldn't be anywhere near the success that I am. I'd be nothing.

I wonder how many other leading lawyers—or experts in other fields—have their secret advisors like my dear jays? My perception is special, but is it unique?

Friday, June 30

Tempest came back. After more than a year, I thought—hoped—she was gone for good. No such luck.

I'm in Santa Fe. Something about the street life here brought her back this afternoon. I was just walking through the art district, window shopping and people watching. Relaxing. Then, completely out of the blue, Tempest chimed in:

"You could do anything here, you know? Nobody knows you from Adam. See that girl over there?" (Anyone my age or younger has always been a "girl" to Tempest. This woman was probably in her early to middle twenties.)

"You could ask her to have dinner with you. I bet she'd say yes. Even if she said no, there are so many others here. Or you could go straight for the action. By eight o'clock, there will be any number of girls on the street that you could take to your room for a hundred dollars. You'd be doing them a favor—they need the money. And you're so vanilla, they'd think it was easy money. Boring, even. You'd be done in thirty minutes; first time in a long time, all that pent up pressure. Why not?"

I didn't answer Tempest. I know better. I've learned that it doesn't matter what I say; it only encourages her. If I ignore her, she eventually subsides into name-calling. As far as she's concerned, I'm a loser. That's the nicest name she ever called me. She had some more choice terms this afternoon.

Fuck. She knows the women I find attractive: thin, almost androgynous, short-haired, animated, and with an impish glint in the eye—what they used to call gamine. Tempest knows all of that, and she's good at pointing them out and stirring things up. This woman fit the bill perfectly; so many of the women here do. It took all my energy to not reply to Tempest—and to not act on her suggestions. I had to go back to the hotel and sit in the dark. I almost drove straight home.

She's right, of course. She always is. All the voices are. That's what makes them so powerful, so dangerous. Every word she said is true. Oh, it wouldn't be as easy as she makes it sound, but I know I could find a willing partner, for a price. It would feel good. God knows it's been long enough. And it would support a local working girl. (Yes, some prostitutes are trafficked or enslaved to a pimp, but most are just marginalized people trying to make a few bucks in a world that offers them no better alternatives.)

So why don't I follow her advice? I don't know. I feel I should have a ready answer—I think I used to, once. Now I just say no, but fuck me if I know why anymore.

There was a time, years ago, when I listened to Tempest—too much. It was especially bad if I'd been drinking. I let her talk me into all sorts of activities better left undone.

Eventually I learned how to keep Tempest at bay. She never bothered me at work. As long as I could stay busy, she would stay quiet, but she haunted my down time. The next most important strategy is not drinking. Oh, I'll have a beer or a glass of wine at lunch if I'm on vacation, and maybe something at dinnertime, but only one. Today was no different: I had a beer at lunch. One beer. Maybe it's the heat. Or just all the beautiful people in this beautiful city.

I'm staying in tonight. Maybe I'll find a book at the hotel gift shop and read. I don't dare venture any further out. Dinner will be ordered in the room. I won't sleep, I already know that. Maybe I *could* sleep if I had a couple drinks, but I still *wouldn't*. Enough alcohol to make me sleep would just ensure that I didn't sleep alone. I want to go out. I want to listen to Tempest. But I can't give in. Damned if I know why anymore, but I can't. It will be a long drive home tomorrow on no sleep, but I can't stay in this town. At least I got to see the opera.

Psychiatric Progress Notes

Patient Name: William "Rip" Taylor

Date: July 6, 2017

Diagnoses:
   Schizophrenia (Paranoid) F20.0
   Tardive Dyskinesia (subacute, drug-induced) G24.01

Medication List:
   Risperidone 4 mg PO SID (QHS)

Physical Findings and Mental Status:
   Vitals: Unremarkable.
   Mental Status: Alert and oriented to person, place, and time.
   Comportment: Well-groomed, alert posture, unremarkable.
   Mood and affect: Cooperative and situationally appropriate.
   Ability to concentrate: Unremarkable.
   Tone and rate of speech: Appropriate and unhurried.
   Danger to self/others: None.

Symptoms:

Mr. Taylor again reports no change in symptoms since intake. Positive symptoms of schizophrenia are reported as remaining manageable and contained to unintelligible voices and occasional visual hallucinations of disembodied eyes and mouths on blank surfaces. Negative/cognitive symptoms and anxiety due to the raptor phobia are reported as unchanged.

Tardive dyskinesia continues to be troublesome to Mr. Taylor and remains his chief complaint.

Interventions:

I again challenged Mr. Taylor's acceptance of any level of positive symptoms.

We briefly discussed adding a low dose of an SSRI antidepressant and/or a benzodiazepine anxiolytic in response to the raptor phobia.

We again discussed adding Ingrezza to his daily medication.

Patient Response to Interventions:

Mr. Taylor was uncharacteristically voluble in denying positive symptoms, responding angrily to any suggestion that they could be a problem.

Mr. Taylor was again very resistant to increasing the dose of his antipsychotic medication. He is unconcerned by the present level of hallucinations, and his delusional belief in their reality persists.

Mr. Taylor also was resistant to adding either an antidepressant or anxiolytic. He objected first on the basis of feeling mentally slowed due to overmedication until I pointed out that SSRIs are often prescribed to *treat* the negative symptoms of schizophrenia.

He then objected on the basis that the threat of the raptors was real and his response was proportionate to the threat. He stated (calmly) that "artificially relaxing my concerns would likely just make me a victim." He admitted that he had never been attacked by any bird of prey, nor did he know any person who had been; however, he considered that irrelevant to their perceived threat, in defiance of any logic.

When pressed about adding an antidepressant to his medications, Mr. Taylor stated that SSRIs had been unsuccessfully tried in the past, though this is not mentioned in his history. Given that his early records are spotty and incomplete, I must take him at his word on this, though I remain doubtful of his veracity.

Mr. Taylor responded very positively to the introduction of Ingrezza to treat the tardive dyskinesia. He considers the TD his chief complaint and is anxious to try anything that would mitigate its symptoms.

Clinical Impressions:

Mr. Taylor's aggressively defensive response to challenges about hallucinations and delusions is troubling. It may just reflect frustration with my repeated challenges, but I suspect rather that he has had more breakthroughs than he is willing to admit.

Despite these concerns, Mr. Taylor's schizophrenia appears otherwise stable at this time. His residual symptoms are concerning, as is his apparent attachment to them, but they appear nominally manageable at current levels. I am concerned, however, that any further shift may upset this delicate balance.

Mr. Taylor appears overly concerned with any neuroleptic sedation. This concern is likely a product of the demands of his profession and his misperception that his cognitive deterioration from schizophrenia is instead due to the medication. This will need to be monitored and likely challenged going forward.

Plan:

Introduce Ingrezza at 40 mg daily, with instructions to watch for adverse effects and discontinue use if any significant ill-effects are observed. This dose will be maintained for two weeks and then evaluated. If it appears well tolerated, dosage will be increased to 80 mg daily, as per standard dosing recommendations.

No other change to medications at this time.

Next appointment in two weeks.

Rx:

Risperidone 4 mg PO SID (QHS), Q 30

Ingrezza 40 mg PO SID (QHS), Q 14

Signed:

JoAnne Filtner, M.D., Ph.D.

Friday, July 7

Tempest has left the building, and it's about damned time. I think I can finally write about it all now.

I ended up spending three days in Santa Fe, though I had planned to stay longer. I drove out on Tuesday, went to the opera on Wednesday, and stayed on to enjoy the art scene for a few more days. I had intended to come home on Monday before the holiday.

The drive out was spectacular, and the first couple days were glorious, at least until Tempest showed up. Glorious, but hot. Highs were in the low 90s and it was sunny every day. Even with the elevation and dry air, it didn't cool down much in the evenings, remaining warm and pleasant.

The mid-summer heat seemed to put everyone in a dull torpor. The mutterers kept to themselves while I drove to Santa Fe, their voices lost in the road noise. Even when I got there they were mostly quiet. There weren't many eyes in the hotel room, and they just watched at first. *Lucia di Lammermoor* was as beautiful as I'd hoped. The mutterers stayed quiet and let me enjoy it. I thought it was going to be a great vacation.

After the show, though, the tension started to build. There were more eyes on my hotel room wall that night, watching and waiting. There were mouths, too, and they were talking to me. No words, of course, there never are, but I could see them talking and I knew something had to be coming. The next day there were more, and the mutterers began to get louder and take on an ominous edge.

It was like the opera I had just seen. Lucia is a tragic heroine, and the first two acts set up her inevitable descent into madness. As the opera unfolds the tension builds and builds until finally it culminates in the famous mad scene in the third act. I didn't know what was coming, but I could feel the storm brewing. The mutterers knew, of course, but they weren't telling.

Thursday I spent visiting the galleries and stores in the art district. It should have been a relaxing time, but I couldn't shake the sense of impending... something. I didn't know what. By Friday morning I knew it was going to strike soon, whatever "it" was. It was Tempest, of course. She made her appearance Friday afternoon. I wrote about that earlier.

I drove home first thing Saturday after a sleepless night. Tempest had kept me up, but it wasn't just her. The mutterers had swelled in a great *crescendo* as soon as she showed up, and stayed *fortissimo* all that night and all the next day. It was the mad scene all over again, but it went on and on without relief. At least I didn't have to worry about falling asleep on the drive back; the voices made sure of that.

Mara and Kala didn't make the trip, of course; three hundred miles is a bit far for them. They said they'd be watching here while I was gone. They greeted me when I got back Saturday afternoon, but just for a short visit and then they were gone. I haven't seen them since. They could tell something was up. I think they've been lying low while Tempest was here.

I thought Tempest would let up as soon as I got back to the Springs, but that proved to be wishful thinking. I quit drinking entirely. I went on long solitary hikes in the sweltering heat. I stayed in and listened to Wagner at his most bombastic. I caught up on my law review reading. It took days, but it seems she has finally shut up again. I haven't heard from her since Tuesday.

I didn't tell Dr. Filtner any of this yesterday, of course. She would have had me committed and I'd be bombed out of my mind on whatever high-powered medication she felt was justified, regardless of how I might feel or what I might say. So I said nothing to her. Everything is rosy. I don't know if she really buys that, but at least she didn't mess with the Risperidone this time. She tried, though. She'll probably insist on it at the next visit, no matter what I tell her.

Dr. Filtner is one of those shrinks who is hell-bent on eliminating all the "easy" positive symptoms: the voices, the faces. She has no concept at all that they are real nor that it is a gift to see them, even if, as with Tempest, the gift comes with a price. No, she wants to beat them down to nothing. Leave me drooling and tied into a chair, maybe, but "free of visual and auditory hallucinations." Bullshit!

Despite her zealous assault on my perception she does nothing to treat the negative symptoms—the depression and anxiety—nor the cognitive symptoms—the slowness of thought and the memory problems. There's never been any interest in treating those, not by her or anyone else. There are no meds available for them because no one cares if we can't think, can't feel, can't dream. All they care about is silencing the voices, with no consideration of their source or their value. They beat us down by chemically mashing our brains to a pulp and call it a win. They call the drugs "antipsychotics"—they'd be more aptly described as "anticogitants," destroying all thought. I hate them.

But I need them, too. Without something to knock the edge off, this special perception gets too intense. Max and Tempest and the others give me no peace. The non-stop voices reduce me to an immobility as profound as anything the medications do, and the glaring, judging eyes give me no peace. So I compromise. I tell the shrinks just enough to get the medication I need and tell them it's a "cure." I have to lie to manage my own medications because they won't listen to my real needs.

I know I'm not the only one who does this. I've talked with others that share my diagnosis. If you can get them in a private setting and feeling comfortable enough, they'll all admit playing the same game. Playing the docs. Staying alive despite the pressures from both sides. Finding that balance. Learning how to shape what they can, and how to cope with the rest. It's always an adversarial relationship, not just with the schizophrenia, but with the doctors as well.

Some of them try street drugs—hell, I did so myself right out of law school. But the drugs don't keep the voices down. They might help you not care for a while, but that's not the same. And the risk is too great, especially lately with all those horrible deaths from Fentanyl and other high-powered opioids. And the benzos—Xanax and the like—sure, they take the edge off the anxiety and fear, but they take the edge off everything else, too. And getting off of them can be harder than kicking heroin, from what I've heard. No, I'll stick to the Risperidone. Better the devil you know.

I did start the Ingrezza last night, at least. Forty milligrams, which is half the normal adult dose. I'll be on that dose for two weeks and then, barring complications, will move to the full eighty milligrams. I take it once a day, in the evening with the Risperidone. I don't feel any difference yet, but it's too early to tell. If this can get the tardive dyskinesia under control without messing with anything else, it would be a miracle. Personally, I don't put much stock in miracles, but we'll see. Dr. Filtner seems hopeful, anyway. At least she's good for that much.

Fuck. Now the nighthawks are out and I heard a barred owl a few minutes ago, that characteristic Here Comes the Bride rhythm. They're hunting tonight. I'll be safe inside, but what about Mara and Kala? Stay safe, my only faithful friends.

Wednesday, July 12

Still no major cases showing up. All the junior partners are booked full now, though. There's an interesting *pro bono* case that I may take. I'm due to take one—it's been months since I did any charity cases. This is one to feel good about, and it might even do some lasting good as a precedent, assuming I can win it. It's a simple prostitution case, or it should be.

The woman charged is in your typical survival-sex situation. She has a GED but no college, has a minor rap sheet—one count of shoplifting (stealing food), and another of resisting arrest, both settled, and has no job (other than prostitution—no legal job). She's Hispanic, though her English is good, and she has no real support system. She has a brother who is a migrant worker, following the harvests, and parents back in Mexico that she sends money to whenever she can. She has her green card, but has received only limited benefits. As is too often the case, prostitution is her only practical choice for income; no one wants to hire a person in her unfortunate situation. She lives in a run-down apartment with another girl with a similar background and profession. They barely manage to pay rent and keep the lights on, and at least half their food is obtained by dumpster diving.

None of this is her fault. She is doing the best she can, whatever it takes to stay alive and to help her parents out. The fact that she can save enough to send $50 most months is amazing, and she should be rewarded, not punished. Unfortunately, our laws essentially make poverty illegal. She got busted by an undercover cop for prostitution—she was desperate for any income and didn't fully vet him like she normally does with a new client. Simple enough: prostitution is a class 3 misdemeanor, no jail for a first offense; pay $100, and you're out the door. That's bad enough, money she can't afford for the victimless "crime" of basic survival, but for some reason, the prosecution decided to pull out all the stops.

Because both she and her roommate turn tricks in the apartment, the state decided to slap her with Keeping a Place of Prostitution (a class 2 misdemeanor, probably $500 and a month in jail for a first offense). That's devastating enough, but then they added a Pandering charge—a class 5 felony with mandatory jail time—claiming she forced her roommate into prostitution to be allowed to stay in the apartment.

Jesus Christ! The poor woman is just trying to live, and trying to help another woman in the same situation. She's not hurting anyone, she's not coercing anyone, she's not defrauding anyone; she's just trying to earn a buck the only way our crummy society allows her to.

So yeah, I think I'm going to take this one. Mara and Kala approve, but I don't think there's much they can do to help this time. I think I can get her to agree to a plea bargain where she would plead no contest on the basic prostitution charge in return for the prosecution dropping the other two charges. I'm not as sure I can convince the DA to go for that. I don't understand why they pressed the other charges in the first place.

I won't recommend that she accept anything beyond that, though. I'm almost hoping the DA refuses the bargain and it goes to court. I feel like I can at least get a hung jury if not an outright acquittal in today's political climate. A jury would probably convict her on the prostitution charge, but, if I do my job right, split or acquit on the other two.

It will come down to the jury selection. We definitely want a jury trial for this—no magistrate's ruling. And if we do get a hung jury, I will let the DA know that I will continue to defend this woman for as long as it takes. I'm pretty sure they won't want to incur the time and expense to try her again. This is a case worth taking.

Mike won't like it, of course. He doesn't really like that we take *pro bono* work at all. He doesn't himself; he just donates to Legal Aid, and only the minimum the Bar Association recommends. I don't do a lot, myself, but I make sure I do at least the recommended 50 hours a year, and usually more like twice that.

Mike grouses, but he lets me. This case won't require a lot of time—the facts are pretty straightforward, it's just the pitch that needs to be tuned.

Friday, July 14

Well, I said that Mara and Kala couldn't help with this *pro bono* case, but boy was I wrong! They explained why the DA's office is going all out on this case:

Me: So I'm taking the *pro bono* case. It's a simple one, but worthwhile. I don't think you can do much to help with this one.

Mara: We can help.

Kala: We always help.

Mara: We've been watching her apartment for a long time.

Kala: Months and months.

Mara: Lots of people in and out.

Kala: She has lots of friends.

Mara: Or her roommate does.

Kala: They both do—visitors come when either one is home.

Mara: Ooh, yes, that's true.

Kala: Almost all men.

Mara: Some women.

Kala: Not many though.

Mara: No, not many.

Kala: And none stay long.

Mara: More than a few minutes.

Kala: But less than an hour usually.

Mara: Usually. Sometimes longer.

Kala: But not often.

Mara: We've seen lots of the visitors before.

Kala: And so have you.

Mara: Two anyway.

Kala: Two?

Mara: Well, one frequent visitor.

Kala: Oh, yes.

Me: I have? Do I want to know? Who was it?

Mara: The one you call "the fucking DA."

Kala: Right, that's the one.

Me: Wait, you're telling me that the DA—*the DA*—frequently visits the apartment?
Mara: Yes, the fucking DA.
Kala: He's been going there as long as we've been watching.
Mara: Every week.
Kala: Except one. He skipped one.
Mara: But all the rest, sometimes twice.
Me: Well, isn't that interesting. He stays a short time like the others?
Kala: Yes, less than an hour.
Mara: But not much less.
Kala: But there was another one.
Mara: But he only went once.
Kala: And left quickly.
Mara: Five minutes?
Kala: No, more than that.
Mara: Not much more.
Kala: No, not much.
Me: Who was it?
Mara: Chief Pastoro
Kala: That's what you've called him.
Me: The chief of police?
Mara: I don't know. He wears a coat with lot of shiny things on it.
Kala: But not when he visited her.
Mara: No not then. But when he's talking to lots of people.
Me: Well, I'll be damned. The DA *and* the chief of police.
Kala: But the chief only went once.
Mara: And left right away.
Kala: And a week later they arrested her.
Mara: That's right, a week to the day.
So I talked to my client (who I won't name even here, thank you), and she cried and was clearly terrified. I assured her that everything she told me as her attorney was privileged, and then explained that meant it was safe, that neither of us would ever have to talk about it in court. She admitted that the DA had been

a regular client. And he tried to set her up with the Chief. She checked him out like she always did, found out who he was, and refused to see him. When he showed up anyway she told him to get out of her apartment and stop harassing her. Good for her!

The chief left, but not without threatening to bring her down. He put beat cops on her block round the clock, which scared off most of her clients. Even the DA wouldn't see her. She was going broke fast. That's when the undercover cop propositioned her, and she took it without checking because she was just that desperate. A classic set-up.

She's terrified of what the police will do. She sees them as holding all the power. I had to stifle my laughter and point out that it was she that held the power now. She had dirt on the DA and the chief. Dirt they can't afford to have come out in court. It would hurt them far more than it would hurt her. Normally, she would be right: nobody would believe her, and opening her mouth about it probably would get her locked up, or worse. But it's not just her now. I know the truth, and not from her telling me. And that makes all the difference.

I'm not sure how to negotiate this yet, but clearly we have leverage. There's no way this case will ever go to court, I'm sure of that. I'll have to find a way to guarantee her safety going forward, but the fact that I know what's going on will help. They could probably arrange to make her vanish easily enough, but I'm not so easily disposable.

I will have to be clear with the DA that she wasn't the source of this information—that I found out by other means (if he only knew how!)—but that she has confirmed it when I confronted her with what I knew. That way he won't be able to discount her story; I have it independently. I don't need to tell him how I know it, since we both know it's true. I can imply that there are pictures to back this up, pictures I'll retain in case anything more happens to her or her roommate.

I don't know what I'm going to tell Mike. He won't be too picky—it's a win, after all—but he will wonder how I got all the charges dropped. I think it's best not to tell him any details.

Hopefully he'll trust me enough when I tell him it's better that he doesn't know. It really is better that way.

It's funny. I don't give a damn what she does. Survival sex isn't a sin, it's a job, and a miserable one at that. I think the World Health Organization is right: sex for money between consenting adults should be decriminalized. Most of the problems associated with it—the real problems, not any moral judgements: the violence, the trafficking, the abuse—exist only because the work has been forced underground. It's not anything intrinsic about the work itself.

So I don't care at all what my client does for her living. I don't really care that the DA or the chief of police use the services of a prostitute. That's their private affair. None of that matters to me. But they can't see it that way. Even if they could, the public, bless their prurient little hearts, would never forgive them. The very pressure they have put on prostitution, all the stigma and punitive laws, it's all come home to roost now. They are hoisted on their own petard.

Oh my! This has gotten the voices fired up, of course. And Max has let me know I'm about to cut my own throat. It's a gamble, that's for sure. He's right: if this goes south, I'm ruined. Even if everything works out, I'll have a mark on my head forever—a mark known only to the DA and the chief. Dangerous. But, damn it, it's the right thing to do. Max can go to hell (I'm sure he'll meet me there). Let the mutterers fume; I've got to do this.

Monday, July 17

I don't normally meet with the District Attorney. When working out a plea bargain, I meet with one of the prosecutors who work for him, whoever will be trying the particular case. That's the way it worked years ago when I was one of those prosecutors, too, working for this DA's predecessor.

This morning, though, was different. I called him first thing. Well, almost first thing. It took me quite a while to work up the nerve. Max was telling me it was the end of my career, and the wordless voices were working themselves into a frenzy. When I finally did call, I had to fight the urge to shout over the angry turbulent mutterings of my private Greek chorus.

Me: Good morning. I need to meet with you regarding the —— — case.

DA: I'm not familiar with that case. You need to talk with the prosecutor. You know the drill.

Me: No, I need to talk with you, sir. And I believe you *are* familiar with the case, and I know why.

DA: Excuse me?

Me: I know you've seen the defendant on a weekly—or more—basis for some time now. We both know why, and what it will mean if word gets out about it.

DA: I assure you, I have no idea what you are...

Me (interrupting, God help me!): Come on, sir, let's not play games.

DA: I don't know what this person has been telling you, but whatever it is, it's baseless. No one will believe her.

Me: Her? So you do know who I'm talking about. And for the record, she didn't tell me, sir, I found out on my own. We both know exactly what I'm talking about.

DA: Are you threatening me?

Me: I would never threaten you sir. And if you would really prefer, I will discuss the matter with the prosecutor. But I believe it would be in your best interest for me to discuss the matter

privately with you, and I would like to afford you that opportunity.

DA: I don't know what lies that whore told you, counselor, but
I have nothing to discuss.

Me: Thank you for confirming that you know what we are
talking about, sir. As I stated already, the defendant is not the
source of my information, though she has confirmed it. Reluctantly, I might add.

DA: And just what is the source of this supposed information?

Me: I'd really rather not disclose my sources, sir. I'm sure you
understand. I'll just say that they are beyond reproach and I trust
them implicitly.

DA: And what do you intend to do with this information you
claim to know?

Me: That, sir, is up to you. If the matter goes to trial, I am
prepared to make it a matter of record.

DA: Sworn testimony of whores and other criminals, I pre-
sume?

Me: I'm not prepared to divulge the nature of what I may reveal at this time. Suffice it to say that I possess evidence that
would reflect badly on those connected to the case.

DA: Meaning me.

Me: If you say so.

DA: What do you think you know?

Me: Do you really want to discuss it over an open telephone
line, sir? I personally have no problem with that, but I want to
respect your privacy.

DA: I doubt that.... Very well. Come to my office at ten. Bring
your evidence.

Me: I will see you at ten, sir. But my evidence remains mine
for now. I will tell you what I know to be true, and you can judge
for yourself if you want the manner of my knowing to be revealed
in court, based on its accuracy and detail.

DA: I won't be bullied, Taylor.

Me: I wouldn't dream of it, sir. I'm merely trying to look out
for your best interests.

DA: I doubt that, too. I'll see you at ten.

Me: Goodbye, sir. See you then.

I hung up the phone and glanced at the wall. It was covered with eyes, half of them wide with alarm and the others deeply enraged. There were several gaping maws, too. My hands were shaking and my knees felt weak. I had an hour and a half before my meeting with the DA, so I went for a walk, hoping it would help calm me down.

Max joined me on my walk—I was pretty much expecting that.

"So, shithead, you put your foot in it this time, didn't you? Suppose he calls your little bluff? What then? Are you going to tell the court that everything you know came from two birds? You pretend to have evidence, but you don't have shit. You can put the whore on the stand, but nobody will believe her, or her roommate. You're screwed six ways from Sunday."

There was more, of course. I didn't reply. What could I say? He was right. It didn't help with the shakes.

At precisely ten o'clock I showed up in the DA's office with nothing but a pad of paper with some notes on it. The walls in his reception area were full of eyes that I tried to ignore. Max had wound down, but I could feel he was just waiting to lay into me again. I felt a wreck, but I somehow managed to hold it together.

The DA came out as soon as his executive assistant let him know I was there, and ushered me into his office. He told the assistant that he was not to be disturbed for any reason until I left. The EA didn't bat an eye. Good man, that.

As the door shut behind me, I noted the soundproofing around it. This wasn't the first private conversation held here, certainly. He guided me to the small meeting table at the far end of the room from the door. We sat facing each other across the table.

DA: So, you have something to share with me?

Me: I do, sir. I know that you have had frequent assignations with my client at her apartment. *(I made as if to check my notes, though I knew this speech by heart. I had rehearsed it several times this morning.)* You went there weekly, mostly on Tuesdays, sometimes twice in a week—Fridays, generally. You missed one full week a couple months ago, I believe you may have been on vacation then, out of town with your wife? You stay for about 45 minutes each time, and leave a bit lighter in the wallet but presumably satisfied in other ways.

DA: You believe this information?

Me: I have every reason to believe it, sir. I know it to be true.

DA: And you can prove it?

Me: Are you willing to risk that I might?

DA: I'm not admitting anything, but suppose I drop the felony charge....

Me: That's a start, but not nearly enough, sir. I know also that you tried to interest our chief of police in the services of my client. You made the appointment for him, but she found out who he was first, and did not let him in. They exchanged words, and he responded by effectively shutting down her business, starving her out. When she was desperate enough, he sent in an undercover, and that was how you got your charges.

DA: An interesting theory.

Me: More than a theory, sir. It's true, every word of it. I believe you already know that.

DA: You have pictures?

Me: I have evidence. The nature of that evidence will be apparent when it is brought out in court, if that should prove necessary. I hope it will not.

DA: What are you proposing?

Me: Drop all charges and have the police turn their usual blind eye to her business dealings. Indefinitely. I will follow up with her periodically and will be watching for any sort of retaliation. The nature of my information is such that it could be brought forward at any time, you know.

DA: What is she to you? Why are you doing this? Looking for some free tail for yourself?

Me: I am not interested in her services. She is a client. That should be enough. I am doing this because it is my job to defend my clients regardless of their circumstances... or those of their accusers.

DA: You're not defending her. You are telling me to drop the charges. You've got a lot of damn gall, counselor.

Me: No, sir. I'm most definitely defending her, and at the same time providing you a favor. I'm offering to sit on my information indefinitely if you will drop the charges *and* instruct our dear police chief to cease any interest in my client, her roommate, and their source of livelihood. Failing that, the matter will be brought to trial in open court.

DA: That's no favor. I can't tell the chief what to do. He doesn't work for me.

Me: I understand that, sir, but you can let him know the nature of the information I hold, and I'm sure you can discuss with him what will happen to both of you if that information were to come out in open court. A trial where I think I can guarantee the press will be present. I fear I would have to call both of you as material witnesses. That would be sure to get somebody's attention.

DA: He'll tell you to go to hell.

Me: That's probably true, and it wouldn't be the first time, but it would be unfortunate. For him and for you. As for me, I'm fine either way; I expect to be consigned to hell, anyway. I feel confident that my client will also be fine either way, at least compared to the chief... and you. I'm sure you can impress the chief with the need to concede this battle.

DA: That was a threat.

Me: Merely an observation. As I said, you are free to doubt me if you think my information is flawed. But as we both know, it is accurate, and given that I'm ready, willing, and able to present it in trial, I believe you and the chief would be best served by acceding to my offer.

DA: Hmmph. I will talk to him. I can't promise anything, mind you. But I understand your offer. I'll get back to you.

Me: I need not remind you, sir, that time is of the essence.

DA: You need not. I'll get back to you by end of day tomorrow at the latest.

Me: That will do nicely, sir. Thank you for your time.

DA: Hmmph. You'll hear from me.

I stood up to go. As I turned my back on him to walk toward the door, he spoke up again.

DA: And counselor?

Me (turning): Yes, sir?

DA: I appreciate your discretion.

Me: Of course, sir.

How did I ever have the balls to do that? I haven't stopped shaking since I left the DA's office an hour ago. I think I actually managed to scare Max, too. He hasn't harassed me, anyway. Even the muttering chorus was shocked into silence for a bit, but they're back now and clearly pretty agitated by all this. We'll see what tomorrow brings.

Wednesday, July 19

As of this morning, I hadn't heard anything back from the DA. The mutterers had grown more and more agitated since Monday afternoon, and the eyes and mouths had multiplied. I'd even caught a few words amongst the jumble: "disaster," "payback," "stupid," "prison," that sort of thing. Max was talkative, too, after he got over the initial shock of my performance with the DA. That did nothing to help me remain calm.

"Well, you've put your foot in it this time, shithead. Trying to pressure the DA *and* the police chief? How dumb can you get? They won't stand for that, you know. They will own you. You will never win another case. You won't even get any clients. You'll lose your job, your home, everything. You might as well start praying they just put a bullet in your head. That's not so unlikely, you know. It would be easier for them and less painful for you than any of the other shit they can do to you. What they *will* do to you. You poor dumb motherfucker. You did this to yourself." That was typical. There was lots more of it.

Mia was there, too. She hasn't spoken to me in years, and I thought she was gone. "Billie, you poor boy. You're being very brave facing things so much bigger than you. I only hope bravery is enough. You know I'm always here for you. No matter what happens, I'll be here. Remember that. Remember me!" Her usual infantilizing pabulum, full of comfort but devoid of solutions. Her mothering always managed to make me feel worse rather than better. Oh, Mia, why have you come back?

I was very nervous about not receiving any word from the DA. He had promised to get back to me by end-of-day yesterday. I felt certain he was calling my bluff. Well, not a bluff, but my "evidence" isn't exactly admissible in court. I didn't dare call him again; he'd hear my fear. At around 10:30 this morning, in desperation, I logged on to the court website to check on the case and see if anything had changed... and the case was gone. Not dismissed, just gone. I don't know how that was done, but it's like the charges never existed. The police records show that my client was arrested, but now show that she was released without charges. No record of the arraignment at all. Everything is just gone.

I was more than a little shocked by this. Obviously records can be corrected when there has been an error, and I'm guessing that's how this was done, but I've never seen a complete erasure like this. I've heard of it, of course, in other cities, but never here. I suppose that's all the response I'll get from the DA or the chief on the matter. Discretion taken to its limit. That's fine—they know I will be watching. My client should have nothing to worry about. I hope.

I'm less certain about myself. Did I really manage to intimidate the District Attorney so thoroughly? Were he and the chief of police so completely cowed? How would that play out for me? Max carries things to extremes, but his image of a bullet to the back of my head doesn't seem so far-fetched. And, of course, I can't tell anyone about this. Certainly not Mike. Not the whole story, anyway.

I did tell my client, of course. I called her up around 11:30, after I had verified as well as I could that everything was truly gone. I just asked her to meet me for lunch. I saw a lot of wide eyes and actively speaking mouths on the wall as I did that, but I did my best to ignore them. Fortunately she agreed right away to meet me.

Tempest was harder to ignore. As soon as I hung up the phone, she spoke up. "She's going to be real grateful, you know. She's going to feel like she owes you a lot—she *does* owe you a lot. And she only has one coin to offer, you know. Are you going to be heartless and turn her down? It would make her feel better. It will make you feel better. There's no reason not to. You don't even need to ask, honey, just don't say no."

I have to admit she did make a tempting argument, but the last thing I needed was to give the DA or chief the opportunity to counter my evidence with some of their own. No, I will only be meeting my client in very public locations, and everything will be very professional. My profession, not hers.

The lunch meeting went well. She was thrilled with the news once she realized what I was telling her and that it was all true. I couldn't blame her for thinking I was playing a cruel joke on her at first. I hardly believed it myself. I'd seen the charges with my own eyes yesterday. She'd heard the judge state the charges at her arraignment. Now there was no record of any of that.

I explained to her that part of the deal was a blind eye from the police toward her activities—that her apartment was now the safest place in the city to carry out her business transactions. And I promised her that I would be available, *pro bono*, if anything changed. I told her I wanted to meet with her regularly and publicly so they could see that I wasn't going to let it go. So that they knew they couldn't just make her vanish while I wasn't watching. We agreed to lunch every two weeks for now, perhaps lengthening the time later. She has my card and I gave her my private cell number and told her to call any time, day or night, if she had any legal hassles.

I spent the whole lunch looking around for anyone watching us. Anyone from the DA's office, or maybe off-duty cops. I didn't see anyone, but that doesn't mean they weren't there. I had purposely chosen a busy and noisy restaurant near her—Gino's—both to be seen and to have the paradoxical privacy that a quiet conversation in a noisy restaurant provides. Even though I didn't see anyone, I'm sure we were noticed. That's not a bad thing.

And Tempest was wrong; she didn't make any offers. I'm sure if I had asked, she'd have been only too willing, but she had enough self-respect to keep everything businesslike. She did cry when she realized this was all behind her—who wouldn't?—but she recovered quickly. I got a hug from her after lunch was done, and a quick kiss on the cheek, but it was friendly and chaste.

I'm still nervous, waiting for the attack I'm sure is coming, but I guess the DA and chief are nervous, too. Maybe this mutual angst will eventually lead to some sort of lasting détente. I can only hope. Meanwhile, this counts as another check in the win column. I told Mike the charges had all been dropped—close enough to the truth—with a bare minimum of my time. He didn't press for details, and I didn't offer any.

Tomorrow is my appointment with Dr. Filtner. The Ingrezza seems to be helping. Despite the tension of the last few days, the tics seem no worse. Normally I would expect all this uncertainty to exacerbate things, but I've been pretty steady at the same level as before. I'm excited to go up to the full dosage.

I'm less excited about increasing the Risperidone, but I'm sure she is going to press for that, too. I have to admit the recent activity from Max, Tempest, and now Mia all make me less inclined to fight her about it. They have been distracting for sure, and reminiscent of the bad times before Risperidone. If I could be a little less aware of them, that would be enough. I don't need the dullness and fog that come with that, though. And I can't risk being unable to understand Mara and Kala, as has happened before. I'm especially wary now when I'm looking for a new case. This is when I need Mara and Kala most.

Psychiatric Progress Notes

Patient Name: William "Rip" Taylor

Date: July 20, 2017

Diagnoses:
Schizophrenia (Paranoid) *F20.0*
Tardive Dyskinesia (subacute, drug-induced) *G24.01*

Medication List:
Risperidone 4 mg PO SID (QHS)
Ingrezza 40 mg PO SID (QHS)

Physical Findings and Mental Status:
Vitals: Unremarkable.
Mental Status: Alert and oriented to person, place, and time.
Comportment: Well-groomed, alert posture, unremarkable.
Mood and affect: Cooperative and situationally appropriate.
Ability to concentrate: Unremarkable.
Tone and rate of speech: Appropriate and unhurried.
Danger to self/others: None.

Symptoms:

Mr. Taylor reports positive symptoms of schizophrenia are unchanged and manageable. Negative and cognitive symptoms also unchanged and manageable.

Mr. Taylor reports that he sees some improvement already in the tardive dyskinesia, though this was not evident to me. He states that he has greater control over the involuntary tics.

Mr. Taylor reported no side-effects of the new medication (Ingrezza) other than possibly some dry-mouth, which was of no real concern to him.

Interventions:

I continued to challenge Mr. Taylor's conception that any level of positive symptoms (visual and auditory hallucinations) was acceptable. I pressed him to list all of the hallucinations he was experiencing, and encouraged him to monitor them and bring a list at each appointment.

We discussed at length a moderate increase in the Risperidone dose since the Ingrezza was well-tolerated.

We discussed increasing the Ingrezza to 80 mg daily as planned.

Patient Response to Interventions:

Mr. Taylor is unusually resistant to extinguishing all hallucinations, even beyond what is sometimes seen with long-duration schizophrenia. Body-language and voice cues suggest that he is withholding information about positive symptoms.

Mr. Taylor reported that this is a stressful time at his work. His last case involved some personal risk that he could not (or would not?) elaborate upon, and he is now preparing to start a new case. He was overtly amenable to listing his symptoms, but I anticipate both compliance and accuracy being issues.

Mr. Taylor remains quite resistant to increasing the dosage of the antipsychotic medication. He continues to be overly concerned with any cognitive or sensory dulling from the medication despite my assurances to the contrary. He also fears worsening of the tardive dyskinesia from extrapyramidal side effects. My recommendation of doubling his risperidone dosage was met with a flat refusal, as was any consideration of an alternative medication. He stated, "My career is too critical to play around with dosage willy-nilly. It wouldn't be fair to me or my clients. I know how to cope with things as they are, and I don't want to mess with that." After a lengthy and sometimes heated discussion, he grudgingly accepted a modest increase in the Risperidone dosage.

Conversely, Mr. Taylor was very enthusiastic about increasing the dosage of the Ingrezza. As noted previously, he considers the tardive dyskinesia his chief complaint and is excited to do anything to moderate its effects.

Clinical Impressions:

Mr. Taylor is resistant to any change that affects his primary diagnosis (schizophrenia). Attachment to hallucinations and delusions is not uncommon in patients with a long history of active symptoms, but it will need to be addressed if he is to make further progress towards a normal life.

He appears to be managing his symptoms adequately, though not without some distress. Paranoia and anxiety do not appear severe at this time, though they are definitely present. I would characterize his mental status as "fragile stability" and believe steps must be taken to make his position less precarious.

Ingrezza appears to be well-tolerated and possibly even marginally effective at this early stage.

Plan:

Increase the Risperidone dosage from 4 mg to 6 mg daily, and also increase the Ingrezza dosage to the maintenance level of 80 mg daily, both medications taken in the evening before bed. Effects of both will be monitored at future appointments, with an eventual goal of complete extinguishment of hallucinations and delusions (Risperidone), and a marked decrease in extrapyramidal symptoms (Ingrezza).

Next appointment in two weeks.

Rx:

Risperidone 6 mg PO SID (QHS), Q 30
Ingrezza 80 mg PO SID (QHS), Q 30

Signed:

JoAnne Filtner, M.D., Ph.D.

Friday, July 21

Max and the others have left me alone since my last entry, and even the mutterers seem quieter. It's too soon for that to be the meds, so they must be plotting something. Whatever they are planning, I'm thankful for the respite, and hopeful that things will remain like this for a while. I have noticed more hawks circling than normal, though. They are watching me. They must know about the new threat hanging over me and are just waiting for something to happen. Opportunistic bastards.

I started on the full 80 mg dose of Ingrezza last evening, and also an increased dose of Risperidone—6 mg instead of 4. I'm excited about the first, but worried about the second. This morning the brain fog did seem a little bit thicker, but that may have been my imagination. As usual, it had mostly lifted around mid-morning, and I was able to get things done after that. Usually the dulling is worst for the first couple weeks after I increase dosage and then eases as I adjust. It had better!

Dr. Filtner is still talking about increasing the Risperidone even more or maybe trying something new, and she also talked about adding an antidepressant. I haven't told her about Max or any of the others, but I think she senses something. I really don't want to mess with the meds any more than she already has. It took too long to find this balance point. We'll see how the present increase goes—I'm nervous enough about that.

I spent today putting the *pro bono* case to bed, including a sealed envelope I placed in the file. This envelope contains a description of all the events prior to the arrest as I understand them. Just that. No description of the source of this information, of course, and nothing about the discussion I had with the DA. And no evidence—what evidence could I leave? Instructions on the outside of the envelope indicate it should only be opened by me. That sort of thing is uncommon, but not completely unheard of in certain sensitive cases. Those instructions aren't binding of course—the files belong to the firm—but they should be respected as long as I'm around. If something does happen to me, it would only be opened by Mike or maybe one of the other senior partners. I may change my mind and remove it later, but for now it feels like an insurance policy.

There has been no communication from either the DA or the police chief, but I really am not expecting any now. I checked again today and the charges are still gone from the system. I included a screen shot showing that (with today's date) in the sealed envelope.

It's tough knowing exactly how to characterize this case. I have to record what I did and account for my time, especially since it's *pro bono*, but it now looks like I was working on a non-case. Not even dropped charges. It has the appearance of me responding to a first phone call after an arrest, as there is no official record of anything beyond that. While that's unusual, it's not really suspicious. If noticed, it would raise some eyebrows and make people wonder what the connection was, but not much else. I can't write up any sort of explanation, either—at least not a true one. I can only hope nobody pays much attention to the case at all. As long as everything stays quiet, nobody will. But what a keg of gunpowder to be sitting on!

Next week I'll start interviewing for the next case, but I'm taking Wednesday off to go to Central City Opera's performance of *Carmen*. It's gotten great reviews, and I'm excited to hear what they do with it. I glanced at some of the case files today, and there are several interesting cases. I'm sure it will take through Tuesday to even finish talking to the potential clients, more likely going into Thursday. I told Mike I'd try and have a decision by the end of the week. He'd like it sooner, of course, but as quickly as this last case wrapped up, he's not really complaining.

Mara and Kala stopped by this evening, as they often do, but they seemed troubled and left fairly quickly. They wouldn't tell me what was bothering them, but it's unusual to see them acting uncomfortable. Out of character. Perhaps it's the increased hawk activity lately. It's hard to know whether they are responding as birds or as something more. They seemed distant or distracted, and that scares me—whatever the cause.

With the new meds, I'm not going to make any plans for this weekend (not that I often do, anyway). I'll try and sleep more and get past the start-up side effects of the new dose so I'm better able to function on Monday. That's the theory, anyway. I must admit I'm feeling tired already, and I haven't even taken tonight's dose. A quick dinner, then, and something light before bed, maybe a little *Don Giovanni*. Mozart usually provides me a good rest.

Monday, July 24

Well, after a weekend spent mostly in bed, I'm feeling a little more energetic today. The morning was still tough—lots of mental fog. But time and coffee worked their magic and I felt more or less human by 10:30. Unfortunately, my first interview was at 9 at the county jail, when I was still staggering like I'd just come off a three day bender. It's good the guards know me, or I might not have gotten in to see my potential client. I'm sure he thought me a little slow, and wondered if he might be better off with a public defender—not that he would be eligible for one. Too well off, so he has to hire an attorney, either us or someone else.

Ah well, his wasn't that interesting a case. A simple assault when he was more than half drunk. So was the other guy. Doesn't look like there were any witnesses to the start of the fight, so who knows who started it? They both got arrested and are facing the same charges, and neither one has any prior convictions. I'd bet dollars to donuts they'll both get off with a self-defense plea claiming the other one threw the first punch. They may even both believe that. Frankly, any one of our junior partners can handle this case, and maybe the expense of that defense will teach him a lesson. Probably not, though, if experience has taught me anything.

By the time I got back to the office for the second interview, I was feeling more lucid. I think the Ingrezza is starting to help, too. The chewing and lip smacking seem much reduced to me, and there are fewer arm jerks. Just that damned blink. The tics have become a significant liability in the courtroom. Even if the judge and prosecutor know what it is and are used to it, it affects the jury. Sometimes I can use that to my advantage, but too often it works against me. My clients deserve better. It's still early, though, and hopefully the Ingrezza will do more as time goes on.

From the file, the second interview looked like it could be interesting. Embezzlement charges—something you don't see every day—and a woman as the defendant, which is even rarer.

Most embezzlers are men. After meeting with her, though, I wouldn't touch it with a ten foot pole. She didn't exactly admit guilt, but it's clear she did it and is just foolish enough to think she'd get away with it. The prosecutor has her dead to rights. The most she can hope for is some sort of plea bargain to give dirt on somebody else, but she doesn't have much to offer that way, either.

I'm going to advise that nobody take the case, but I doubt that will fly. It might not be a bad one for a new attorney to learn negotiation tactics; negotiating to mitigate a loss, which is sometimes all you can do. That's a hard lesson, but an important one. Unfortunately, the clients never appreciate your efforts, which just makes it harder.

The afternoon cases were both dull. Worth defending, certainly, but not anything I want to pursue. Hopefully, someone else can pick them up. I think one attorney could handle them both, as neither looks like it will require a lot of legwork. As long as the trial dates don't collide, it should work out. Even if they do, most judges will grant a continuance for that.

I'm definitely going to have to have some interviews on Thursday. Tomorrow is full, and there are a couple more potential clients I want to visit with beyond that. I'm not going to let it interfere with *Carmen* on Wednesday, though. Maybe I could come in for the morning, but I want to have time to relax in Central City before the show. If I leave right after lunch, that might just work, but nothing later. And as much as the drug fog is kicking my butt in the mornings, I'm going to have to drive home after the show and before taking my meds which will make for a late evening. Given that, Thursday probably won't start for me until the afternoon. Maybe I'll just spend the night there—if I can find a room. We'll see if I make my Friday deadline for deciding. I'm not giving up my *Carmen*, in any case!

There was no sign of Max or Tempest or any of the others this weekend or today, and the mutterers were pretty quiet, too. Just the usual eyes and mouths—they'd frown and scowl whenever something struck them wrong, but it would pass quickly. They didn't multiply, either, which was a nice switch from the recent past. I'm not sure if they're more relaxed or if they're plotting something. Where do they go when they aren't here, anyway?

That's the good news. As for the other, Mara and Kala stayed away all weekend. There were other jays at the feeders, and the usual other birds, but not Mara and Kala. They came to the window this evening as usual, but there was hardly any conversation—just a lot of calls and croaks. What few words there were I found disturbing:

Kala: You're hard to find.

Me: I'm right here where I've always been.

Mara: The place is here, but you aren't.

Kala: Yes. We thought you were gone.

Mara: But we saw the other birds.

Kala: So you must be here, but we couldn't find you.

Mara: Not until we were right here.

Kala: Until we could see you.

Me: What do you mean? You find me without seeing me?

Mara: Of course we do.

Kala: We always know where you are.

Mara: Almost always.

Kala: But not now.

Mara: And there was before...

Kala: But not for a long time.

Mara: Until now.

Kala: You're hiding.

Mara: Hardly there at all.

Kala: But we see you.

Mara: Just barely.

Me: I'm right here. I've been here all afternoon. I'm not hiding, I promise you.

Kala: Maybe not.

Mara: But we couldn't see you.

And from that point on they just cawed and shrieked—I couldn't get any more words from them. They ate a few more cashews and flew off still noisily calling back and forth, but without a word to me. The damned falcon screamed right after they left, too, which gave me a fright, but he sounded distant, and it was more a scream of failure or fear, I think.

I'm worried that this is related to the increased Risperidone. The last time my meds were adjusted, things were similar. I still saw Mara and Kala, who came and fed as usual, but they had nothing to say to me. I thought they resented the change—they always seem sensitive to my mental state, somehow. No matter; they came back once I stabilized on the 4 mg dose. But now it's happening again. And this is the first time they've said anything about not finding me. Like it's something different about me, rather than their choice not to speak.

Am I losing my special gift? Does the quieting of the voices spread to Mara and Kala, too? They are different—I know they are. For one thing, I both see them and hear them, and for another, so does everyone else. Oh, the other people don't understand them—that's either my unique talent or it's theirs to direct their words just to me—but others acknowledge the jays, commenting on how greedy or noisy they are. Maybe that gift of understanding is tied up with the perceptive ability to hear Max and the rest, and to see the eyes and mouths on the walls. I can't afford to lose Mara and Kala. If this doesn't resolve, I'll have to go back to 4 mg, whatever Dr. Filtner says. I'd sooner cut my 6 mg pills in half and take just 3 mg than do without my friends and advisors.

I'll give it a little time, a couple weeks, maybe. After all, my perception did come back last time after I adjusted. I'm just interviewing right now, and regardless of what I pick, it will probably be a bit before the case heats up. I prefer to confer with Mara and Kala before I choose a case, but my instincts have generally been good. The jays haven't contradicted my initial assessments in a year or more. But I want an interesting and worthwhile case, and that means I will want... no, I will *need* their help.

Damn these doctors and their single-minded worship of blind uniformity! Just once, I'd like to find one that would help me be my own self instead of trying to cram me into their inflexible mold. They keep wanting to fix me. I'm not broken, dammit!

Tuesday, July 25

I don't know if it's just the meds or if I'm coming down with something, but today had a really rough start. I could barely make coffee this morning. I'd wander into a room and have no idea why I was there. I ended up cancelling both morning appointments, which means I probably won't make my Friday deadline. I just hope I'm good enough to drive the two hours to Central City tomorrow. The fog did lift around noon, though I still feel like I'm moving through molasses.

I pulled myself together enough to make the afternoon interviews. One case looks pretty interesting, a larceny case that seems a bit of a reach for the prosecution. The defendant, Butch Marner, was one of two people who work the late shift at the warehouse for Wilderness Experience, a high end chain that caters to well-off climbers, hikers, kayakers, and campers. Marner and his coworker would gather the orders that came in during the day from each of the retail stores and assemble the inventory to be trucked out to the stores before they opened the next day. They also placed the wholesale orders for all the merchandise needed to keep their warehouse inventory up. Typical supply-chain stuff. The day shift took care of receiving the inventory from the suppliers and stocking the warehouse, checking everything off against the orders the night shift had placed. With all the retail stores, it takes two people a full overnight shift to get all the orders gathered, palletized, and ready to deliver during the next morning.

During the annual inventory of the warehouse, the auditors discovered a problem. A store that had been closed the previous year was still placing orders. There were, of course, no deliveries occurring to the store (since it didn't exist), and the store's inventory was never checked (ditto), but the ordered merchandise disappeared from the warehouse every night, just as if. As a result, roughly $750,000 worth of inventory had been ordered, received at the warehouse, and supposedly delivered to this non-existent store. A clever little scheme that avoided the normal day-to-day checks and balances, though it was inevitably caught during the annual inventory when the recorded deliveries to the stores were matched against their sales.

Marner claims to know nothing about the scheme or the closed store. Curiously, his coworker, Rick Palermo, disappeared about a week before the inventory—just didn't show up to work one Monday and hasn't been seen since. You would think that Palermo would be the obvious suspect, especially since his car—a large SUV—was found abandoned near the Utah border. But the police got a search warrant for Butch Marner, and found a few pieces of the same type of equipment that had been purloined. Marner claims he bought it legitimately, but he doesn't have the receipts (who would?). It's only a couple boxes of climbing equipment, nothing like the cases and cases that had disappeared. It's pricey stuff, but as an employee he gets it basically at wholesale.

As far as I can see, they arrested and charged Marner just because he's around. Unless they have something more, it should be easy to show that Palermo could have done the whole deed himself and then bailed shortly before he knew he'd be found out. Marner assured me that that must be what happened. Not at all your typical case, but one that should be a straightforward win unless something surprising comes up, as it too often does.

There don't appear to be any witnesses nor any surveillance equipment at the warehouse, so I don't see how the state can make its case in the absence of Palermo. I hope to check it out with Mara and Kala—they'll know if he's as innocent as he claims or not—but I have a good feeling about him, somehow. At least I don't sense anything bad, which is as good as it usually gets.

Mara and Kala didn't show up at all today—not too unusual, though I wish they were here, especially as I'll be gone tomorrow. They might find me at home before I leave for Central City, but if not, I won't see them until Thursday at the soonest. I decided to stay overnight in Central City and was able to get a room at The Vintage. I didn't book anything early for Thursday anyway, and I'm wondering now if I should just take the whole day off. If this morning brain fog keeps up, it won't be safe to drive until noon anyway. Mike won't be happy, but he'll just have to deal with it. He was gone by the time I made the decision—he had a late afternoon at court and didn't come back to the office. I left him a note. Normally I'd ask in person, but since I'm not here tomorrow.... This will give him a chance to cool off, anyway.

While the brain fog is bad, the meds do seem to be helping. Max and company haven't uttered a peep, and I'm not even sure they're paying attention to me. Even the mutterers are barely audible now and easily lost amidst the background noise of the air conditioning and city sounds. There was only a single pair of eyes watching me most of the day. That, and one inexpressive mouth that came and went. If anything, this might be working too well. I'm hoping it's the meds that are doing this and not some sort of plot for something bigger coming soon. That's happened before. This feels different, though—less foreboding, maybe. Still, their absence is a little disturbing. I prefer the devil I know.

Wednesday, July 26

The opera was amazing! I've never seen a better live performance of *Carmen*. I'm in heaven! Emily Pulley was fantastic in the title role: I've never seen a more sultry performance. And Adriano Graziani as Don José built and built his character until everyone in the audience was on fire. Michael Mayes was delightfully comic as Escamillo. It was just everything you could want musically and theatrically. The March of the Toreadors was maybe a little understated, but that had more to do with the physical limitations of the stage than anything the actors or director could have done. I am so glad I made the drive up here.

The drive itself was challenging. The day was warm, and by the time I was leaving at 2 PM (after another very difficult morning) a storm was brewing. It stormed the whole first half of the drive, just bucketing down rain, which made for some unnerving miles on I-25. It let up for a bit once I got close to Denver, but then a second storm caught me driving into the mountains on I-70. I was a nervous wreck by the time I arrived. I checked into the hotel and just relaxed there until it was time to go to the opera, rather than hiking or enjoying the town.

I seem to have outrun Max. Normally he would have been chiding me through any kind of rough drive like this. Or maybe it's the meds. Either way, he left me alone again today. And there is just the one pair of eyes, looking out from the wall of my hotel room as if they are bored to death. They stayed away from the opera, thankfully, and there weren't any mouths trying to sing along like I've seen in the past. That can be amusing, but it's awfully distracting.

I'm physically tired—I think partly the meds, but mostly the nerve-wracking drive—but I'm so mentally fired up by the opera, I don't know that I can sleep. I think I'll head down to the bar for a nightcap and see if that can't help me get to sleep.

* * *

Update: Back in the room. The bar was having a karaoke night, and I couldn't handle the inept singing to brainless country tunes. Not when I still had Bizet arching through my brain. I got a brandy to go (not exactly kosher, but a 100% tip works wonders), and I am going to enjoy it right here in the quiet of my room—not quiet at all as I replay the highlights of the evening in my head. I took my meds already, swallowing them with brandy.

Thursday, July 27

OK, these mornings are getting old. Today was a little better, but I still wasn't really human until probably 10:30. I'm glad I decided to take the whole day off, even though Mike will doubtless give me a hard time about it tomorrow. I spent the morning bringing myself to something like consciousness with lots of coffee, and then spent a couple hours walking around Central City and feeding the local birds in the park. There were jays there that could have been Mara and Kala's twins, but they didn't say a word—just squawks and squabbles fighting over the cashews.

It was hot there, even with the altitude, so I was pretty well ready to be done by three o'clock. I drove back through threatening skies and occasional patches of wet pavement, but no real rain. Much easier on the nerves than yesterday's drive through the storms. I didn't even stop by the office, but came straight home. After I relaxed a bit, I went out to the yard a little before sundown. The feeders were empty from a day's inattention, so I filled them and hand-fed the braver birds while the hummingbirds zinged around and fought over their late dinner. No sign of Mara and Kala, but they may have figured I was gone for another day. I went inside about 30 minutes after sundown when the night hawks began to scream and all the daytime birds had gone to roost.

I made some dinner—Stouffer's lasagna to the rescue!—and looked over my notes for tomorrow's interviews. A couple possibly interesting cases, but I'm still intrigued by the Marner larceny case. I wish I could consult with Mara and Kala. I expect I'll see them tomorrow. It would be unusual to go that long without them paying me a visit. I miss them.

I don't miss Max and company, though. I'm pleased—and just a little nervous—to say they've still been leaving me alone. The mutterers were mostly quiet again, too, though there are three pair of eyes now watching me write this. Still, that's less attention than there often is, and they don't seem too unhappy. If anything, they seem kind of bored. I'm almost wondering if I need to do something to entertain them. Almost. Well, no, not really. If they stay bored, maybe they'll leave me alone.

I still have *Carmen* in my head—I won't even listen to anything else just so that I can savor the memories of that glorious performance. It's sure to be the highlight of the summer, if not the whole year.

Friday, July 28

Today's been like one of those bad news, good news, bad news jokes. The bad news is that I woke up in a complete brain fog when the alarm went off. It must have taken me two or three minutes just to figure out how to turn it off. I forgot to make coffee before taking my shower—almost forgot to shower, to be honest. As a result I was late to my first appointment, something I never do and hate myself for having done this time.

The good news is that once I got there I started feeling more clear-headed. So maybe the brain fog is improving as I get adjusted to the new med dosage. I was able to concentrate pretty well on the interviews, well enough to know that I wouldn't bother with them. None of these cases were as interesting as the Marner case, and the afternoon ones were real train wrecks. I'm advising against the firm taking either of those, and the morning interviews are fine for junior partners—walks in the park, really.

The bad news was that Mike came by at 4:30 pressuring me to make a decision so I can start on the new case first thing Monday. I don't know why he's so gung ho when I've been turning cases over so quickly, but he was really riding me. I told him I had to do a little more research, but that I'd have a decision on his desk before I left the building.

The good news is that I was pretty sure I knew what I wanted, so Mike's ultimatum wasn't so bad. I like the Marner case. He may be guilty, of course, but if so, he hides it well. It feels like it should be an easy fight to win the case, but something tells me there's a reason the DA brought the charges. They must have some reason to think they can make them stick. I don't know what they know, but there must be something. Presumably it will come out in discovery. I smell a good fight!

The bad news—the really bad news—is about Mara and Kala. I held out from just telling Mike I was going with the Marner case so I could consult with Mara and Kala this evening before committing. They showed up about a quarter to six, pretty much as usual. At least I'm assuming it's them. It definitely looked like them, and they came right to my office window as usual. But these were just ordinary jays. If it *was* Mara and Kala, they had nothing to say to me. When I talked to them they'd both cock their heads and listen, just like normal, but then they'd just squawk back and forth at each other afterwards between bites of cashews. No words for me, not one.

I'm afraid the meds have robbed me of them. This happened before, but it was temporary. I can only hope it's temporary this time. I can sense this is going to be a challenging case, and without them, it will be a lot more so.

It's almost a full week before my next appointment with Dr. Filtner. If Mara and Kala aren't back by then, I'm going to be pushing hard to drop the dose back on the Risperidone. There's a court date of August 7, a week from Monday, for discovery, with the actual trial scheduled for a week later on Wednesday, August 16. Those dates could shift, of course, depending on what gets found during discovery, but time is definitely of the essence here.

The good news, sort of, is that I'm being left almost completely alone otherwise. The mutterers are nothing more than easily ignored whispers now. Any background noise at all drowns them out entirely. And there's just been the one pair of eyes, and they've been only casually interested in me all day. At times I think they were sleeping; at least, when I looked, the eyes were closed. Could that mean they were listening instead? I haven't seen ears, but I'm not sure I would. Somehow, the eyes have reacted to conversations in the past. It could be the meds, but I feel like there's something else going on. Something building that I can't quite sense.

I don't have the feedback I'm used to, and it's driving me crazy. I have no way to prepare for what my special chorus will bring me. Because they will bring something. They never go away entirely. They'll be back, and if I don't have some warning, it could be a major mess. Damn Dr. Filtner for messing with things!

And now, the worst news is that it's dark. The big hawks and that damned peregrine are gone to roost, but the night hawks are out, and so are those deadly silent owls. If Mara and Kala have been stricken dumb, how will that affect their ability to escape these predators? They've eluded fate for so long—twice a normal lifetime!—but if they are compromised now, who knows? I fear for them and thus for myself.

Well, there's nothing more to it. That must have been Mara and Kala that stopped by this evening, but either they have lost the gift of language, or I've lost the gift of understanding. Either way, it's a disaster. I'll leave the note on Mike's desk saying I'm taking the Marner case, and we'll see what the next week brings. I'm going to spend the weekend resting and seeing if I can't at least get the brain fog behind me a bit. Hopefully Mara and Kala will visit this weekend and be back to their normal talkative selves.

I have a bad feeling about this.

Sunday, July 30

Disaster! Mara and Kala—or at least two jays that look just like them—visited both yesterday and today. Lots of squawking back and forth, and apparent listening to me, but they said nothing I could understand. Not a single word. I might as well be listening to the buzzy hummingbirds. They acted like they were as frustrated as I was, and they were certainly vocal, but if they can understand me, that's the only direction in which we communicated.

I was in tears by the time they left both days. And both days they left in a hurry when a northern harrier drifted overhead. The alarm went up from whichever bird saw it first, and all the rest of the birds left in a flash. I haven't seen a harrier in a long time, and they were never common here. I hope this doesn't mean they've moved in and claimed this as their territory. Dangerous birds, and brutal hunters. Unlike most hawks, they cruise back and forth low above the ground when hunting. I can see why all the birds flee in fear when they see them. I had to go inside myself for fear it would dive at me in my useless fear. Not because I'm prey—I'm far too big for that, I know—but just because they could. They are well named, these harriers.

Normally when something this bad happens, Mia is there to comfort me with her useless but soothing platitudes. Not a peep from her, either. I was spared Max's haranguing, but I'd even welcome that over this silence. Even the mutterers were struggling to be audible, and the lone pair of eyes would just fade in and out, seemingly without seeing me. My whole world is going dark. All the things that make me *me* are disappearing. My only faithful companions for the last twenty-plus years. Gone.

My head is clearing more, at least. I think I'm going to have to get up a half hour earlier if I'm going to function at work—maybe have a second cup of coffee before going in—but if I do that, I seem able to function more or less at par. Once I get moving, things seem to roll along. And the Ingrezza has made a definite difference. There are still tics, of course. I don't think anything can entirely eliminate them, but I am experiencing a lot of relief now.

Even that feels like a loss, though. As much as I hate the tardive dyskinesia, and as much as it has compromised my life, it remains part of what makes me unique. And now it, like the rest, is abandoning me. I may be more "normal," maybe even more "healthy," but what does that really mean? I'm less me. I'm not the person I know. I don't have the abilities I once had, even if I am free of some of the hurdles I've faced. Instead of dealing with problems I know and have tools to cope with, I'm faced with new challenges that I can't even recognize or name. I don't know who I am and can't even guess at what to bring to bear against these new issues.

I don't even know what I want. I have lost my tether. I'm spinning free, adrift with not even a star to navigate by. I'm sure Dr. Filtner would be thrilled to read this—as if I'd share it! She'd think everything was going great and that I was finally getting "relief" from my symptoms. She, who has never experienced the gifts of schizophrenia, sees it only as an illness. Something to be cured or at least treated. Symptoms in need of relief. But this is not relief. This is torture. This is no different than waking up in a different body or with no memory of the past. This is Kafka's *Metamorphosis*. I am an insect now. Completely unrecognizable, utterly without power, and with no hope of improvement. I am nothing but despair. I am a puddle. I am nothing.

Fuck the meds! This is going to be a long week. I only hope things start getting better soon. I have no more words.

Monday, July 31

I'm a wreck, but at least I'm a productive one. So much of my life is gone now. Work at least fills the time and keeps my mind off my loss. I managed to keep busy during the day, which was great while it lasted.

I set my alarm a half-hour earlier than normal and had a second cup of coffee before leaving my apartment. As a result, I got to work at my usual time and was more or less able to function. The fog, at least, is getting back to something bearable.

Mike came in not long after I got there and wanted to talk about this new case. He has had previous dealings with my client, as a witness in another case. Mike said Marner's a pretty rough customer, and he wouldn't put it past him to have done the robbery. I guess he knows my proclivity for defending only the innocent, and he wanted to make sure I was really down with it. Backing out of a defense part way through can't help but be prejudicial towards the client, and is about the worst thing an attorney can do.

I couldn't exactly tell Mike that I had reservations because my best informants, who just happen to be Steller's jays, aren't talking to me. I allowed that Marner may have participated, but I suspected his role was more the innocent fall guy given Palermo's abrupt disappearance. Mike knows I have a soft spot for that kind of victimization. He nodded and told me to be careful. I assured him I would be. I always am, right?

I got to work finding out everything I could about all the parties involved. Marner had a rap sheet—he admitted as much when I interviewed him—but there was nothing major on it. A couple disorderly conducts, a misdemeanor assault, and a no-contest plea to shoplifting less than a hundred dollars. The last conviction, the assault, was about a year ago. It looked like a bar fight that got out of hand, nothing more.

As Mike said, he was a bit unsavory, but there isn't anything that really points to this scale of larceny. Rather, it makes him the perfect victim as a fall-guy, taking the heat for the theft so that nobody will be looking too hard for Palermo, who turned out to have a similar record of minor infractions.

I checked with the Colorado and Utah State Police, and there had been no sign of Palermo yet, just his abandoned car. No credit card activity, either, and his bank account was untouched—all $137.42 of it. That wouldn't have been worth cleaning out compared to the money he had presumably earned from fencing the pilfered goods over the last year.

I spoke with the owner of Wilderness Experience. He was remarkably helpful, considering I'm defending the person charged with stealing from him. He says he's just interested in getting to the bottom of it, which I heartily agree with. He indicated their records showed that the nonexistent store had been placing orders for the climbing equipment throughout the past year, starting right after inventory was completed and to the tune of about $15,000 of inventory each week. He promised to send me a spreadsheet with all the details.

This definitely makes it sound like an inside job. Somebody knew the company's practices and schedule, and picked the ideal time to do this. Starting right after one year's inventory and closing it out right before the next required internal knowledge. It pretty much has to be either Marner or Palermo (or both), but there is no way to tell which from what I can see. Palermo was the more junior employee, by a few months, but they'd both been working this job for about two and half years.

The goods that were stolen were mostly small metal fittings used in technical climbing: carabiners, belay devices, that sort of thing. These were not your usual sport equipment, but the high-end equipment used by elite climbers: rescue-rated lightweight fittings that are expensive at least as much for the potential liability from their failure as the expense of their construction. They are easy to fence or unload online and would bring good money for the amount of space they took up. There's a good reason Wilderness Experience keeps them in locked cabinets behind the registers that require a manager to open. Again, this points to a well-planned inside job.

But why would the DA chose to prosecute Marner alone? He must have figured it would be impossible for Palermo to have done it all without Marner at least finding out, if not helping. Just moving all the volume of merchandise should have been noticeable. It's possible the inventory got diverted and never arrived at the warehouse, but the paper trail is solid from the vendor to the warehouse, and each item is checked into and out of the warehouse inventory. It really does look like all this stuff got moved out bit by bit throughout the year. Could Palermo have done all that unnoticed as Marner claims? I'm going to have to prove that he could.

The owner confirmed that the wholesale cost was about three quarters of a million, and the retail prices well over a million (nice markup!). The goods would probably fence for something between those values, or they might be sold piecemeal through eBay and the like for something closer to retail. All in all, a likely million-dollar-plus haul.

That could easily be worth the risk to someone so inclined, even if you have to go on the lam as Palermo apparently has. Staying hidden costs money, but not that much. There are plenty of places and ways to disappear if you don't live too high. This was definitely more money than either Marner or Palermo were ever likely to see otherwise.

Those are the basic facts I learned today. I'll meet with Marner again either tomorrow or Wednesday and get more details from him. I hope to meet with Palermo's contacts, too, and start building a witness list. I need to find out more about Palermo. If he was buddies with Marner, he probably was pretty rough, too, so I should be able to paint him as a potential thief.

I worked through most of lunch, just breaking long enough to grab a polish sausage from the food truck. I took it back and ate it at my desk while I reviewed all the materials I had for the case. I was undisturbed, not only by my coworkers, but by all my own distractions. The deafening silence from the various voices continued, and the few eyes that came and went seemed barely interested in me. If I stared at them they would fade away in just a few seconds leaving only blank wall where they had been.

There was a single hawk circling overhead when I grabbed my lunch, but other than that, the raptors seemed to be leaving me alone, too. No harriers, and even the resident peregrine was nowhere to be found. I thought about leaving early, before Mara and Kala would usually come by, but I got busy and lost track of time. They—or their imposters—tapped at my window as usual, but again not a word was spoken that I could understand. I couldn't tell if they seemed agitated by this, or if it was only my own shock and dismay. After about five minutes I couldn't take any more and shooed them off. I closed the window, put my head on my desk, and bawled.

I don't even remember driving home. I haven't eaten dinner, and I'm not hungry. I'm writing this to fill the hole that is ripped in my heart. I am desolate. I can't wait until my appointment on Thursday. I just want my life back. The real me that nobody else can see.

Wednesday, August 2

Tomorrow is my appointment with Dr. Filtner. I have to figure out what I'm going to tell her. I can't go on like this. I left at noon today because I couldn't cope with the silence, but I ended up back at work in the afternoon because it was just as quiet wherever I went. I don't recognize the world anymore. I haven't had a good night's sleep in I don't know how long, and I'm barely eating, except when I gorge myself on junk. As often as not it all comes back up, anyway. My coworkers are beginning to notice. But how do I explain this to the doctor?

She'll ask about my symptoms. Do I tell her the voices are haunting me more? That I'm seeing and hearing new hallucinations? She'll just up my Risperidone, or worse, move me to something more powerful. Do I tell her the truth, that everything is gone? She'll consider that a success, a sign that she's accomplished what she set out to do. No matter that she has ruined my life. I'm now just as blind and deaf as any normal neurotypical joe. Hurrah for normality.

Fuck.

Fuck, fuck, fuck!

The one bit of good news I have is the Ingrezza. It is definitely making a difference, and even she will be able to see that. I'd love to keep on that, but I have to cut back on the Risperidone. Discovery is on Monday, and the trial itself starts just two weeks from today. I could maybe petition the judge for a continuance, but Judge Hobart is notoriously strict about that, and I'll need good and specific justification. He is a firm believer in keeping the wheels of justice turning. Normally I'm in favor of that, but I don't know how I can face a trial when I'm like this.

I guess I can tell Dr. Filtner that the side effects are too severe. The dry mouth and stomach problems—even though they are gone. I can talk about the brain fog, though that's abated for the most part, down to something not much worse than before. She doesn't believe it exists, anyway. If I don't take my dose tonight, but take it in the morning, I'll be extra foggy, but my appointment is at 2. I can't really afford to take the entire day off with the case coming up, and I'm not sure I'll be able to even get to the appointment at 2 if I take the meds too late. I can fake the fog—God knows I've faked the reverse often enough!—but that's risky, too.

I think that's my only option, though. I've got to get my dose back down to 4 mg. I've got to get my life back. The silence is torture. How do neurotypicals even stand it? I think I finally understand the horror of solitary confinement. I'm there now. It is Hell.

It's not even 8:00, but I'm spent. Feeding the birds does nothing for me now; it's just mechanical. Mara and Kala keep coming by—or at least some pair of jays does—but I can't stand listening to them just squawk, and I soon chase them away. Why won't they speak to me? Hell, I'd welcome even Max's abuse now. I haven't even seen any eyes in my apartment tonight. I haven't seen a mouth in days. I'm going to take my meds with four fingers of Scotch and try to sleep, though the abyss of my vacant mind makes that nearly impossible.

What have I become?

Psychiatric Progress Notes

Patient Name: William "Rip" Taylor

Date: August 3, 2017

Diagnoses:
Schizophrenia (Paranoid) *F20.0*
Tardive Dyskinesia (subacute, drug-induced) *G24.01*

Medication List:
Risperidone 6 mg PO SID (QHS)
Ingrezza 80 mg PO SID (QHS)

Physical Findings and Mental Status:
Vitals: Pulse moderately elevated (86), otherwise unremarkable.
Mental Status: Alert and oriented to person, place, and time.
Comportment: Slightly disheveled appearance, pale and with dark circles under his eyes.
Mood and affect: Agitated and defensive.
Ability to concentrate: Extreme focus despite agitation. Hypervigilant.
Tone and rate of speech: Rapid and direct.
Danger to self/others: None.

Symptoms:
Mr. Taylor reports no positive symptoms at all since his last appointment (though his manner and behavior belie this), and he denies that this indicates any change from his previous visit. When pressed specifically about unintelligible murmuring or breakthrough voices and visual hallucinations of eyes and mouths he was immediately defensive and aggressively denied any change, stating "if I said something different before, it was just a way of speaking. Nothing is different."

When discussing negative symptoms, Mr. Taylor indicated that he had a significant increase in somnolence and "morning fog." I asked "if you are sleeping more, then why do you appear to actually be sleep-deprived?" He replied that it must be due to the changes in his medications. He also stated that the tension of working while dealing with these effects was leaving him "really stressed out."

Mr. Taylor seemed noticeably calmer when discussing the symptoms of the tardive dyskinesia, noting that he continued to see improvement and denying any side effects.

Interventions:

I opted not to challenge Mr. Taylor's attachment to his symptoms at this time, given his already agitated state. I attempted instead to address his obviously degraded appearance since his previous visit.

We discussed the risperidone dosage including continuing to increase the dosage. We also discussed the possibility of a brief voluntary hospitalization so that we could better monitor his medication and its effects, including possibly trying an alternative antipsychotic.

We also again discussed adding an anxiolytic (e.g., Xanax).

Patient Response to Interventions:

Mr. Taylor denied that his appearance or deportment was significantly different than his previous appointment, becoming quite agitated and defensive (even aggressive) when pressed about the matter.

Mr. Taylor was strongly resistant to any increase in his risperidone, or any transition to another medication. Voluntary hospitalization was "off the table." He indicated that he was in the midst of an important case with a tight timetable and could not possibly be "out of circulation" for several days. He did acknowledge the need for some dosage of antipsychotic, as he is unable to function without it, but he argued that he was much better served at the lower dose of Risperidone despite his current manifest pyschosis. He repeatedly asked to return to 4 mg of Risperidone, with increasing agitation each time. He was palpably upset with my decision to maintain the Risperidone at 6 mg.

He refused to consider adding an anxiolytic or any other new medication, indicating that if it was prescribed it would go unfilled unless "you lock me up and shove it down my throat."

Clinical Impressions:

Mr. Taylor's condition is markedly degraded and of significant concern. Regardless of his denial and despite the increased dose of Risperidone, it appears that he is presently in a psychotic break. This is not totally unexpected given the previously observed fragile nature of his disease management. This break is most likely induced or at least exacerbated by work-related stress.

I considered involuntary hospitalization, but decided he fell short of the guidance for Baker Act commitment at this time. Nevertheless, I believe hospitalization would be best for him at this point, and it may prove necessary if his condition worsens.

It is possible that his distress is the result of a decrease in the positive symptoms. This has been occasionally observed with long-duration schizophrenia: when patients finally receive an appropriate therapeutic dose, the change in mental state is difficult for them to accommodate at first. This usually resolves fairly quickly, though in some cases it may take up to six months.

It is worth noting that, despite his agitation, Mr. Taylor was better able to maintain eye contact and to focus on the discussion without distraction. I take this as further indication that the risperidone is having the desired effect, reducing the primary hallucinations, and that this psychotic break is transitory in nature.

It is encouraging that Mr. Taylor acknowledges the need for antipsychotics, even in his current state. I am confident that if I continue to prescribe Risperidone at this dose (or even a moderately elevated dose) that he will be compliant and take it rather than do without entirely. He has stated that he has no store of Risperidone beyond the current prescription, and antipsychotics are not generally available as street drugs or through other gray-market sources.

Plan:

Risperidone will be maintained at 6 mg daily. I will prescribe another 30 days to avoid his running out before the next visit, as I feel that would be very detrimental to his condition.

Ingrezza will be maintained at 80 mg daily.

Next appointment in two weeks to reassess progress.

Rx:

Risperidone 6 mg PO SID (QHS), Q 30

Signed:

JoAnne Filtner, M.D., Ph.D.

Thursday, August 3

Fuck Dr. Filtner! She was completely unwilling to listen to me today, and refused to lower the dose of Risperidone despite everything I said. I made it very clear that I could not function at the 6 mg dosage, but she prattled on about giving my system time to adapt to the increased dosage and blah, blah, blah. Argh! A typical shrink, convinced that the only goal is to reduce every patient to such a medicated state that they are unable to complain about anything. They may be unable to function, but that doesn't matter; at least they aren't complaining. No compassion. No understanding. No ability to listen. A complete waste of time and money—but unfortunately the only source for the Risperidone I need.

I suppose I should begin looking for another psychiatrist. I hate going through that, though. We have another appointment in two weeks. I'll try again then, I suppose. Surely she must listen to me eventually. See that the 6 mg dose is leaving me unable to function. I must figure out how to convince her. Damn her! She should be working to help me, not forcing me to find ways to work around her.

She's keeping me at 6 mg, and I filled the new scrip right away, even though I still have two weeks' worth from the previous prescription. She seemed to forget that, and I wasn't going to remind her. I also bought a pill splitter at the pharmacy. Starting tonight I'm going to cut the pills in half and take just 3 mg. Fuck her and her bull-headed notions! If she won't listen, then I'll just have to take things into my own hands. I cannot function as I am now, devoid of everything that makes me *me*. I don't know what the loss of 1 mg from my earlier dosage will be, but it can't be worse than what I am facing now.

I got nothing done at work today. The appointment ate up the afternoon, and I was unable to focus this morning in the silent prison that my office has become. All I could think about was the loss of my abilities. I was sure that the mutterers would have something to say about all this, and expected a lot of angry eyes and stern mouths, but there was nothing.

I fed the birds in the park during the lunch hour, but they were just birds, with none of the personality that even the simplest sparrows normally held. The jays were there—the ones that used to be Mara and Kala. They ate what I fed them and argued amongst themselves. They might have been talking to me, but who can tell? They said nothing I could understand and seemed interested only in the food.

I felt awful, but I couldn't even cry. Not out of fear of being seen, but because even that would require some passion, some intensity of existence that I now lack. I even forgot to look up for the raptors. They must not have been present, or the birds would have fled, but how could I be so unaware of my tormentors? I can't even fear properly.

I should have gone back to the office after the appointment, but I couldn't face it. I knew I wouldn't get anything done, but would just stare at the pages in front of me. I need to be tracking down everyone associated with the missing Palermo, finding out what the police know, trying to figure out the angle the prosecution will take. Doing my job. But even the simple satisfaction of doing my job well is gone. Even justice, precious justice, leaves me empty. And I couldn't bear the jays coming by, silently begging for food, offering me nothing in return.

Discovery begins Monday, so I just have tomorrow to prepare. Fortunately, as the defense counsel I don't have to provide anything. The more I know going in, though, the more I can learn about what the state has to back their case: witness lists, any depositions they've taken, that sort of thing. Why do they think they can pin this on Marner with Palermo missing? Tomorrow I'll check again with the Colorado and Utah State Police to make sure Palermo hasn't turned up. I will keep digging, of course, but unless the prosecution has more than I think they have, this will be a win based on their lack of proof. Whatever. I'll take it.

I watched the Ingmar Bergman film of Mozart's *Die Zauberflöte* tonight. Normally the fiery passion of the Queen of the

Night and the solemn power of Sarastro move me deeply. To-night: nothing. I was more drawn by the faces of the audience at the beginning and intermission. Funny, I'd never noticed them much before. I'd been too distracted, I suppose. Even the surreal scene of the third challenge, where Pamina joins Tamino walking through the writhing bodies signifying fire and water just seemed banal this time. Instead of identifying with it as I usually do, it all seemed mechanical and contrived.

Has the Risperidone taken even opera from me? Am I left without anything that I can recognize as my own? An empty life, devoid of passion? No! I will not accept that. I'm going to go split a bunch of pills and then go to bed. I hope I can sleep with the reduced dose. Maybe some brandy will help. Maybe a lot of brandy. At least I might feel something then, even if it's just drunk.

Monday, August 7

Today was the discovery meeting in the Marner case. The DA thinks it was a joint operation by both Marner and Palermo. The evidence they presented was mostly things I already knew. The only bit of surprising information came from an interview the DA conducted with the auditors of the store's inventory system. To enter orders from the stores, someone has to log in on the computer system, and there was a record of that with every order. Those records show both Marner and Palermo placing the orders to the phantom store—one night it might be Marner, another Palermo. From the records, it appears that one of them took the task of placing all the orders each night.

The prosecutors did not disclose any evidence to show that either of them had moved the stolen goods, however. Neither Marner nor Palermo showed a big boost in income, nor any online records of listing stuff for sale. In addition to the few bits of similar material found in Marner's possession when they conducted the search, there were also loose pieces of equipment and box labels in Palermo's car. The prosecution confirmed there is still no trace of Palermo. They listed a few witnesses that I haven't spoken to yet, so that might turn up something, but it still seems like a pretty weak case to me. I'll have to talk with Marner about the computer records, though. If he did enter the orders from the non-existent store, that will be awkward, at least.

I have a week to put together my defense. Trial got moved up to next Monday, the 14th due to another case being settled before trial. Technically, that's too soon after discovery, but Judge Hobart asked if it would allow adequate preparation time, and I assured him it would. There's really not that much to put together, as far as I can see. The state's case is weak, so it should be easy to introduce doubt. I'll know more tomorrow after I talk with Marner.

I managed to hold it together through the whole process—I'm not entirely sure how. I've halved my dose on the Risperidone for

the last four nights, and I'm still not seeing any change. If anything, things have gotten worse. The mutterers are absent (or at
least silent), the eyes and mouths are gone, none of the things
that I have been told are unreal are there. Just blank space and
silence. And worst of all, nothing from Mara and Kala. The jays
keep coming, pretty much as always, but they only squawk to
each other, nothing to me. I am isolated and bereft.

Oddly, though, I don't even feel the loss as strongly as I did.
Am I adjusting to this, as Dr. Filtner hoped? Or am I so medicated
that I just can't feel any emotion now? I suspect it's the latter. I
am getting nothing from my music, either. Recordings that con-
sistently moved me to tears in the past now leave me flat. I can
appreciate the quality of a performance, the acoustics of the hall,
that sort of thing, but it's cold and analytical. No beauty, no passion. Dead.

I guess that may be good for work—there are certainly fewer
distractions getting in my way. But there's also none of the drive
to accomplish justice that I used to have. I hadn't realized before
now how much of an emotional investment there was in my
work. The job pays well, of course, and is intellectually stimulat-
ing, and all of that is still true. But that isn't what got me there
in the morning, or kept me there late at night. It wasn't even the
knowledge that I was doing something good; it was the *feeling* of
it. A passion I recognize now only by its absence.

Who knew that a life so free of pain could be so not worth
living?

Wednesday, August 9

I am finally seeing a glimmer of improvement after reducing my Risperidone dose. The world is still mostly silent, but there's a sound almost like a gentle breeze blowing that I was aware of today in the office. Just the slightest hint of a murmur. Small as it is, I am excited by it. An excitement I haven't felt in a week or more. Perhaps there is a little color coming back into the world—it is not all muted shades of gray. Sadly, that's all I can see, though: a hint that things might someday improve. There's no sign of Mara and Kala, my trusted companions and guides, though. Not the real Mara and Kala. There's only the raw physical manifestation of the Steller's jays that so gladly relieve me of cashews and remind me of what I've lost.

And how I miss them! Preparing a case like this without their input feels so unnatural. I realize now that this is how most attorneys must function. It is much harder and much less certain. I think I have a solid defense forming, but I don't know. I always had the certainty of innocence before, which made any defense so much stronger. (Not to say that the innocent are never convicted—I'm not that naïve.) How do my colleagues stand it?

The matter of the computer logs was easily resolved, at least. According to Marner, whichever one of them got there first would log on to the system—just a single computer console that they shared—and that session would stay logged in through the entire shift. Yes, they were supposed to log out each time they left the terminal and log in again when they sat down to enter something, but that took time in a shift that was already too full of work. The logs are evidence, but weak and easily overcome. I should have no problem convincing a jury that anyone would take that shortcut. How many of us do the same thing all the time?

I can't prove that Marner didn't participate in the fraudulent orders and consequent larceny, but I don't have to. I only have to prove that it's possible he did not. So far there is no evidence that proves that Palermo didn't do the whole thing on his own, and there is his absence to indicate a likelihood that he did.

There remains an intriguing open question of what happened to the stolen equipment or the money from its sale. Neither Marner nor Palermo seem to have any ties to it—I have found no evidence of where the merchandise might have been stored or of how it might have been disposed of. While a day or maybe even a week's worth of the pilferage might have easily fit in a car, the grand total of nearly a year's steady orders would take up quite a bit of room. But where? It's possible it may have all been sold, but how? And what happened to the money? Neither Palermo nor Marner seem to have been living particularly well nor sitting on any large sums.

Is it possible that one of them could have moved the equipment out every week without the other knowing? I asked Marner about that. Palermo was a smoker, and took several breaks each shift to stand outside the warehouse and smoke. He always did that outside the door leading to the parking lot, where there was a cigarette butt station—there was no smoking allowed inside the building.

Marner didn't pay much attention to Palermo's comings and goings—he was too busy doing his own job. It seems possible that Palermo could have loaded his pockets each time he went out, depositing the items in his car before coming back in. There was no video surveillance either in the warehouse or outside. (I bet there will be soon!). I admit this seems like a stretch, but there's no proof it did not happen. The physical volume of the stolen goods was not huge—it was the price per item that made the take so high.

To accomplish this would require stealing roughly $15,000 worth of goods each week. That would mean taking out a thousand dollars' worth on each smoke break (figuring three breaks per shift, five nights a week). Tomorrow I'm going to go to Wilderness Experience and buy $1,000 worth of precisely the items that were being moved. If I'm right, I should be able to secret that all about my person even wearing a suit. I can make a strong case by walking up to the bench to enter in evidence with completely empty hands, then producing it all out of my pockets. A little theatrical, maybe, but that's the sort of thing a jury remembers.

I haven't told Marner I'm going to do that. I want him to be as shocked as anyone—that reaction will help, too. I'm sure I'll be cautioned by the judge for it, but that won't hurt the case. With that demonstration, I think I can poke sufficient holes in the state's argument to win an acquittal, or at the very least a hung jury.

The weather has been hot lately, but even with the resulting thermals there are few soaring raptors. I've seen the peregrine falcon a couple times over the last week, but not often. And either they are all much less vocal, or I am just not noticing it. I did hear an owl last night, though. Great horned, I think. Far from the terror that it used to strike in me, I found myself smiling at it. At least it was something familiar. Maybe the Risperidone fog is lifting after all. Tomorrow will be a week on the reduced dose. It took a couple weeks for the increased dose to take full effect, so maybe the decrease will take the same. I can only hope!

Friday, August 11

Trial starts Monday. I think I'm ready. I think Marner is ready, too. I've got him cleaned up and got him some good clothes to wear at court. Nothing too fancy—he was a night-shift worker in a warehouse, after all. A suit would be inappropriate for him, the wrong image for the jury. Instead he'll wear plain decent clothes: khakis and button down shirts, dark socks, and a nice pair of leather shoes, functional, not fancy. We got him a good conservative haircut, and he'll shave each morning before court. He looks like a fine upstanding citizen, no matter what his past record might be. Looks matter more than facts to a jury, after all. Everyone knows facts can be distorted, but seeing is believing. Hah!

The state will focus on the relationship between Marner and Palermo, trying to paint them as not just coworkers, but buddies who did everything together. Two of their witnesses will make those sorts of claims. I've got three who will say just the opposite. Both men are generally loners. No family to speak of. They did some things together—drinking and playing pool—but they spent most of their time separately. Neither had any family to speak of. Marner was into hiking and climbing, and I have plenty of trail records and gym records to show that he spent most weekends outside or in training, and not with Palermo.

The computer entry issues are easily dismissed with the kind of lazy security that is all too common. The physical movement of the stolen material will be graphically explained by my little theatrics. I have $1,342 worth (retail) of climbing equipment that I purchased the other day, and I can carry it in my suit pockets with no particularly noticeable bulges, clinks, or rattles. I spent the entire day today walking around the office with it all in my pockets and not one person noticed, even when I asked them if my suit looked OK. It's an assortment of different items, too, all of them on the list of things that were stolen. I admit I got some strange looks from the sales agent at the store when I bought them, which amused me. Maybe he'll read about it later and put things together. I didn't offer any explanation, in any case.

Unless the state has some real surprises—unlikely since they didn't reveal anything in discovery—I should have reasonable doubt for everything they can raise. Objectively, I believe I have an adequate defense against a pretty weak case. Not enough to prove innocence, but that's not my job. Proof is the prosecution's job; mine is just doubt. So why am I so nervous? I feel less confident about this case than any I can remember.

The answer, of course, is that I don't *know* that my client is innocent. With Mara and Kala's help, I've always been able to show reasonable doubt by simply telling the truth. I could clearly show what plausible things may have happened, because I knew they *did* happen. I was always confident that I was serving justice. Now I am uncertain and uneasy.

That uneasiness is oddly comforting. At least I'm feeling *something*. Lately there's been far too little of that. I feel like I'm starting to be more myself—less a half-dead foreign inhabitant in my familiar old body. I listened to Wagner last night—*Das Rheingold*—and I'm looking forward to *Die Walküre* tonight. Looking forward to it! Not as just an intellectual exercise, but as beautiful music. The whispers have grown some, too, I think. Still nothing recognizable as even muttering, but a susurration that at least reminds me of my old Greek chorus. I thought I caught some eyes glancing at me today, too, just out of the corner of my eye. Whatever they were disappeared as soon as I looked at them, but I could feel it: something was there—something watching, waiting to return.

There were more birds at lunch today, too. That might be partly the weather (still hot) or the relative dearth of raptors lately—I suspect they've all moved up-slope to avoid the heat. The jays that I thought were Mara and Kala haven't been around either of the last two days, though. Off on their own corvid adventures, no doubt. Perhaps they've found someone more receptive than me. I hope they return soon. It would be unbearable to lose them now, just as I'm starting to recover some sensitivity again. If only it would come more quickly.

The Ingrezza seems to have done what it's going to do. At least I haven't seen any more major changes. The disruptive tics are much reduced and easier to control. I still can feel the chewing and grimacing happening, my tongue sometimes has a mind of its own, and the hard spastic blinks—well, I don't know if those will ever go away. But it's much less obvious now. Less distracting to others, I think. I look forward to that advantage in the courtroom. Perhaps that was my curse I bore to counteract the boon of Mara and Kala. Now things are shifting and I'm losing both. I'd welcome the return of the tardive dyskinesia, though, if it would just bring back my feathered counselors. How I miss them!

Sunday, August 13

The oddest thing happened this afternoon. I was relaxing out-side after having had a good hike during the day. I'd driven up into the foothills after a late breakfast, up highway 15 a ways and then off along an unmarked jeep trail I know. There's a wide spot where I can park and then just hike—no trail, but easy enough to navigate. I've hiked it enough that I can't get lost there. I walked for probably three and a half hours, maybe ten miles of distance with a lot of elevation shift—it felt good. Physical activity has always been a good way of clearing my mind before a trial, and I needed it now more than ever.

I was high enough in elevation that it was a little cooler—the sweat evaporated quickly in the slight breeze and kept me cool. The area was overrun with ground squirrels, busy with their own purposes and caring little about me, just curious enough to see if I was going to feed them before darting off in search of... what? Seeds? Sex? Or maybe they were just doing what I was doing and moving for the simple pleasure of moving. I drove back after the hike and got home around 3:30. I fixed a snack—the food I had eaten before the hike was wearing pretty thin. After eating I went outside again, just into the yard around my building.

I was gathering my thoughts, mentally preparing for tomor-row's start of the trial, when the two jays that I think are Mara and Kala joined me. One of them—Mara maybe?—had a piece of paper in its beak. That's not uncommon—like any corvid they are drawn to things that are bright or shiny or might make good nesting material. Sometimes they've even brought me shiny beads or buttons, laying them in front of me without any expla-nation. This time, though, Mara—I think it was Mara—very deliberately hopped over to where I was sitting on the ground, not ten seconds after landing, and stuck the paper in my pocket. As soon as that was done they both silently took off and they haven't been back.

I'd never seen them do anything like that before. I pulled the paper out of my pocket and looked at it. It was just a piece torn from a magazine by the looks of it. Glossy paper. One side had a piece of a picture of something I couldn't make out. The other side had just a single word: "DON'T." Big and bold, in black capital letters on a white background, probably part of an advertisement. But precisely that word. All of those letters, and no pieces of any others. "Don't."

What could that mean? It may mean nothing. It could be just a quirky random behavior like any bird might do. But if this is Mara and Kala, and they are unable to talk to me—or I am unable to comprehend them—could this be their attempt to give me a message by other means? "Don't."

I had no notion that they could read. That was never evident before. God knows if they had been able to read street signs it would have made my last trial easier! But this scrap was so clearly this single word; just it and nothing more. A simple command. "Don't."

Don't what? There are so many things it might be. Don't keep altering my Risperidone dose against doctor's orders? Don't keep taking the Risperidone? Don't go hiking? Don't defend Marner? Don't do some particular part of the defense? Don't what?

I'm nervous. I'm beyond nervous; I'm scared. I would have welcomed a positive communication—oh, how much I would!—but this...? A firm admonition. "Don't." An instruction. A commandment. But what does it mean? Don't what?

And why fly off before I could even read it? It's like they didn't even want to try and explain it. A puzzle I have to figure out on my own, without their help. "Don't."

A contradiction. Firm and direct, and unquestionably deliberate. But without any clear meaning other than... what? Displeasure? Warning of danger? Is it a plea, or an order? How could anyone know? Just "Don't."

After they gave it to me, I definitely heard a change in the background noises, too. The mutterers are coming back, I'm sure of it now. They were amused by this conundrum. Laughing amongst themselves. They get the joke that I don't. They know what it means. "Don't."

When I came in, I definitely caught a pair of eyes in the hall. They vanished quickly, but not before I saw them watching me. Looking to see if I got the message. I got it—physically. But I don't understand it. Or rather, I have too many understandings, too many possibilities. An imperative verb, but missing a direct object. Don't what? Don't which? "Don't."

I'll be up late, I'm sure. Hoping that Mara and Kala return, maybe with another scrap for me. Or at least able to somehow answer my questions. This will haunt me at the trial tomorrow. I won't be able to keep myself from pondering if anything I do is what I shouldn't. "Don't."

Trial starts at ten. I'll be meeting with Marner at nine—enough time to make sure he looks presentable and fix anything that needs fixing. Enough time to do any last coaching, reminding him what to say and—more importantly—what not to say. What not to do. How not to act. Just don't.

And if I don't see Mara and Kala before the trial, what then? What do I do? Or more to the point, what don't I do? What is this message that is so important that they found a new way to pass it to me? A word that, if it can't be spoken, can at least be delivered in writing. In half-inch tall black capital letters on a glossy white background. One word. Four letters and an apostrophe. One syllable. "Don't."

Monday, August 14

I'm finding myself again.

The Marner trial opened today. After the usual opening statements, the prosecution started its case. No real surprises. They called the chief information officer of Wilderness Experience as the first witness to explain the particulars of the system used in the warehouse. They had him describe in detail the logging that is done on all the orders and the checks that are made. I was able to cut some of that short by stipulating that the larceny had every appearance of being an inside job conducted by one or more night-shift workers. I don't think they were expecting that.

There were two set of eyes on the wall directly behind the judge that were watching me through the whole proceeding. The first eyes that I could look at since reducing the Risperidone dose. I was happier to see them than they were to be seen, apparently. They appeared stern, as if they were just waiting for me to fail. After my stipulation they relaxed briefly, but then were noticeably angry when I stood up to cross-examine the witness.

My cross-examination invalidated the evidence of the system logs. The computer expert admitted that it was based on signing into the system, with nothing enforcing signing out other than a thirty-minute inactivity timeout—something that basically never happened during the busy shift. I had him explain the process of signing out, signing back in, and navigating back to the appropriate screen in detail, every keystroke and mouse click. Described that way it sounded tedious, and the prospect of Marner and Palermo doing that over and over during the night when they were already overworked came across as ridiculous.

I asked the CIO if it were possible that one person could log in at the beginning of the shift and stay logged in throughout even though both of them used the system. After stating that that was against the company policy, he agreed that it was possible. I pressed him further, and he admitted that the logs showed that

that was exactly what happened. Each night had one, or at most two logins (presumably after a timeout), and so all the transactions were logged to that one person, regardless of who actually made the entries. Strike one for the prosecution.

I'd been focused on the witness and the jury during the cross-examination, but when I sat back down the eyes had each added a mouth to complete their visage. They were not happy expressions. I felt I'd done a good job, but they clearly disapproved. The mutterers were definitely present, also. They were still hushed compared to the past, but it was clear that they were riled up about something. Anxious at least, possibly angry or outraged. It was hard to read their tone, but the effect was disconcerting.

I felt encouraged by their presence, though, after the weeks of silence—at last, I was beginning to feel like I knew who I was. I could do without the interference during the trial, but it was still grounding somehow. It felt like being on a sailboat after a long period of being becalmed in the doldrums unable to make headway, and now I could see a storm coming up. A storm that would give me a real challenge. A storm that might even wreck the boat, but at least I would be active and the boat would move. There was the risk of disaster, but also the possibility of improvement, instead of only deadly stagnation.

The prosecution next brought up Marner's criminal history, such as it is. I was able to counter with Palermo's similar history. Both have been convicted of misdemeanors, neither of felonies. Marner may not be the person you'd want to date your daughter, but he wasn't a monster, and he wasn't any worse than Palermo. Strike two for the prosecution, and that brought us to the lunch break.

Marner seemed reasonably confident and collected, so I left him on his own while I went outside to escape the eyes in the courtroom. I had brought a small bag of cashews in my briefcase and took them out with me, hoping that I might see Mara and Kala. Hoping I might be able to make some sense out of last evening's strange encounter. I was not disappointed in the first as they flew to the bench where I was sitting just a few seconds after I sat down.

They squawked back and forth, their attention clearly focused on me, but there was nothing I could recognize as words. They ate the cashews I provided, but that wasn't their only focus, they seemed concerned with me. They gave every impression of trying to tell me something, but I couldn't understand what it was. I asked them what they wanted me to do. I begged them to talk to me. I asked for clarification on last night's cryptic "Don't." Each question produced more animated calls from both of them, but nothing that provided any guidance at all.

Are they forever lost to me, or are they just slow coming back? One of them, Kala maybe, would occasionally fly off a little ways and pick for a few seconds at a newspaper that was lying discarded on a nearby bench before returning. They were trying to communicate, clearly, but I wasn't holding up my end. I went back into the courthouse feeling no more enlightened than when I'd come out.

When the trial resumed, the prosecution called a series of witnesses to speak to Marner's character and to the nature of the work he did. They succeeded in painting him as dull and coarse, even resentful of the people who bought the products he sent to the stores. Privileged types who had thousands of dollars to spend on hobbies while he struggled to make rent. It was effective in establishing motivation, no question about that, but nothing they offered applied any less to Palermo. A foul tip; still strike two.

The eyes and mouths were there still, watching and judging. They did not multiply and did not seem any more concerned than earlier, but I still felt clear disapproval from them. The muttering undercurrent would get louder whenever I stood up, sounding alarmed and anxious but also distant.

After these witnesses established motivation, the next witnesses were used to paint a buddy relationship between Marner and Palermo. The prosecution wanted to show that they knew each other's business and shared their activities, while my cross-examination shot holes in the depth of the relationship. Sure, they got along as coworkers and were friendly when things brought them together, but they each lived their own lives with their own interests. Another foul tip, keeping them alive and at bat but not really advancing the case.

I was afraid the prosecution was going to raise the issue of moving the merchandise—I hadn't expected that this early and had not taken the opportunity to load up my pockets with the evidence to present. The trial was moving faster than I anticipated. Fortunately I was able to stall a bit during cross-examinations and they didn't get there before the end of the afternoon. I expect they'll raise it tomorrow and I'll be ready for them.

I talked with Marner briefly after the proceedings were done. He appeared only slightly nervous, more calm than most defendants after the prosecution has had a full day of making their case. I told him to be prepared to take the stand tomorrow—I expect they will call him and try to trip him up. He claimed to be ready and looked forward to setting the record straight. I urged him to remember the coaching and not offer the prosecution anything more than precisely what they asked. Short answers are always best. He should stick to his story, never embellish it, and offer as little information as possible. The time to sing is when I am leading the chorus, not the opposition! Hopefully he'll remember that when he gets on the stand, unlike so many defendants before him.

My attention when talking with Marner was only half on him, and half on the eyes behind the now empty bench. I could tell Marner was wondering what I was looking at, but I couldn't escape their judgement and clear disapproval. I was glad to leave the courtroom and their forbidding gaze.

I went back to the office to get the merchandise I planned to enter into evidence tomorrow and to collect any messages that might be waiting. There were eyes and a mouth on my office wall but they were seemed content to just watch me. As I was leaving

I thought I heard Max say "Shithead!" but it was faint and unclear. It might have been something from one of the other offices, or even my imagination, but it sounded like Max's voice and his favorite epithet for me. In any case, it was just that one word.

I picked up a take-out order of tikka masala with rice and naan on the way home—I hate cooking when I'm in court—and ate it standing in the kitchen while listening to the first act of Verdi's *Macbeth*. The mutterers are definitely coming back, but they couldn't compete with the opera, and I enjoyed the opportunity to lose myself in the music and the rich taste of my dinner. After I had eaten and cleaned up, I grabbed the cashews and went outside. The sun had already set behind the mountains, but there was still a little light in the sky. The gathering darkness seemed fitting for the second act of *Macbeth*.

Mara and Kala showed up just as Act 2, Scene 3 was finishing. The next scene comprises Banco's aria *"Studia il passo."* Both of them listened intently, which they'd never done before. They still had no words for me, but it was clear they understood the significance of the opera, even though it was in Italian. They watched me through the aria, as if it could somehow speak for them. They were particularly agitated at the end of the aria when Banco is murdered in front of his son. At the conclusion they squawked excitedly and then flew off.

What was their fascination with the music? Is it something peculiar to this scene? Banquo is a character in Shakespeare's *Macbeth*, called Banco in the opera. Sung by a bass, Banco plays a small but important role, appearing alive in the first act, murdered in the scene they reacted to, and returning later in that act as a ghost to haunt the newly-crowned king, Macbeth.

I went back inside and listened to the rest of the opera, concentrating on Banco's character. He is a potent force even though a small role, and ultimately his descendants, nine generations later, are revenged upon the murderous Macbeth, finally ascending the throne Banco was wrongly denied after the king's death. This felt like it was important, but I didn't have all the pieces.

"Don't." And now the murder of Banco. What are they trying to tell me?

Tuesday, August 15, 5:30 AM

Methought I heard a voice cry "Sleep no more!
Macbeth does murder sleep." The innocent sleep.
Sleep that knits up the ravell'd sleave of care
The death of each day's life, sore labour's bath,
Balm of hurt minds, great nature's second course,
Chief nourisher in life's feast.

Macbeth, Act 2, Scene 2, lines 32-37

I've been up all night. I listened to two different versions of Verdi's *Macbeth*, and read the Shakespeare play clear through, focusing on the scenes with Banquo's ghost. I've been trying to figure out what Mara and Kala are telling me. I'm beginning to have a theory, but it's almost too wild to believe.

What if the role of Macbeth in this little drama we call life is played tonight by Butch Marner, the role of Banquo/Banco by Richard "Rick" Palermo, and his ghost by the pair Mara and Kala? King Duncan will be played by Wilderness Experience, and I suppose that would mean that I am playing the role of Macduff, and Justice plays the role of Malcolm, with Lady Macbeth played by simple human greed.

Confused? I'm not surprised. In the play, Macbeth, spurred on by his wife, murders Duncan, the king of Scotland. He manages to throw suspicion on Malcolm, Duncan's son, who flees the country, and so Macbeth becomes king in turn. Banquo and his son are a threat to this, however, as they have a better claim to the throne than Macbeth, so the Macbeths murder them, too. Banquo's ghost haunts and torments Macbeth, driving him quite mad (see the above quote). Macduff ultimately challenges and defeats Macbeth and Malcolm is restored as king.

Got it? No? OK, consider this. Suppose Marner and Palermo both did the robbery—or maybe just Marner, it doesn't matter. And either Palermo threatened to confess or Marner was worried he wouldn't keep quiet or would try to move the merchandise too quickly. Maybe Marner just got greedy, it doesn't matter. Palermo is "missing," presumed to be on the lam for the theft. What if instead he is dead, murdered by Marner?

I have no evidence of this, of course. Neither does the state, or they would have charged Marner with murder instead of larceny. They may have some suspicions along these lines, but if they lack solid evidence they wouldn't press the charges so they wouldn't have to reveal anything in discovery. Getting Marner convicted of larceny at least keeps him around so he can't flee while they look—if they even are looking. They obviously won't tell me that. Without finding Palermo, dead or alive, this whole crazy idea will be very hard to prove or disprove.

The mutterers have been active all night, swelling in volume every time I'd make a connection. They were clearly agitated, but I couldn't tell if they were angry with me, or just generally upset. The eyes and mouths have been following me all night, too, grim and expectant, perhaps waiting for me to decide what I am going to do before they express judgement. Even Max finally weighed in, though rather cryptically. When the idea that Palermo might be dead instead of on the run first hit me he said quite clearly "Well, shithead, that's quite a notion, isn't it?" That was his only comment, and the first that I'm sure of in weeks. Snide and sneering as always, but is he mocking me for coming up with the idea, or for being so slow to come to it?

This is a long reach from Mara and Kala's interest in an aria. It's a stretch to even think Mara and Kala know what was going on in the opera. It's in Italian, after all. Even if they somehow understood that isolated aria, would they know how it fits into the story of *Macbeth*? It would be far more reasonable to suspect they were just showing they are aware of me, even if I am not of them, with nothing deeper intended. And yet....

Let's not forget, I am responsible for Mr. Marner's defense—I am expected to work to clear him of charges, not to add new ones. It would be against all manner of legal ethics for me to pursue this idle speculation. Every person, guilty or innocent, is entitled to a competent defense. This is fundamental to the practice of law. I am that defense. Guilty or innocent, my duty is to defend Marner against the charges leveled against him. I know this.

And yet... this is Mara and Kala.

Regardless, now I have to get ready for court. The prosecution will likely finish today, and I'll need to be ready with my "evidence" planted about my person. Depending on how quickly they finish I may or may not start my defense this afternoon, so I have to be ready for that, too. All on no sleep at all.

Very well. *Lay on Macduff, and damned be him that first cries "Hold, enough!"*

Tuesday, August 15, 9:00 PM

Second entry for today, at more my usual hour. And what a day it was—sleep deprivation makes everything so much more interesting!

As expected, the prosecution raised the issue of the "impossibility" of Palermo moving all the equipment—almost two tons by their calculation—without Marner knowing about it. They called one of the day-shift workers as a witness, asking him if he thought it possible. I, of course, objected to this as requiring the witness to speculate, and so they weasel worded around it and got him to say he wouldn't know how to smuggle two tons of stuff out of the warehouse without anyone noticing. The perfect setup.

During cross-examination I first had the witness confirm that he couldn't see any way that the material could have been smuggled out without notice. I then asked about the smoking policy at the warehouse. He looked confused but answered that smokers were allowed three five-minute breaks per shift to smoke, but they had to do it outside. I asked where outside, and he answered that most did it near the door from the parking lot because of the butt-disposal station. I confirmed that it was three breaks each shift, so fifteen per week. He agreed and added "or more, some guys take more than their three." Bless him!

I told the judge I had some items to enter as evidence. Walking up to the bench empty handed the judge even asked me if I had forgotten to bring the evidence. Thank you, your honor! I proceeded to empty my pockets onto the bench over the objections of the prosecution and was duly chided by the judge for grandstanding and theatrics, but I made my point. I had weighed the items beforehand, of course, so I was able to state that they weighed four pounds, ten ounces. At twenty trips per week—fifteen smoke breaks, plus a trip to the car at the end of the shift—for fifty weeks, that amounted to four thousand six hundred twenty-five pounds. Over two tons. It was easily possible to move the material, especially as the witness had already alluded to more breaks being possible. Strike three for the prosecution.

They had little else to offer and closed their argument somewhat lamely, I thought, arguing how much easier it would have been for both workers to have worked the scheme together, which was true enough but didn't prove anything. They argued how unlikely it was that one could have moved the merchandise week after week without the other noticing, even if they weren't involved, though I had already demonstrated clearly how it could be done.

Then it was my turn to call witnesses after a late lunch break. I should have been thrilled at this point. I hardly had to make any case at all. I only had to show the jury how the prosecution had failed to make theirs. A slam-dunk. But the eyes had been angry all morning, and the mouths had scowled and angrily mouthed words at me during my cross-examinations. The mutterers had been building up an angry chorus all morning, too, and even Max got in the act when I sat down after entering the evidence in.

"Well, shithead, that was a lively bit of theater. Very nearly got yourself tossed out for that, didn't you? The judge was pissed. Are you proud of yourself, you little shit? Do you know what you accomplished? You poor dumb motherfucker."

I managed to keep a neutral expression, but I couldn't escape rehashing last night's speculation. Was I defending a man guilty of not only the larceny he was charged with, but murder as well? I had no way to know. It didn't matter (or shouldn't at any rate). My job is to defend Marner. That is my clear duty as his defense attorney. Everyone deserves a competent defense, right? And yet, what if...? Can I stand by, a knowing party to such a perversion of justice? The legal ethics are clear—I can and I must—but that makes this no less of a moral dilemma.

When we broke for lunch, I told Marner not to worry, that the prosecution had failed to make their case. He seemed pleased but still uptight—typical of anyone in his position. I should have stayed with him, but I quickly went outside hoping to find Mara and Kala waiting for me.

They were there, squawking and nervously flitting about, seeming quite agitated. I told them about what had happened and they listened intently. Then I told them my crazy theory from last night based on their clue, and they became even more animated, squawking loudly at each other and, it seemed, at me. At times I almost found words amidst their squawks, but nothing I could clearly make out. It seems the communication is beginning to open up again, and none too soon.

If only I had some more time! I don't see any way I can stretch my defense past tomorrow before turning it over to the jury. Even if I take the whole day, the jury might still return a quick verdict. If not, the trial will certainly end early Thursday.

I could possibly plead illness and get a continuance, but that would be risky. Judge Hobart would reasonably expect another lawyer from the firm to complete the case, especially in light of how it was going so far. Mike would take a dim view of any such action, to say the least. I am running out of options.

I begged Mara and Kala for anything they could provide to tell me how to proceed, any evidence of the murder, if murder it was. They squawked back and forth quite a bit after that before flying off. I struggled to understand anything they were saying, but couldn't quite make out any words. I was sure there were words in there—more than just the usual assortment of noises a jay makes—but what they were eluded me.

As I walked back to the courthouse I could hear the mutterers debating over something, as wordless as ever, and Max let me have it with "You're so fucking close, shithead. But you just can't do it, can you? You are nothing on your own, and even with help you can't cross the finish line. You dumb fuck, why not just give up?"

I gave a long opening statement, going over all the points made by the prosecution and refuting them in detail. This should rightly be done in the closing statement, but the judge allowed it, for a while, anyway. Explaining that, while the state had shown a possible interpretation of the facts of the case, that's all they had done—one possible interpretation among many. They had failed to prove any of the key points of their case beyond a shadow of a doubt—beyond even some very serious doubt.

That a crime had been committed was not in question, but the prosecution had failed to prove who had committed the crime. They could not refute that the fraud and larceny might have been performed by only the missing Rick Palermo—and there was his absence to indicate that it was.

The prosecution objected that Mr. Palermo was not on trial here, Mr. Marner was. But, as my defense was based on the alternative interpretation that Palermo had perpetrated the larceny completely on his own and without Marner's knowledge, the judge overruled it. I recalled the computer expert from Wilderness Experience and asked how the phantom store had come to exist. He admitted that a very real store had closed two years ago but it had not been completely removed from the system. I asked how that had not been discovered in all that time, and he revealed that, unless there was activity from the store, nothing was set up to catch it. Nobody created this problem; it just happened, and it was lying there waiting for someone to take advantage of it.

I effectively demonstrated that the software was not as airtight as the prosecution made it out to be, but actually I was stalling, and the judge and prosecution both knew it, though they had no idea why. The peanut gallery of mutterers, eyes, and mouths knew it, too, and not one of them was happy. I wasn't too happy about it myself, but I didn't know what else to do.

In any case, I stretched things until three thirty, and the judge decided to end the day there, as I indicated my next witness could take a while. I was thinking of calling Marner himself, even though this was clearly not in his (or my) best interest. Our defense was solid without his testimony, and putting him on the stand would open him up to the prosecution's cross-examination. I was frankly surprised they hadn't called him themselves. He was on their list at discovery—but one never knows what they might be thinking and there is no requirement to call all the possible witnesses. Even so, I didn't doubt for a second that they had some juicy questions lined up if I would be so foolish as to put him on the stand.

I could say tomorrow that matters had changed overnight and I had decided not to call my (fortunately unnamed) witness. That, too, would irritate the judge and maybe some jurors if they realized that this meant an extra day of jury duty that they might have avoided. No matter; it shouldn't affect the conclusion—I hope.

I drove home, stopping on the way to grab some Kung Pao chicken and rice—not because I really wanted it, but because it was quick. I put it in a bowl and took it and chopsticks outside to eat. I had just finished wolfing it down when Mara and Kala flew in. They were quite animated, and Mara had a large piece of a trail map in her beak which she laid flat on the little table I was seated at, holding it down with one foot and calling continuously at me.

The scrap was too small for me to identify what trail it showed, and that didn't seem to matter. I looked for any words on the map, but that seemed to irritate both jays, and there was nothing there that connected for me, anyway. Finally I asked if they wanted me to get my maps and they both started making a racket and fluttering back and forth between the door and where I was seated. That was what they wanted.

I took my empty bowl into the apartment and came back out with my folder full of maps that I use to plan hikes. Some were specific trail maps from the various parks and resorts in the area, and others were USGS topographic sections, mainly of the foot-hills and nearer mountains to the west. I pulled them out one at a time, hoping the jays would know what they were looking for. It took quite a while—I have a lot of maps.

The Cascade topo map, northwest of the city, provoked their interest. Could jays read maps? It seemed that Mara and Kala could, anyway. Mara repeatedly pecked at a point on the map, between Wellington Gulch and Williams Canyon, at about 8,800 feet elevation. I had hiked some in that area, but the point Mara kept tapping was not on any established trails that I knew—just a random point in the middle of the national forest land. It would be accessible from the Williams Canyon trails over ground that didn't look too steep, according to the map. There was no way to get there before dark, though, nor in the morning if I wanted to get back in time for court. I wasn't about to try off-trail hiking it in the dark.

Could my theory be right? I tried asking Mara and Kala, and they seemed excited and just on the verge of speaking, but nothing I could be sure I heard. I asked if that was where Palermo was and they went crazy, squawking and fluttering and pecking at that same point in the map. On a whim, I tore off a piece of blank paper, and wrote "Banco" on it. Kala took it from me immediately and put it down, right on the spot on the map Mara had been pecking at.

I couldn't think of any way to be more sure. Not without words. I marked a small "X" on the map where Mara indicated, and she pecked at it continually. If I struggled, I thought I could catch the word "Yes" over and over from both of them, but I couldn't be certain. It may have just been my imagination letting me hear what I wanted to hear. I asked every way I could if this was where Palermo was, and if he was dead. "Yes." Maybe.

Was it enough? And what could I do with this information if I did believe it? It finally got too dark to really see, and I could think of nothing more to ask. Mara and Kala were agitated, but it was clear they needed to leave—it was far later than they would normally be out, and I feared for their safety. I gathered up my maps and told them I would figure something out and went in. They fluttered around me until I actually went inside.

Riding the elevator up to my apartment, Max finally chimed in again. "So what now, shithead?" What now, indeed? Well, for the immediate now, sleep. I can barely keep my eyes open. Another sleepless night is impossible. As for tomorrow... I have no earthly idea.

Wednesday, August 16

Well, I've torn it now. I don't even have a word to describe this day.

I woke up before the sun, about 4:30, with a pounding headache. I'd had a restless night, in and out of dreams that I couldn't remember, waking in abject terror more than once during the night. I awoke to Tempest, of all voices to hear, crooning in my ear, begging me to find a hot girl and just skip court. "Everything is going to shit anyway, you know. You might as well enjoy yourself while you watch the world burn." Tempest always has the worst advice.

I took some Excedrin and made coffee and sat down to figure out what I *was* going to do. It was not going to be what Tempest was suggesting; I was certain of that. I gradually realized it wasn't the only thing I was certain of.

I was certain that Mara and Kala were telling me that my theory was right. Marner, my client, killed Palermo, either to keep him quiet or to claim all the money. And the body is hidden just a little ways west of here, up in the wilds of Pike National Forest, not far from Palmer Reservoir. As for the car? Presumably Marner drove it himself and dropped it there, probably hitchhiking back—he couldn't risk anyone he knew finding out he'd made the trip.

So my client, whom I am defending on charges of fraud and larceny, is not only guilty of those crimes, but also of murder. I know this—I'm quite certain. I may be crazy, but I'm sure of it. I trust Mara and Kala, and I know I'm interpreting them correctly. But I have no evidence, and even if I did have evidence, I am ethically and legally bound to defend my client. What could I do?

I went outside at first light, but Mara and Kala were nowhere to be seen. I hoped they'd made it back to their roost without incident, but I really wished they were here, even though I had no idea what more I could ask them. I stayed outside anyway, if only to avoid the judgmental eyes in my apartment. It didn't help.

I arrived at court purposely late, leaving little time to say anything to Marner before the bailiff told us to rise. Not knowing what I was going to ask, I called Marner to the stand. That granted me a shocked expression from both the prosecution and the judge, and a "What the hell?" from Marner. The judge asked me if I really intended to call my own defendant to the stand. I assured him I did, and looked everywhere but at Marner, though I could feel his scowl burning into me. After he was sworn in, it went something like this.

Me: Mr. Marner, have you ever driven Mr. Palermo's car?

Marner, hesitating: Yeah. Once or twice, I guess.

Me: When was the last time you drove it?

Marner: I don't remember.

Me: Did you drive it on the weekend before Mr. Palermo failed to report to work?

Marner: I didn't see him that weekend. Not since the end of the Friday night shift.

Me: You're sure about that?

Marner: What? Yeah. I'm sure.

Judge: Mr. Taylor, are you badgering your own witness? What is the meaning of this line of questioning?

Me: Your honor, please indulge me a bit further. I have some new information I would like to explore with this witness.

Judge: You are aware he is your client, Mr. Taylor?

Me: Yes, your honor.

Judge: Would you like a few moments to confer with him before proceeding?

Me: No, your honor.

Judge, after several seconds of silence: Very well. Proceed, Mr. Marner, at your own risk.

Me: Thank you, your honor. Mr. Marner, you like to hike, is that correct?

Marner: Sure. Hiking and climbing, both.

Me: Were you hiking the weekend Mr. Palermo disappeared?

Marner, hesitating again: I'm not sure. Yeah, probably.

Me: Do you remember where?

Marner: No, I'm not even sure I was out, now that I think about it.

Me: Do you ever hike in Pike National Forest?

Marner: Sure—all the open land around here is part of Pike.

Me: Do you hike near Palmer Reservoir or Wellington Gulch?

Marner: What are you getting at?

Judge: Yes, Mr. Taylor, what are you getting at?

Me: Your honor, please, a few moments more.

Judge, hesitating: Very well. The witness will answer the question.

Marner: I guess so. I've been to the Reservoir.

Me: Were you there the weekend Mr. Palermo disappeared?

Marner: What the hell are you doing?

Me: Please answer the question.

Marner: Judge?

Judge: Mr. Taylor, this is quite irregular. You are badgering your own witness over a matter that can't seem to help your case.

Me: One more question your honor.

Judge, after a long hesitation: One more question Mr. Taylor. Make it a good one.

Me, after walking to the desk and retrieving the Cascade topo map from my briefcase, and pointing at the X I had marked last night: Mr. Marner, did you hike to this point on the weekend Mr. Palermo disappeared, and did you leave something there?

Marner: What the hell? I'm not answering that!

Judge, banging his gavel: Mr. Taylor, I will see you in my chambers. Now! This court is in recess.

A few moments later I was alone with Judge Hobart in his chambers. He didn't sit and didn't offer me a chair.

Judge: Mr. Taylor, suppose you tell me just what the hell you think you were doing out there?

Me: Your honor, the prosecution should be here to hear this also.

Judge: I'm asking you.

Me: Please, Judge, bring Tom in.

Tom Biddle was the prosecutor. I'd first met him when I worked for the DA's office. He was just clerking there then, fresh out of law school. A good man and a sharp attorney—I'd faced him a couple times before in my present role.

The judge shook his head, but opened his door and called for the bailiff to have Biddle join us. No one said anything for the minute or so before he walked in.

Biddle: What's happening, Judge?

Judge: That's what I'd like to know. All right, Mr. Taylor, you have the prosecution here. Would you mind telling us what the hell is going on?

Me: Your honor...

Judge, interrupting: We're not in court, Mr. Taylor. No need to be formal, just spit it out, and quickly.

Me: Yes, sir. *I took a big breath and let it out slowly.* I now believe my client is not only guilty of larceny as charged, but also that he murdered Mr. Palermo, deposited his body in the woods at or near the point marked on the map, and then drove Palermo's car to where it was found, all to throw suspicion off of himself.

Judge: Mr. Taylor, that is an extraordinary claim, especially coming from the defense. Do you have evidence to back that up?

Me: Not that I can present at this time, sir. I would suggest that you check the car for any indication that Marner may have driven it to where it was found, and maybe some indication that he hitchhiked back here. And search the location I marked on the map. I think you'll find Palermo's body there, though I can't say where exactly, or in what condition you'll find it.

Biddle: Is this some sort of joke? Rip, what are you saying?

Judge: If it is a joke, it is not at all funny. Mr. Taylor, what the hell are you doing?

Me: What am I doing? Slitting my own throat, most likely. But I stand by what I said.

Judge: That sounds like an accurate assessment, Mr. Taylor. How am I supposed to proceed? You are the defense attorney. Can you see any alternative to a mistrial?

Me: No, your honor.

Biddle: Rip, are you out of your mind? Are you off your meds?

Me: Maybe, Tom. Out of my mind, that is. But I have to do this.

Judge: What you have to do, Mr. Taylor, is defend your client. You know that. You're not some dewy-eyed first year law student, all principle and no understanding. You have a legal and an ethical duty to your client.

Me: Yes, sir. But I also have an ethical duty to justice.

Judge: No, Mr. Taylor, you do not. That is not your responsibility. That is not even my responsibility. The juridical process is what assures justice, as best we know how. You know that. Your responsibility in that process is the defense of your client. The best defense you know how to give. What you are doing is wrong, Mr. Taylor, whether or not your story proves true. Wrong in every sense.

Me: Yes, sir.

Judge: Mr. Taylor, I am finding you in contempt of this court and declaring a mistrial. You have acted against the interests of your client in direct contravention of all legal ethics, and you have interfered with the business of this court. I don't see how this can be anything but "conduct prejudicial to the administration of justice" and "conduct intended to disrupt a tribunal."

Me: Yes, sir.

Judge, shaking his head: I will have to file this with the state Supreme Court you know, Rip. They'll suspend you, at least.

Me: I know, sir. Tom, tell me you'll check this out?

Biddle: Yeah, of course. I'll get the State Police right on it. Can you give me that map? Rip, I don't know what you did, or why, but... Jeez, man.

That may not be exact, it's a lot to remember, but it's close. At least Max had the decency to stay silent through all of this. Even as I left the courtroom all he said was, "Well, shithead, you screwed the pooch rightly there. Didn't think you had it in you. Fuck of a way to handle it, but you get points for having the balls to pull it off. I'll be damned if I know what the fuck you'll do now." Me too, Max, me too.

I left the courthouse without speaking a word to my erstwhile client. I was just glad Judge Hobart hadn't thrown me in jail. Professional courtesy, I guess.

This was all before lunch. I called Mike from the courthouse and told him I had to see him right away, in private, in his office. He told me to come in—he hadn't heard what happened yet. I was honest with him about what had happened. It was all a matter of record, after all. He lit into me in a way that made Judge Hobart seem like a kindly old grandfather. I'll spare the gruesome details, but needless to say I'm out of a job. I'll at least have my license suspended; I may even be disbarred.

Mike fired me immediately. He was furious, especially when I told him I had no real evidence to back my claims, just "what the birds told me." He glared at me as I cleaned out my desk and then escorted me out of the office personally, taking my key and pass card.

His last words to me were: "Rip, you've done a lot for this firm. You've won some amazing cases, and you were well rewarded for it. But you undid all of that today. The harm you've done is beyond calculation. If I could take back all the bonuses I ever gave you I would do it in a heartbeat. As it is, you'll get your final base pay in the mail, and don't expect anything from this trial that you so royally screwed up. Not a cent."

"I understand, Mike. I'm sorry," I replied.

"Now get the fuck out of my building."

This will make the headlines tomorrow, I'm sure. Maybe it won't be too bad in the public's eye if Marner comes up guilty. That will depend on how it plays out and how the press handles it. Regardless, it will reflect badly on the firm and I'm sorry for that. It will make any guilty party think twice before signing on with the firm—and let's face it, most of the folks we represent are guilty. I feel awful about doing that to Mike.

So I'm screwed. And my client is screwed, but justly so. They held him over on suspicion of murder pending investigation of my claims. If I'm wrong, I'll not only lose my license but I'll be sued for all sorts of things by Marner, and rightly so. Fortunately, truth is absolute defense for slander. I only hope my insurance will cover any malpractice claims that may arise, guilty or innocent.

Now I get to figure out what to tell Dr. Filtner tomorrow, starting with "don't bother filing today's visit with insurance." Fired with cause means I don't even have the option for COBRA coverage.

Fuck.

Psychiatric Progress Notes

Patient Name: William "Rip" Taylor

Date: August 17, 2017

Diagnoses:
   Schizophrenia (Paranoid) *F20.0*
   Tardive Dyskinesia (subacute, drug-induced) *G24.01*

Medication List:
   Risperidone 6 mg PO SID (QHS)
   Ingrezza 80 mg PO SID (QHS)

Physical Findings and Mental Status:
   Vitals: Mildly elevated pulse (92) and BP (144/90), otherwise unremarkable.
   Mental Status: Alert and oriented to person, place, and time.
   Comportment: Well-groomed, alert posture, unremarkable.
   Mood and affect: Cooperative with elevated mood, possibly hypomanic.
   Ability to concentrate: Somewhat distracted.
   Tone and rate of speech: Inappropriately exuberant, slightly hurried.
   Danger to self/others: None.

Symptoms:

Mr. Taylor reports no significant symptoms of schizophrenia, saying this is unchanged. (Note this is not consistent with observation. See Clinical Impressions.)

Mr. Taylor reports significantly diminished extrapyramidal symptoms from tardive dyskinesia, consistent with observation.

Interventions:

I spent time exploring Mr. Taylor's elevated mood (see Clinical Impressions) without directly challenging it. We discussed his financial situation and future prospects.

I pressed Mr. Taylor about his compliance with medications given the inconsistency in his affect with respect to his previous visit.

Patient Response to Interventions:

Mr. Taylor at first denied that his mood was significantly different from his previous visit, but then acknowledged that he had been under considerable stress because of the case he was defending at that time. He indicated that he now had none of that stress since he was no longer employed as an attorney. He acknowledged that being unemployed was "concerning" and that his uncertain future was "awkward," but showed no real distress from these events even when pressed.

Mr. Taylor was quite emphatic that he was taking all his medications and never missed a dose. He was adamant that he took his medications as prescribed, and he attributed any change in behavior and affect to the change in his circumstances and possibly acclimatization to the new medication dosage. His denial seemed disproportionately emphatic, possibly indicating untruth.

Clinical Impressions:

Upon arrival, Mr. Taylor's smiled and requested that he be billed directly for this session rather than having the charges submitted to his insurance. When asked why, he shrugged and said, "I'm no longer employed and have no medical insurance at this time." He seemed completely unconcerned about this, despite his work having been his primary focus since starting under my care. There was no indication of either sadness or anger; if anything, he appeared exuberant.

When asked about what happened with his job, he shrugged his shoulders again, smiled at me, and said, "I made the mistake of doing the right thing. I acted for justice instead of jurisprudence and did what any good person and no good lawyer should ever do." He would not elaborate on this, saying, "You can probably read all about it in the newspaper." I will have to look for any stories relating to him and append them to these notes.

Asked if he would be finding another law firm, he replied, "No, I think I'm done with the law for at least a little while. I'll know for sure later. I'll be looking for something else, I guess." As before, this was delivered in an almost off-handed matter, as if it made little difference to him. He indicated that his financial situation was solid and this would not be an immediate cause for concern.

While this easygoing acceptance of his situation is admirable on the face of it, it is a very atypical response for anyone and is inconsistent with Mr. Taylor's personality. It does not appear to be a shallow façade, however, and was quite durable when challenged. In another patient, I would explain this grandiose behavior as a manic or hypomanic response, but Mr. Taylor has no history of mania nor other indications of bipolar disorder.

Mr. Taylor did seem distracted throughout the appointment, frequently looking at blank spots on the walls or missing conversation as if listening to other voices, much as was observed prior to the Risperidone increase and contrary to his behavior 2 weeks ago. My impression is that he is under-medicated, possibly either taking his medication less frequently than prescribed or splitting doses, despite his stringent denial of either.

Mr. Taylor's management of his schizophrenia seems precarious at best. I fear that he is on the verge of a psychotic break. It will be essential to monitor his condition closely, given the extremely stressful changes in his situation.

Mr. Taylor's tardive dyskinesia symptoms seem much reduced since starting the Ingrezza. He confirms this is consistent with his own observations. I observed occasional tongue darting and chewing, and the spastic blinking is little changed, but overall the effect is much reduced. The Ingrezza seems to be having the desired effect.

Plan:

I considered ordering a blood draw for Risperidone levels, but decided against it for now, given Mr. Taylor's present financial/insurance situation. It may be warranted, however, if his present state continues.

No change in dosage of either medication at this time, to allow for a baseline to be established. Ingrezza prescribed to maintain adequate supply.

Next appointment in two weeks.

Rx:

Ingrezza 80 mg PO SID (QHS), Q 90

Signed:

JoAnne Filtner, M.D., Ph.D.

Friday, August 18

Well, at least I know I was right. I got a call this morning from Tom Biddle, the prosecutor in the Marner case. He called just to let me know that the State Police had located a body presumed to be Palermo right where I had indicated, crammed into a rocky depression. It had not been buried, but it looked like it may have been covered with some branches. There wasn't any evidence of humans touching it since it was deposited, but animals had gotten to it. It had been partially dismembered and presumably devoured, which will make identification challenging. They also checked the car out and did find Marner's fingerprints around the headlights and ignition. He'd apparently wiped the steering wheel and gear shift—or maybe he'd worn gloves, but he missed those. Nice of Tom to let me know.

I got a confirmation of that about an hour later when the State Police came to my apartment, asking me to make a statement. There was considerable question about how I knew where the body was located. That knowledge made me a "person of interest" in the investigation. I hadn't considered that, though obviously I should have. I managed to evade the worst of their questions by claiming privileged communication.

I explained that information I found while researching the case led me to be suspicious, and that the evening just before my final court appearance I became certain. When asked what made me certain, I said simply, "That is privileged information that I am not at liberty to reveal." I neither named Marner nor stated the privilege that I was invoking. If they assumed it was attorney-client privilege, that is not my concern. Of course, they may have assumed it was fifth amendment privilege, too. In a way, it was—though not for the crime they think. I'm simply not admitting to the "crime" of having non-human counsel, which could get me locked up, if not in jail, in someplace arguably worse.

Max, of course, chimed in while I was being interviewed. "Well, shithead, you're in deep shit now. What a fuck-up. Never thought about what you were doing. Of course you're a suspect, you dumb fuck. You'll be lucky if you don't spend the rest of your miserable life in prison. Not that you don't deserve it, even if you didn't kill the guy." That sort of thing. I could barely hear the detective's questions over Max and the agitated noise of the mutterers. And the walls were filled with glaring eyes and mouths clearly shouting their disdain for me. I'm sure I must have appeared pretty distracted—but then, interrogation brings out the weird in people, anyway.

They've got Palermo's body, or what's left of it, at the morgue and will be doing a more detailed examination in the next couple days. Tom told me that much. Hopefully that will reveal something more about what happened to him, something that can be positively pinned to Marner and not me. I've got contacts at the Medical Examiner's office, of course, but they wouldn't tell me anything, even if I were to ask. I'm not that foolish. Too much curiosity does not look good.

Marner has apparently stopped saying anything to anyone, to no one's great surprise. He is no doubt awaiting a new lawyer. It won't be from Mike's firm, I'm sure. I won't be completely in the clear until they find some direct evidence of how Palermo was killed and proof that Marner was the sole murderer. I wasn't told that, of course, but it's clear enough now. The police can't rule out that I was in on it from the start and have taken out both Palermo *and* Marner in order to maximize my profits. It would be very helpful if the police could find where the stolen merchandise went. I obviously can't help with that search, as any information I gave would only increase suspicion about my involvement.

For what it's worth, I wasn't arrested, but I was requested to stay available and not leave the state without notifying the State Troopers. I suspect that has more to do with some lingering professional courtesy than any presumption of innocence. They aren't even trying to hide the fact that I'm being watched. There's an unmarked car parked where it can watch both the front entrance and the side fire exit, and another watching the back. I'd be willing to bet my phone is being monitored, too. I doubt they'd have much trouble getting a judge to issue a warrant for that. I'm "free"—but only free enough to hang myself.

Max has been suggesting I do just that, since I got back from the station. "Pack it up, shithead. You dug your own grave this time, so you might as well lie down in it. You dumb fuck. You poor miserable bastard. If it weren't so sad, it would be funny. Hell, it is funny. And to think I thought you might do something good. You had balls, that's for sure, but no brains. You don't deserve to walk around in public, shithead. Locking you up is better than you deserve." God, I hate him. He's right. He always is.

The smart thing for me to do would be to lawyer up, myself. But the little matter of my information source complicates that, so for now I'll proceed *pro se*. Hopefully they'll find something soon, or else Marner will come clean in order to cop a plea bargain and avoid the death penalty. That's assuming he doesn't figure that he can finger me for the crime—I'm sure he has no love for me at this point.

I tried going outside, just to sit and maybe find Mara and Kala, but every time I even considered doing that, I heard a hawk scream. They're waiting for me, too. They sense that I'm prey. Even if they wouldn't attack me, I couldn't subject Mara and Kala to their hungry attention. I've seen what a big hawk can do to birds their size, and it's not pretty. So now it's the middle of the afternoon and I'm holed up in my apartment, afraid to leave. I'm watched outside by the police under suspicion of murder and larceny, and watched inside by my own private judging eyes.

And there's that damned hawk, again! Max is right. I am well and truly fucked.

Saturday, August 19

Not much different today, unsurprisingly. I'm apparently still a suspect because the unmarked police cars are still there watching me. What must that be costing them? Max has been plaguing me pretty much non-stop, and even he has to nearly shout to be heard over the mutterers—if I can even call them that any more. I'm almost tempted to go back to the full 6 mg of Risperidone. Almost. Not really. At least I'm alive; at that dose, I was little more than an animated corpse.

Mara and Kala dove at my window this afternoon, kicking up a racket I could hear even over Verdi's *Aida* turned up loud enough to cover the other voices. I turned off the music and went outside. They quickly flew down beside me and started chattering away—in English. Yes, that's right, I can understand them again!

Mara: Are you there?

Kala: You look brighter.

Mara: We can find you even inside.

Kala: Even if we didn't know where you were.

Mara: Which we did.

Kala: Are you stuck here?

Mara: Where have you been?

Kala: You faded.

Mara: For weeks.

Kala: We couldn't find you.

Mara: And then when we found what looked like you...

Kala: You wouldn't talk to us...

Mara: So we'd talk to you...

Kala: And you ignored us.

Mara: And you were defending that bad man.

Kala: Very bad man.

Mara: We couldn't let you do that.

Kala: But you wouldn't listen.

Mara: We finally found a way.

Kala: Words on paper!
Mara: What a clever idea.
Kala: It was your idea, Mara.
Mara: I thought it was yours.
Kala: Either way, first we had to learn to read.
Mara: And then find the right words.
Kala: "Don't." That was the first.
Mara: Simple.
Kala: Short and sweet.
Mara: But maybe too simple.
Kala: Did you know what we meant?
Me, laughing to hear them again: Not really—there were too many possibilities.
Mara: Too simple.
Kala: Too short.
Mara: So then we had to think...
Kala: ...how to tell you so you'd understand
Mara: But you told us.
Kala: You were listening to it.
Mara: Macbeth.
Kala: What an odd story.
Mara: But beautifully poignant.
Kala: Right on point.
Mara: And then we had to find the right words.
Kala: That was hard.
Mara: Very hard.
Kala: But we succeeded.
Mara: We hunted.
Kala: And we found it.
Mara: "Banquo's Ghost."
Kala: Wasn't that clever?
Mara: You understood that, right?
Me: Eventually, yes. I figured it out.
Kala: But you still kept defending that bad man.
Mara: Why did you do that?
Kala: We thought you must not know.

Mara: Or didn't know what to tell others.
Kala: Most people don't understand us.
Mara: So maybe you can't convince them.
Kala: You needed more.
Mara: So we showed you where.
Kala: On a map.
Mara: That was clever, too.
Kala: Maps are hard.
Mara: Harder than reading.
Kala: Because you have to read *and* understand the lines.
Mara: Easier to just go somewhere.
Kala: Fly there and see it.
Mara: Don't draw it.
Kala: But you can't fly.
Mara: And we couldn't talk to you.
Kala: So we learned maps, too.
Mara: Harder than words!
Kala: But we found it.
Mara: Knew where the body was.
Kala: And knew how to show you.
Mara: And you understood.
Kala: Not our words.
Mara: But our meaning.
Kala: You are clever, too.
Mara: If a bit slow.
Kala: And you stopped defending the bad man.
Mara: And now he'll be punished for what he did.
Kala: Eventually.
Mara: So everything is better.
Me: Not quite. They think I might have done it.
Kala: But you didn't know either of them.
Mara: Not until after the one was dead.
Kala: You couldn't do it.
Mara: We know that.
Kala: And you know that.
Me: But the police don't. They need proof.

Mara: That proof thing again.
Kala: Very silly.
Mara: Why not just use what's true...
Kala: ...and not bother with proving?
Mara: They have the body.
Kala: And the shiny metal stuff now.
Mara: That should be enough.
Me: Wait, they found the merchandise? The stuff that was stolen?
Kala: They found it this morning.
Mara: In a storage yard.
Kala: They found where both bad men put stuff.
Mara: Every week.
Kala: For a year.
Mara: In this big metal building.
Kala: With a bright orange door.
Mara: Big door.
Me: They rented a storage shed?
Kala: That was where they put it.
Mara: Every week.
Me: They must have used a different name or something. Harder to trace, I guess.
Kala: We don't know that.
Mara: But the police were there today.
Kala: We helped them find it.
Mara: They needed our help.
Me: You talked to the police?
Kala: No, they don't understand us.
Mara: But we told them.
Kala: Like we told you.
Mara: When you couldn't understand us.
Kala: Words on paper.
Mara: They figured it out.
Kala: They took all the stuff out.
Mara: Lots and lots of stuff.
Kala: They brought a truck.

Mara: Too much for a car.

Kala: So now they have it, so they know you didn't do any-thing.

Mara: Or isn't that proof?

Kala: Proof doesn't make sense.

Mara: True makes sense.

Kala: One bad man is dead, that is true.

Mara: And the other is in jail, that is true, too.

Kala: And you didn't do anything.

Mara: You aren't a bad man.

Kala: And you aren't in jail.

Mara: Or dead.

Kala: Though we thought you might be.

Mara: When we couldn't find you.

Kala: But you're back.

Mara: And not in jail.

Kala: And not dead.

Me: You're half-right, at least: I'm not dead. And not in jail yet.

Mara: Are you going to jail?

Kala: That would not be good.

Mara: That would be bad.

Me: I hope not. That remains to be seen. Even if I'm not in jail, though, I don't know what I will be doing. I don't think I can be a lawyer any more.

Kala: We're working on that.

Mara: Yes, we have plans.

Kala: Secret plans.

Mara: Secret for now. We can't tell you.

Kala: Not a word.

Mara: Not now.

Kala: But soon.

Mara: Once we know more.

Kala: Yes, more truth to find.

Mara: Good plans.

Kala: Soon.

And with that cryptic message they flew off, perhaps sensing the hawk that cried a few seconds later.

So the police are still watching me—but they have the stolen merchandise. They somehow tracked down the rental shed where it was being stored, presumably by finding the rental records. And from what Mara and Kala said, I guess they were both in it together, and Marner just got greedy, or maybe scared. Hopefully that will fall out to clear me. For now, though, I'm still being watched. And not just by the police. The eyes have been multiplying. At least Max has been quiet since Mara and Kala gave me their news.

Monday, August 21

I got a phone call this morning at 8:30 from the police, asking me to come to the station to answer a few questions. Asking, not sending someone to pick me up—I thought that was a positive start. Max didn't, of course. "Yep, shithead, that's how it works. Make you relax and think you're in the clear so you'll talk freely, then spring the trap. Just try and run or refuse, you'll see." Shut up, Max.

When I went outside to drive there, about an hour later, the unmarked cars that had been there were gone, or at least better hidden. I didn't doubt Max was right, though. I drove to the station and after about fifteen minutes was shown into an interview room to meet with the detective.

"Thank you for coming in, Mr. Taylor. Let's get right to it. You know you're a possible suspect in the theft from Wilderness Experience and the murder of Richard Palermo, correct?"

"Yes, sir. Though I didn't know it had been ruled a homicide."

"It hasn't yet. Not officially, anyway, but we're investigating it as if it were. I don't think you did it, personally, but there's the question of how you knew where to find the body. If you could clear that up, it would be much easier to eliminate you as a suspect."

"I'm sorry, sir. I can't do that. It's privileged information."

"You didn't have any problem divulging that information at the trial."

"On the contrary, I had many problems doing it. It has already cost me my job, and likely will cost me my license and my livelihood."

"But you broke confidence anyway."

"No sir. What I revealed I found out on my own. That was not privileged information. *How* I found it out—that is privileged. I had many problems, but breaking privilege was not one."

"Then why did you do it, if it cost you so much?"

"It was the right thing to do, don't you think? Mr. Marner was on the verge of being acquitted for the theft and no one had any knowledge about the murder. That would have been unjust."

"Since when does a defense lawyer worry about justice?"

I smiled and shrugged my shoulders. "Since last week, apparently."

"Hmmm." He looked at his notes. "Know anything about the U-Store in Fountain?"

"No, should I?"

"Ever been there?"

"Not that I recall. I don't have much reason to go to Fountain."

"Right. So if we found your fingerprints there?"

"I would be very surprised. Are you saying you did?"

"I'm not saying anything one way or other, just asking questions."

"Yes, sir. May I assume that this has something to do with the Marner/Palermo case?"

"Why do you ask?"

"Well, as I understand it, that case is why I'm here answering questions. And knowing something about the case, well.... When I was looking into it, I didn't find any evidence that the stolen property had been fenced or sold. That didn't mean it hadn't been, but it would be reasonable for them to have stored it for a while to avoid suspicion."

"You figured that out, huh?"

"Detective, it was my job to figure that out. And if Mr. Marner had been tried and acquitted for the theft, well, then it would be safe for him to move the goods."

"How do you figure that?"

"Double jeopardy. He was already tried and acquitted. He can't be charged with that theft again. Oh, he could face other charges, but not the larceny charge."

"But you put a stop to that."

"Well, not permanently. It was declared a mistrial. He can be tried again now."

"Part of your justice?"

"It was a consideration. So I'm right then, you found the stolen property at the storage facility?"

"Yeah, alright. We did."

"And the lease on it?"

"Marner leased it—paid in cash. His is the only name on the lease, but the attendant remembers another man with him."

"Palermo?"

"Or you."

"It wasn't me. How did you find out about the storage?"

"How did you find out about the body?"

"I see. I suppose you could say a little bird told me. Two birds, in fact."

"You don't say? Jays?"

I hoped I didn't startle too much at that. "Why do you say that?"

"It's the damnedest thing. We suspected they might have stashed the loot, and I was out checking the local storage rentals in Springs, showing the managers pictures of Marner, Palermo, and you."

"Me?"

"You are a possible suspect. Anyway, there's about twenty different storage lots, and I'd been to all of them. Nobody knew anything. I'd just checked the last one when these two jays—the blue ones?"

"Steller's jays."

"Yeah, them. One was flying all around me, all in my face, and the other was poking at my jacket. They flew off after a few seconds. I thought it was weird, but forgot about it. At least until I found a card in my jacket pocket. A card for the U-Store in Fountain."

I barely stifled a grin. "How unusual! And that's where you found the stolen property?"

"That's right. It wasn't on my list, being outside of the city, you know. But I thought, what the hell, and sure enough, that's where we found it all. And now you talk about the birds."

"It's a common expression."

"Come on. You just about jumped when I said they were jays. But you aren't surprised about what they did." Damn, I did react.

"What are you suggesting, detective?"

"Did you train them?"

I laughed before I could catch myself. "No, sir. If anything, they've trained me."

"What do you mean?"

"They follow me. I feed them. They have me well trained to feed them."

"And they gave you the information about the body?"

"Detective, that would be absurd."

"You said they told you."

"I said two birds told me—a common enough expression for people whose identity is being protected."

"But you know these two jays."

"I know two jays—whether they are the ones who you ran into, I can't say."

"Uh huh. You can't say. Did you give them the card?"

"Why would I do that?"

"Why, indeed. Then where did they get it?"

"Found it on the ground, I would imagine. Jays pick up all kinds of things."

"Mmm-hmm. And then they just happened to put it in my pocket?"

"So it would appear, detective."

"And you don't know anything about this."

"How could I?"

The detective watched me quietly for a moment, no doubt hoping I'd say something more. When it was clear I wasn't going to answer my own question, he proceeded.

"I don't like mysteries, Mr. Taylor. I don't like loose threads and things I can't explain."

"I would imagine that's an occupational hazard for you."

He actually laughed at that. "Yes, well, I guess it is."

"Are there any more questions, Detective? Am I free to go?"

"I suppose so. You don't have anything more you want to share about the case?"

"No, sir. You know all that I do about it."

"I doubt that. But I don't think you did it. I guess you knew we were watching you?"

"It was pretty obvious."

"Yeah. Well, that's done. You're free to go, for now. But if we find anything more that ties you to the case, that could change." He handed me his card. "Call me if you happen to have anything else you want to share, OK?"

"Of course."

"And Taylor?"

"Yes, detective?"

"Watch it with the birds."

That was my morning. I came back home and fixed some lunch while listening to *Die Meistersinger*. In the afternoon I was served with a summons to appear before a Hearing Board convened by the Presiding Disciplinary Judge of the Colorado Supreme Court. I'd been expecting as much, but not so soon.

I'll give this to Judge Hobart, he moves fast. He must have invoked Rule 251.8 for Immediate Suspension of my license. The hearing will be on Monday, September 11. I am ordered to refrain from any legal duties not already in process until the hearing.

Max is right. I'm a shithead, and my career, if not my life, is toast.

Wednesday, August 23

Not going to work every day takes some getting used to. Before, those few times when I've taken an extended vacation, I always had the return to work to look forward to. Even when my license was suspended the first time, back when I was working for the DA's office, I knew in pretty short order that I'd have another position soon on the other side of the aisle. That suspension was only thirty days, too. I'm sure this one will be longer, maybe permanent.

I got a call this morning from the detective I spoke with on Monday. He let me know that Marner had pled guilty to both the theft and the murder of Palermo in return for having the death penalty taken off the table. He didn't go into details, of course, but it was clear they had strong evidence against Marner, so this was his only recourse. He told me that my name had never come up, and there was no evidence supporting my involvement, so I was officially no longer a person of interest in either crime. It was unusually nice of him to tell me that—that's not normal police practice. I suspect he may think I somehow produced the evidence that led to the conviction and used Mara and Kala to deliver it. This was his way of thanking me for the help. I wasn't inclined to disabuse him of that notion.

Speaking of Mara and Kala, they have been acting very mysterious—more so than normal, which I might not have believed possible before now. They keep talking about "secret plans" and telling me not to worry about having lost my job, that these plans will keep me busy. I tried asking whether these plans included getting paid, but they were (deliberately?) vague and unconcerned about that issue. I'm not sure they really understand the human economy, but I've also learned that I shouldn't assume any limitations on their knowledge or ability. They learned to read and use maps when they needed to, and they seemed to understand the plot of *Macbeth* after hearing only the first act of the opera through a closed window. How is that even possible? They seem to know (or learn?) whatever they need to know to accomplish their purposes. Purposes that they keep to themselves.

Those purposes, as much as I understood them, have always aligned with my own so far. Honestly, I built my career almost entirely on their influence. If I ever doubted that, it was made only too clear during their recent absence. Those purposes, while they cost me my job and perhaps my career, were always focused on justice. Mara and Kala, like me, care more about justice than about winning. As much as I can tell anything, though, it seems like they have something else planned now. Here was yesterday's conversation, as near as I can reproduce it:

Me: There you are! I missed you yesterday and the day before.
Mara: We have been busy.
Kala: Very busy.
Mara: No time to visit.
Kala: Working on plans.
Mara: Secret plans.
Kala: Very secret.
Mara: But not for long.
Kala: No, not long. Soon all will be revealed.
Mara: Not all.
Kala: True. Not all. But more than now.
Mara: Much more.
Kala: But not yet.
Me: Can you tell me anything about these plans you have for me?
Mara: No, too soon for that.
Kala: Too much uncertain.
Mara: We are working on it.
Kala: Working hard.
Mara: Much to do, far to go.
Kala: Very far.
Mara: Long trips.
Kala: Which is why we were gone.

Mara: Yes, we weren't here.
Kala: Couldn't visit even if we weren't busy.
Mara: More trips to come.
Kala: Yes, you won't see us for days.
Mara: Several days.
Kala: At least several.
Mara: But don't worry.
Kala: Worrying is bad; it accomplishes nothing.
Mara: We're getting things set up for you.
Kala: Finding the right place.
Mara: Finding the right people.
Kala: Making sure everything is right.
Mara: Everything is just so.
Kala: Just so what?
Mara: Just so right!
Kala: Exactly.
Me: So I will need to travel, too? You're setting something up away from here?
Mara: Oh, yes.
Kala: Can't do this here.
Mara: Not that it's not needed here.
Kala: It's needed everywhere.
Mara: Including here.
Kala: But need is not opportunity.
Mara: Well said.
Kala: Thank you.
Mara: But we are finding opportunity.
Kala: It will be good.
Mara: Very good.
Me: More legal defense work? You know I won't be able to practice law, for a while at least. Maybe permanently.
Kala: We know.
Mara: But we don't understand.
Kala: You told the truth.
Mara: You got the bad man punished.
Kala: You served justice.

Mara: Isn't that the aim of the law?

Kala: Justice. You call your top judges that.

Mara: Indeed.

Me: In the large sense, the law is about justice, but it's also about fairness and a set of rules to operate within, to ensure that fairness is always maintained.

Kala: Is it fair to let bad people go free?

Mara: Or to punish innocent people?

Kala: That seems most unfair.

Me: Sometimes we can't know the truth—who is guilty, who is innocent. The rules generally protect us from doing harm. But sometimes—like in this case—they get in the way of justice.

Mara: This seems very silly.

Kala: If the rules get in the way, you need new rules.

Mara: Or you need to ignore the rules.

Me: These rules are the best we've been able to come up with after centuries of trying. And I did ignore the rules, which is why I can't practice law any more.

Kala: Because the rules are more important than justice?

Me: Ultimately, yes. Yes, they are.

Mara: That seems silly.

Kala: That seems worse than silly.

Mara: True. Much worse.

Me: Well, I guess I agree. My actions say that, anyway.

Kala: Yes, you did good.

Mara: And got punished for it.

Kala: So we will reward you.

Mara: Not punish you.

Kala: You will see. You will do more good.

Me: And this good I do, will I be paid for it? I don't need a lot, but I need enough to have a place to live and food to eat.

Mara: We are working on that.

Kala: Finding the right place.

Mara: The right people.

Kala: Where you can live.

Mara: And do good.

Kala: And get paid for the good you do.

Mara: And not for following stupid rules.

Kala: But that is hard to find.

Mara: Very hard—your systems don't work that way.

Kala: Very true. Things are broken.

Mara: Not everything, though.

Kala: Not everywhere.

Mara: Not all the time.

Kala: You will see.

Mara: You will.

Kala: Soon.

Mara: But not today.

Kala: Not even tomorrow.

Me: OK. But don't take too long, OK? I'm good for a while, but eventually I need to have some idea what I'm doing.

Mara: Patience! We are working as fast as we can.

Kala: Maybe faster.

Mara: How can we work faster than we can?

Kala: By having others help.

Mara: Oh yes, that's true. Faster then.

Kala: Soon. You'll see.

Mara: Soon.

And with that, they flew off to... wherever they are going. Maybe where I'm going. I guess I'll find out when they are ready to tell me. I can't go anywhere until after September 11, anyway, when I have my hearing to determine my fate as a member of the bar. After that, well, we'll see.

Friday, August 25

Mara and Kala are still gone on whatever errand they are pursuing. I haven't seen them since Tuesday. I miss them. I worry about them traveling—I hope they are safe. So many predators, especially in unfamiliar territories.

Which is where I find myself. Not geographically, of course; I'm still at home. But occupationally and even spiritually. *Terra incognita.* I don't do well at waiting without a known purpose. It leaves too much time for my mind to wander. Too much opportunity to listen to other voices. Too few distractions. Too much awareness. If Mara and Kala could at least give me a hint I might at least have something to study, something to learn about. But I don't have any idea what they have planned for me.

Max, of course, has plenty to say about that.

"Well, shithead, how the mighty have fallen. You were doing so well. Standing up for yourself. Taking risks, making sacrifices. And now what? The sacrifice has been made and you are left an empty corpse? You dumb fuck. Get out there and do something. Stand on your own feet!

"But no, you don't stand up. Instead you are waiting on birds. Birds! You're incapable now of doing anything on your own? As soon as the jays come back you trade in your balls? You have to wait for birds to think for you? Is that all you are, a slave to a pair of fucking jays? You are a miserable excuse for a human. No wonder you are done as a lawyer. What a fuck-up. Can't think for yourself. You don't deserve your license. You should never have been admitted to the bar. Those damn birds rule you, and you let them. What a fuck-up. What a shithead."

You get the picture. There was lots more of that. All cruel—cruel because it is accurate. Max sees me more clearly than anyone, including myself. I am a worthless excuse for a human.

Tempest has offered lots of suggestions about how I should fill my time, too. I have to admit I'm sometimes tempted to follow her lead. I can only take so much of sitting here in the apartment listening to opera and the voices in my head, seeing the walls animated only by disdainful eyes and mouths. I've tried going out—going on hikes and long drives. But lately, every time I try to do that, I am pursued by the raptors. Not always the same ones—some days it's red-tails. Other times it's a sharp shinned hawk or a Cooper's hawk. I went up to one of the high lakes and was pursued by an osprey. Walking around the city, it was a kestrel or that damned peregrine. At night, if I venture out, there are the cries of the barred and great horned owls. They are clearly stalking me. Letting me know that I am prey. Just waiting for the opportunity to strike.

So mostly I stay in. But that doesn't stop Tempest. No, she knows all sorts of things to offer. Any number of distractions that will come to me right here in the apartment. And she makes it so easy, so tempting. Reminding me that there is no harm in supporting an independent girl—only good. Helping her survive—purchasing a freely offered service and supporting the local economy. Tempest has all the answers. And she's right, too.

It would be good—except that I don't deserve it. As Max is quick to observe, I'm a shithead and a fuck-up. I don't deserve the happy distractions that Tempest offers. So I keep telling her no. And she keeps offering anyway. If something doesn't happen soon, she'll win. I can feel myself weakening. Falling prey to her gentle but insistent encouragement. Rotting me from the inside as Max chews on me from the outside.

Even Mia is getting into the act these days, usually after Max has had a go at me. So quick to coddle me. So quick to offer useless sympathies. To treat me like a weepy child. Which I am, I suppose, but I don't need to be mothered. I've made it this far without it; I'm not about to go back now. Give me something useful, Mia, not your pity. Your solicitous ministrations accomplish nothing. They can't even give me the pleasure that Tempest promises. They just remind me of how pitiful and puny I really am.

Fuck. This is a messed up entry. Waiting is hard. Where are Mara and Kala? What are they doing? When will I know what the future holds?

Max is right, I am a slave to the jays. I like to pretend that I listen to their suggestions and then make my own decision, but of course whatever they suggest will be what I decide. And why not? Like Max, they are always right. They are the truth I don't deserve. They are the golden opportunity—the only such miracle I've ever had in my life. They are what keep me going. And now they are missing. They said they'd be gone for a while. But how long? Are they safe? Are they OK? When will they return?

Come rescue me, my friends. Before Max and Tempest and Mia drive me completely 'round the bend. It's not so very far a trip, after all.

Tuesday, August 29

It's been a week since I've seen Mara and Kala. Max haunts me every day, several times a day. For hours. I am nothing. I am the shithead he claims me to be. I have given up in defeat at the loss of my most trusted advisors. He's right. I am their slave, and without their attention, I am nothing. Worse than nothing—a blight on the world.

This weekend I let Tempest win, if only to escape Max for a little while. Saturday I called up an independent woman who offers an outcall service. Consuela, she said her name was. That's not her name, of course, but I didn't care. She was my Consuela, my consolation, if only for an hour. I didn't know her, but I knew how to find her from defending others like her. Knew where to look, how to contact her, what to ask for. She was perfect. She gave me the escape I needed, even if it wasn't quite what Tempest recommended. Max was quiet while she was here, but the eyes watched and judged me, and the mouths spat their wordless chastisements. I couldn't look away from them even to feast my eyes on Consuela.

She was very beautiful, my Consuela, but in the end, there was nothing physical. Not for want of her trying. Consuela was sensual and so very willing, everything I could possibly want in a sexual partner. She even offered me little blue pills to help me perform—part of the service, I guess. I didn't take them, though, and didn't even try to do anything more than hold her. Caress her, and talk. And cry. I didn't expect that last one.

The mutterers carried on, of course, but they are just so much noise. Consuela was my balm. I may call her again. What have I got to lose? She certainly seemed happy for the work. Of course, it's her job to seem happy—that's what I paid her for. But I paid willingly, and tipped well. Why not? Good payment for good services rendered, even if not the services either of us anticipated.

Of course, as soon as she left, Max was back. Letting me have it. Berating me for being incapable of doing anything on my own. And he's right.

He brought a friend, too. Or maybe it's a part of him. A thundercloud. My own private thundercloud. Lightning, thunder, the whole works. Max said it was my own creation, but I think he brought it. How could I create anything so powerful as that? It is chaos—that's what Max called it. Chaos. Maximum entropy—the chaos of my existence, spinning out of control without guidance from Mara and Kala. Max said I should enjoy it. It was my creation, after all, the only thing I'm capable of creating. I wish it would fucking go away. It lingers in the corner of whatever room I'm in, up near the ceiling, shooting lighting out the top and bottom and rumbling away in chaos.

I wonder if Consuela will mind it? Maybe she won't see it, if it's like Max and the rest. Can she be that blind? It's hard to miss. How do you obscure a private thunderstorm? Can chaos be hidden? Surely it must be so manifest that others can't miss it.

I have stopped shaving. I have stopped showering. I have stopped caring. I will have to put on a mask of civilization on Thursday, I suppose—for my appointment with Dr. Filtner. Mustn't let her see how I've devolved, after all. Put on the smiles and the happy face. I won't even try to get her to approve the return to 4 mg Risperidone. Keep giving me the 6 mg and I'll keep dividing the pills. I am building a stockpile that way. I might need it if I have to travel. Who knows if she'll give me an advance scrip anyway. She thinks I need more care. She wants to lock me up. She thinks I need to be fixed.

I'm not broken. I'm just worthless. I have manifested my abilities, my special senses, and they have revealed me to be the fuck-up that Max always knew I was. Without Mara and Kala, I am utterly without redemption. I serve no purpose. Chaos. That's all I am. A shithead. A fuck-up. A waste of space. Even Mia has given up on me. She quit coming around after I yelled at her. I told her it was too late to mother me. If she'd been my mother when I was a child, things might be different. It was too late now, and her empty ministrations were just so much piss in the wind. I told her to fuck off. I guess she did.

Maybe I should call Consuela again. But that would mean cleaning up—I have at least that much self-respect left. I don't want her to see how worthless I am—though she must know already. Why should she care? The money is good. I guess it's vanity, empty pride on my part.

The fiction—that is everything. Her fiction, and mine. Falsehood carefully constructed for my pleasure and her survival. Have to play the game. Have to follow the rules. The rules say I care enough to shower and shave and not live in squalor and a sea of trash. Fuck the rules—that's too much to ask. So no, no Consuela. Just me. Me and my chaos, my thunderstorm. And Max. Alone with my truth. My failure.

Why did I even write this? No one cares. No one should. Worthless.

Psychiatric Progress Notes

Patient Name: William "Rip" Taylor

Date: August 31, 2017

Diagnoses:
Schizophrenia (Paranoid) *F20.0*
Tardive Dyskinesia (subacute, drug-induced) *G24.01*

Medication List:
Risperidone 6 mg PO SID (QHS)
Ingrezza 80 mg PO SID (QHS)

Physical Findings and Mental Status:
Vitals: Unremarkable, pulse and BP slightly elevated.
Mental Status: Alert and oriented to person, place, and time once attention could be obtained.
Comportment: Disheveled and unkempt appearance, un-shaven, hair tangled.
Mood and affect: Distracted and combative. Highly labile.
Ability to concentrate: Greatly reduced. Distracted by apparent hallucinations, unable to maintain a coherent conversation past two responses.
Tone and rate of speech: Rushed with occasional "word salad."
Danger to self/others: No explicit threat, but unable to care for himself.

Symptoms:
Mr. Taylor reports that he is suffering no delusions or hallucinations in spite of obvious evidence to the contrary (at one point interjecting "Shut up, Max, and let the doctor talk" despite no one else being present).

He stated that he was taking his medication as prescribed, but when asked what that was, said, "three 'migs' of Risperidone"—half his prescribed dosage. He corrected this to six when pressed, but not until then.

Interventions:

I asked Mr. Taylor for any explanation for his unkempt experience, and he denied that anything was amiss. He replied that he was simply "enjoying his retirement," though there was no sign of joy. I attempted to challenge his mental status but was unable to engage him in any coherent fashion.

I suggested Mr. Taylor consider a brief hospitalization for observation. Once he understood what I was suggesting, he reacted aggressively, denying that there was any reason to even consider such action. After ten minutes of fractured discussion, I excused myself to use the rest room and called 9-1-1 to send paramedics and police for an involuntary psychiatric hold. They arrived within ten minutes while Mr. Taylor was still in the office.

I spent the remainder of the session time filling out the necessary Baker Act paperwork for an involuntary 72 hour hold.

Patient Response to Interventions:

As noted above, Mr. Taylor declined to voluntarily commit himself for observation, but acquiesced to the involuntary commitment when it became clear that he had no other viable options. He complained but did not struggle when strapped to the gurney for his and the attendants' safety.

Clinical Impressions:

Mr. Taylor is clearly in the midst of a severe psychotic break, likely due to the stress of his joblessness coupled with a suspected decrease in dosage of his Risperidone against medical advice. He demonstrates clear evidence that he is unable to care for himself in his present state and in my estimation represents a danger to himself and possibly others.

Plan:

Mr. Taylor was committed to a 72 hour involuntary psychiatric hold at approximately 4:00 PM today. I have ordered a Risperidone level upon admission, and have given orders for Haldol to be administered while gross psychosis manifests, at the discretion of the psychiatric resident on duty. Additionally, Mr.

Taylor should continue his present medications while hospital-
ized.

I will visit him tomorrow in hospital to assess his condition
and revise my orders as needed.

No next appointment scheduled at this time.

Rx:

Haldol 4 mg IM Q4H until gross psychosis subsides, at the
discretion of the psychiatric resident on duty (inpatient medication order)

Risperidone 6 mg PO SID (QHS) (inpatient medication order)

Ingrezza 80 mg PO SID (QHS) (inpatient medication order)

Signed:

JoAnne Filtner, M.D., Ph.D.

Inpatient Psychiatric Report

Patient Name: William "Rip" Taylor

Timestamp: Friday, September 1, 2017, 3:07 PM

Diagnoses:
Schizophrenia (Paranoid) *F20.0*
Tardive Dyskinesia (subacute, drug-induced) *G24.01*

Medication List:
Risperidone 6 mg PO SID (QHS)
Ingrezza 80 mg PO SID (QHS)

Physical Findings and Mental Status:
Vitals: Unremarkable, slightly depressed from baseline.
Mental Status: Drowsy but alert and oriented to person, place, and time once roused.
Comportment: Improved appearance, alert posture, unremarkable.
Mood and affect: Cooperative and situationally appropriate, subdued.
Ability to concentrate: Moderately sluggish but without distraction.
Tone and rate of speech: Appropriate and unhurried.
Danger to self/others: None.

Symptoms:
Mr. Taylor reports that he feels overmedicated and "mentally dead."

Mr. Taylor understands the reason for the involuntary hospitalization but maintains that it was unnecessary. He states that his condition was only "stress" from losing his job and the impending hearing about his law license. He denies any positive symptoms of schizophrenia even during the break other than "some breakthrough voices of no consequence."

Interventions:

A stat drug level for Risperidone was ordered upon admission. Results are inconsistent with 6 mg QHS, but consistent with 3 mg. Mr. Taylor was challenged with this information after he first maintained that he had taken his medication as prescribed.

Haldol was discontinued by Dr. Richardson at 8:00 this morning. Mr. Taylor had received four 4 mg IM doses of Haldol at that time (last at 6:00 AM) for a total of 16 mg in 12 hours. Nursing reports indicate fitful sleep through the night, deepening as the night progressed and the Haldol reached therapeutic levels.

Patient Response to Interventions:

Mr. Taylor initially maintained that he had taken all medications as prescribed prior to this hospitalization. When confronted with the laboratory results, however, he admitted that he had been taking half-doses (using a pill splitter) for two weeks prior. He remained adamant that he would not consent to a return to the 6 mg dose, however, despite the obvious consequences of the reduced dosage. When asked why, he responded, "Because it leaves me like this: medicated to the gills and incapable of any inspiration, creativity, or original thought. In every way that matters, I am dead." This loquacious answer was delivered without hesitation even in his depressed state, which suggests it is a repeatedly traversed thought pattern rather than an unrehearsed response to the question.

Mr. Taylor was completely unwilling to consider any antipsychotic other than Risperidone, nor any dose above 4 mg SID. He was unwilling to consider the long-acting intramuscular form of the medication. He noted that, since he is paying out of pocket now, that he would not hesitate to find another psychiatrist who would "listen to [him]" if I did not comply with his wishes. He was unmoved when I noted that another psychotic break would result in another involuntary hold, assuring me that it would not happen.

Clinical Impressions:

Mr. Taylor appears to be past the gross consequences of a psychotic break stemming from a reduction in antipsychotic medication against medical advice. He is subdued from the neuroleptic effects of the Haldol at this time.

It is my judgment that 4 mg of Risperidone is an insufficient dosage to fully mitigate his psychosis, but in light of his defiant non-compliance with a higher dose and refusal to consider long acting (biweekly intramuscular injection) Risperidone or any other antipsychotic medication, I am forced to comply with his wishes for now.

Plan:

Mr. Taylor will start on 4 mg Risperidone in addition to the 80 mg Ingrezza with this evening's dose as noted above. Discharge instructions include a prescription for 4 mg Risperidone SID (QHS) Q30.

I will authorize his discharge following his examination tomorrow at the discretion of the psychiatric resident on duty. If he is not discharged at that time, he will need to be discharged no later than noon on Sunday in compliance with the 72 hour hold.

Next appointment will be scheduled post-discharge.

Rx:

Risperidone 4 mg PO SID (QHS), Q 30

Signed:

JoAnne Filtner, M.D., Ph.D.

Saturday, September 2, 2017

Fuck Dr. Filtner and fuck psychiatrists and the entire fucked-up medical industry! A fucking 72-hour hold? I was discharged at noon today, after almost two full days in the psych ward, and after being doped to the gills with fucking Haldol. 16 mg total! Jesus Christ, it's a wonder I could even talk after that. I'm still only half here.

Everything is quiet. No Max, no Tempest, not even the mutterers. No eyes, no mouths. And no Mara or Kala—even as mute jays. I am physically alive, but mentally I am just a shell. I can barely come up with words to put here.

At least the bitch agreed to reduce my Risperidone to 4 mg, but only because I gave her no choice. She knew there was no way I would stand for 6 mg, and that it was either 4 mg, or 3 mg by me my dividing my dose—and I find a new shrink. It won't last, though. She made that clear. She intends to raise it one way or another. Well, good luck with that, bitch. If I can't live my life with all my faculties intact, what's the point of living at all?

I'm going to skip my dose tonight and just start the 4 mg tomorrow so I can maybe get back to my life more quickly. I agree I need something—my sensitivity and perception are overwhelming without something to check them, but that doesn't mean they should be obliterated entirely.

Fuck. I'm going back to bed.

Sunday, September 3

Barely a week until my hearing. I need to get back on my feet.

I woke up to silence again this morning. Is this how "normal" people live? God, how do they survive it? Not just not seeing and hearing all that is out there, but not feeling, either. I am incapable of passion—not joy, not sorrow, nothing. Well, almost nothing—I am managing to be angry with Dr. Filtner still, though I credit that to extreme provocation.

By noon the silence was overwhelming, and music failed utterly to move my soul. What fate could be worse than that? I went for a hike in the foothills. I think I walked for about four hours, though I honestly don't remember much of it. By the end of the walk, though, I was beginning to feel a little more like myself. What I thought was the breeze rustling the aspen turned out to be the susurrations of the mutterers beginning to return. I discovered this when I got into my car and shut the door and the sound continued. I guess the Haldol didn't do any permanent harm.

It's 8:30 now, and they have gotten a little louder, but it is still an indistinct rushing noise, and not anything discernable as speech, however muffled. Max and the others are still gone, too, as are the eyes—though I'm starting to see... something... out of the corner of my eye.

No sign of Mara and Kala, either. There was a jay that scolded me at one point while I was walking, but just one, and it was clearly just guarding its territory. Once I walked on, it left me alone. Where are you, my friends? What are you working on? Are you safe? When will you return to me?

I don't know about the Risperidone—I'm tempted to give it another day. I'm clearly still overmedicated. I know the Risperidone takes a while to build, though, as well. I think I'll skip it one more night and start it tomorrow. Hopefully things will continue to improve.

It really is criminal that I—that all of us—have to fight for our own treatment and definition of health. How do psychiatrists pretend that they know what is best for us? They aren't in our heads. They don't know what we face. They think that their pitiful existence is something to be desired, and the more we don't actively color beyond their lines, the happier they are. So they medicate us until we are zombies incapable of coloring at all. We scratch ineffectually at the paper and they call it progress. "See? No stray marks." No marks at all, dammit. They look at the beautiful creations of our exceptional minds, and they see only disorder and chaos. Creativity that must be stamped out. Perception that must be obliterated. Heaven forbid that anyone see further or more clearly than them. Their world is too small to allow for the likes of us. Well, fuck their world!

I'm going to try listening to something simple and light. Something more technical than passionate. Mozart, I think. *Cozi Fan Tutte*, maybe. That's light and easy; maybe I can at least enjoy that. That, and a bath. And a glass of wine. Maybe two glasses. And then we'll see what tomorrow brings.

Tuesday, September 5

I took a 3 mg Risperidone last night—one half of one of the 6 mg tablets I was prescribed earlier. Things still aren't back to where I'd like them to be—I feel dull and befogged. I filled the 4 mg scrip and will take those once I'm thinking a little more clearly. I almost didn't take anything, but I don't want to wait too long to start and end up being overwhelmed again. The last thing I need is to miss my hearing because I'm in another damned 72-hour hold.

Ideally, I'd like to learn to just live with my reality, pure and unadulterated. Just knowing that Max and the others *can* be silenced weakens their hold a bit. It's not that they are any less real, or any less correct, but they don't hold all the cards anymore. It is possible for me to control them, to silence them, to banish them from my reality—if I am willing to pay the cost. That cost is the loss of my sensitivity and my creativity; my ability to think, to reason, and to synthesize. Ultimately, the cost is the loss of myself—of everything that is uniquely me. I become an empty shell, physically resembling me but without any soul. That cost is just too high.

So instead I play the balancing game—giving up a little of my soul in order to have enough quiet space to actually use the mental gifts that are uniquely mine. I suppose it's like percussionists wearing earplugs to protect their delicate and superior hearing—that special sensitivity that enables them to produce the most dynamic effects in the orchestra. If they played without some dampening, it would overwhelm their sensorium, leaving them unable to function. At the same time, they can't cut out all sounds, or they wouldn't be able to play as an ensemble, or even hear their own contributions.

For now, that means 3 or 4 mg of Risperidone. Over time, who knows?

The murmurers are definitely back. I can no longer mistake them for wind or rain, though I can't make out any words.

They're fairly calm now, not too anxious, but there is a sense of anticipation from them. Something is coming. No sign of Max since the psych ward debacle, but the eyes are back. Just a few, and they fade away if I focus too long on them, but others appear at the edge of my vision, quietly keeping watch. Observing and abiding, for now.

I still haven't seen Mara and Kala—not only have they not spoken to me, but the birds themselves have been gone. It will be two weeks tomorrow since they flew off to points unknown. They promised to have answers "soon." How soon? Did something happen to them? I hope they return before my license hearing, at least.

Ah, yes, my hearing. I feel like I should prepare for it. Not being armed with a solid bastion of facts and legal references when going before a judge feels completely wrong, but I don't know how I can prepare for this. I know the relevant statues; they're simple enough. The facts are well known, a matter of court records. What else is there? The Hearing Board will decide whatever they will. I doubt I'll be able to influence things much—especially as I don't regret my choices or actions. We are called the "justice system," after all. Shouldn't justice trump jurisprudence? Maybe they are right, and I'm not fit to be a lawyer—but if so, I believe it is because I have a superior moral compass.

That sounds awfully conceited. Maybe it is—maybe I am. Or maybe I've just been in my own head space too much. Time to get out, get some fresh air, maybe take in a concert. Something—anything to halt the churning of my own mind.

Thursday, September 7

Plenty of changes since my last entry. Most importantly, Mara and Kala are back. They didn't stay long and they looked haggard. They came this afternoon while I was sitting outside listening to *Tosca* on headphones. I was so lost in the music that Kala had to peck my hand before I realized they were there. I nearly broke the headphones ripping them off, I was so happy to see my friends again.

Kala: Did you forget us?

Mara: We thought you couldn't see us again.

Kala: Except we could see you.

Mara: It wasn't like when you were hard to find before.

Kala: Though it was, a little.

Mara: You're not all here.

Kala: Hazy.

Mara: Fuzzy around the edges.

Kala: But here.

Mara: Definitely here.

Kala: And we are, too.

Mara: Now.

Kala: We just got back.

Mara: We were far away.

Kala: Farther than we've ever been.

Mara: And still not far enough.

Kala: Well, far enough to learn.

Mara: Yes, far enough to learn, but not see.

Kala: No, we have to let others see for us.

Mara: But they do. They help.

Kala: Others see things like we do.

Me: I've been so worried about you! Where did you go? Who did you talk to?

Mara: We followed the sun.

Kala: But left, too.

Mara: Yes, left of the sun.

Kala: Days and days.
Mara: Into the desert.
Kala: Following the river.
Mara: We had to.
Kala: It was the only water.
Mara: And not much.
Me: Which river? Did you follow the Colorado? How far did you go?
Kala: Who knows?
Mara: Many miles.
Kala: To the big water.
Mara: Yes, the wall that holds the water back.
Kala: There were lots of those.
Mara: Yes, many, most in the mountains.
Kala: But then none for a long time.
Mara: Very long. After the mountains were gone.
Kala: And the river got bigger.
Mara: We flew and flew.
Kala: The trees ran out.
Mara: Even the grass ran out.
Kala: We kept flying.
Mara: Deep into the desert.
Kala: Following the river.
Mara: Then we came to this big lake.
Kala: The biggest we've seen.
Mara: It was held by a big wall.
Kala: All of those walls were big.
Mara: But this was the biggest.
Me: Lake Powell? You flew all the way to Lake Powell? That's got to be five or six hundred miles!
Kala: Yes, it was very far.
Mara: We flew and flew.
Kala: And it was still only half way.
Mara: But far enough.
Kala: Yes, far enough.
Mara: We saw many things.

Kala: Heard many things.
Mara: Talked to many other birds.
Kala: Learned many things.
Mara: Learned what we needed.
Kala: Yes, now we know.
Mara: It is time.
Kala: Time to make things happen.
Mara: Almost.
Kala: Yes, not today.
Mara: Today we rest.
Kala: And tomorrow.
Mara: And there are things to do here.
Kala: Yes, connections to make.
Me: Are you being deliberately cryptic? Tell me what you're planning.
Mara: Not yet.
Kala: Almost.
Mara: Soon.
Kala: Very soon.
Mara: Not today.
Kala: Not tomorrow.
Mara: You will like it.
Kala: But you will have to trust us.
Mara: Yes. Trust us.
Me: I do. You know I do.
Kala: Yes, we know.
Me: I can't do anything big for about a week, anyway. I have to go to my hearing on the 11th.
Mara: Yes, we know that, too.
Kala: That's why we hurried back.
Mara: Yes, but too much hurrying.
Kala: Too much flying.
Mara: We go now, to rest.
Kala: We'll be back.
Mara: Not today.
Kala: And not tomorrow.

Mara: But soon.

Kala: Very soon.

Mara: You'll see.

And with that, they flew off. Max, of course, had to chime in—yes, Max is back now, too.

"So now you're trusting your future to the birds, shithead? Didn't you learn anything from how they screwed up your life so far? You fight so much for your own control, and then you give it up to a pair of birds? You really are fucking nuts."

I could hear his smile, though. Max just can't pass up an opportunity to needle me, even when he agrees with me. And I can tell that in this matter he does agree. I wish I knew why.

So Mara and Kala flew all the way to Lake Powell. And there they met with some mysterious contacts, presumably other birds from even further away. And it's all for some mysterious purpose that involves me. I have to say that my curiosity is piqued.

Not today, and not tomorrow, so Saturday at the soonest. And my hearing is on Monday. After that, who knows?

Who knows? Mara and Kala, apparently. And they're not telling. Not yet, anyway. "Soon."

Sunday, September 10, 6:30 PM

Mara and Kala finally came back today—the day before my hearing. Max had been riding me all day yesterday that they weren't coming back, that I was on my own. He just about had me convinced that tomorrow was going to be the beginning of my rapid descent into personal and professional oblivion. He may still be right.

And today Tempest has been after me to just skip the hearing, go out in a blaze of hedonistic glory, spending all my money on a blow-out bacchanal with booze, women, drugs and, at the end, a bullet. She, at least, is not going to get her way. I hope.

Mara and Kala were considerably more upbeat, though hardly illuminating.

Mara: Tomorrow is your silly hearing.

Kala: They know you told the truth.

Mara: What else could you do?

Kala: You had to tell the truth.

Mara: Especially when everyone else didn't know.

Kala: Exactly! Spreading truth.

Mara: Always good.

Kala: Not always.

Mara: Not always. But usually.

Kala: And good then.

Mara: Yes, very good. The bad man got punished.

Kala: When he would have gone free.

Mara: You were a hero.

Kala: And for that they punish you?

Mara: Very foolish.

Kala: We will look after you, though.

Mara: Like we always do.

Me: You could have looked after me better by keeping me from taking that case in the first place.

Kala: But we couldn't find you then.

Mara: And when we did, you didn't listen.

Kala: We tried.

Mara: And it turned out best, anyway.

Kala: Yes, with someone else he would have gone free.

Mara: But you made it better.

Kala: With our help.

Me: We'll see how much better I made it. I expect to lose my license tomorrow. What am I supposed to do then?

Mara: You don't need a license to live.

Kala: We don't have a license.

Mara: But we live.

Kala: And so will you.

Me: But how? Unlike you, I need to have money to live on.

Mara: Yes, so many foolish things you humans need.

Kala: Very foolish. But we understand.

Mara: Do we?

Kala: Mostly.

Mara: Enough.

Me: I hope so. When will you tell me about it?

Kala: We start today.

Mara: That's why we're here.

Kala: But only start.

Mara: Yes, there is much to do.

Kala: First steps.

Mara: But they are ready.

Kala: Indeed.

Mara: Are you ready?

Me: Are you kidding? I've been ready for weeks!

Kala: No, you've had things to work through.

Mara: You weren't even able to hear us.

Kala: And not because we were far away.

Mara: You went away again.

Kala: Not physically.

Mara: No, that was us.

Kala: But in the way you do.

Mara: And you're only just now all the way back.

Me: So tell me already!

Kala: Yes, we'll tell you.
Mara: And you'll have to trust us.
Kala: That is important.
Me: I do, I promise. I trust you. Tell me!
Mara: Impatient, isn't he?
Kala: Jumpy.
Mara: Irritable.
Kala: But we'll fix that.
Mara: Yes. Right now.
Kala: You know the shelter?
Mara: For people who don't have houses.
Kala: Or apartments.
Mara: The homeless shelter.
Kala: In the city.
Me: St. Andrew's Mercy Mission? I know where it is, yeah. What about it?
Mara: You need to go there.
Kala: You need to meet someone there.
Mara: Ruthie.
Kala: Yes, Ruthie. Talk to her.
Me: Who is Ruthie? Does she work there? What is this about?
Mara: She works there.
Kala: But she stays there, too.
Mara: It's her home.
Kala: Because she doesn't have a home.
Mara: Except the shelter.
Kala: You need to talk to Ruthie.
Mara: And she is expecting you.
Me: What? Who is she? What do you mean she's expecting me? Did you talk with her?
Kala: No, we only talk to you.
Mara: Well, we talk to lots of people.
Kala: But only you listen.
Mara: We talked to Ruthie.
Kala: But she didn't listen.
Mara: But we told her anyway.

Kala: So she's expecting you.

Mara: Only she doesn't really know it.

Kala: Or who you are.

Mara: Or why.

Kala: But she is expecting you.

Mara: Sort of.

Kala: In a way.

Mara: Tell her about us.

Me: What? I don't tell anyone about you. Talking about you will get me locked up and medicated to where I can't hear you anymore.

Kala: Yes, most people don't understand.

Mara: Almost no one.

Kala: But Ruthie will.

Mara: Yes, Ruthie will understand. We looked hard for her.

Kala: She's the one.

Mara: And you need to meet her.

Me: How do I find her? Just go to the shelter and ask?

Kala: Yes, everyone there knows Ruthie.

Mara: She lives there.

Kala: She works there.

Mara: Everyone knows Ruthie.

Me: And what do I tell her?

Kala: Tell her about us.

Mara: Tell her we sent you.

Kala: Tell her the truth.

Mara: Always tell her the truth.

Kala: Yes, very important.

Mara: Don't hide the truth with Ruthie.

Kala: She will understand.

Mara: Will she?

Kala: She will. She knows.

Mara: Yes, she knows. Kala is right.

Kala: I am.

Mara: She will understand.

Me: So I'm supposed to go to the shelter, talk to someone named Ruthie, and tell her you sent me, because she's expecting me? That's insane! Do I do this before my hearing, or after?

Kala: Either, but don't wait too long.

Mara: She might forget.

Kala: Forget that she's expecting you.

Mara: So soon is good.

Kala: Before your hearing.

Mara: Yes, that is best. Before.

Me: And I just tell her about you, and that you sent me?

Kala: Yes. She will understand.

Me: That's crazy. I can't just tell people about you. You don't understand how people react to that sort of thing. I could get locked up in a hospital again and medicated to where I can't hear you anymore. People don't understand you, don't understand that I can talk with you. They think that makes me crazy. Sick. They want to lock me up and bury my brain in medicine. Kill my soul. You don't know what you're asking. I am really uncomfortable about this.

Mara: You said you trust us.

Me: I do.

Kala: Then go talk to Ruthie.

Mara: She will understand.

Kala: She won't lock you up.

Me: This is more justice? Someone else I need to protect?

Mara: No, this isn't about others.

Kala: This is about you.

Mara: You and Ruthie.

Kala: Yes. Good for both of you.

Mara: Ruthie will protect you.

Kala: And you'll protect her.

Mara: Trust us.

Kala: Talk to Ruthie.

And off they flew. So now I'm getting dressed to head out. Tell me, what does one wear to an evening outing at the local homeless shelter? An assignation with the mysterious "Ruthie" who seems to be both a resident and a worker there. And who is expecting me—except she isn't. And I'm supposed to tell her about Mara and Kala, the two jays who talk to me.

What could possibly go wrong?

Sunday, September 10, 9:30 PM

So I went to the St. Andrew's Mercy Mission. An older building in a seedy neighborhood. I got there a little before 7:30 and they were just finishing up dinner. The door was propped open and I was met there by a neatly dressed Hispanic woman. She looked at me with barely concealed judgement.

"Can I help you? Dinner is done."

"I'm not here for dinner."

She looked me up and down again before answering.

"Uh huh. So what you want, then?"

"I'm..., well, I'm looking for someone. Is there someone named Ruthie here?"

"What business you have with Ruthie?"

"I'm not entirely sure, to be honest. Someone told me to meet her here."

"Someone."

I nodded.

"It's Sunday night."

"I know that."

"And this is a church mission."

"I know that, too."

"And you're lookin' for Ruthie because someone sent you?"

"That's right. Could I speak with her, please?"

"And you won't say your business with her?"

"I'd rather speak with her."

"Uh huh."

"May I?"

"She ain't goin' out again tonight."

"That's fine. I'd just like to speak with her."

"You a cop?"

"No. I'm a defense attorney, but that's not why I'm here."

"So why are you here, Mr. Defense Attorney?"

"To speak to Ruthie."

"Because someone sent you."

"Yes."

"And you won't say what it's about."

"I doubt you'd believe me."

"Try me."

I swallowed. Here it is. Mara and Kala told me to be honest.

"OK. I'm here because a pair of Steller's jays named Mara and Kala told me I should come here and talk with Ruthie. They said she is expecting me, but she doesn't know it."

"You're right. I don't believe you."

"Yeah, well, I told you."

"Uh huh. You got a better story?"

"Probably, but Mara and Kala were very clear I should only tell the truth."

"You crazy?"

"I have schizophrenia."

"Uh huh. That I believe."

"So may I talk with Ruthie, please?"

"You're seriously asking me that?"

"Yes. I would very much like to speak with her if she's here."

"Oh, she's here. She's cleanin' up. Tell you what. You see that bench there?" She pointed to a city bench on the sidewalk at the front of the Mission. "You wait there. I'll tell her what you said, and if she wants to talk to you when she's done, she'll holler at you."

"And if not?"

"Then she won't."

"How long should I wait?"

"That's up to you. Why don't you ask the birds?" She laughed, not hiding her amusement at my expense.

"I'll wait here. Thank you for telling her."

"Uh huh." She shook her head, and closed the door. I heard it lock. I went over to the bench and sat, wondering if I would be back in the psych ward soon.

After about fifteen minutes, the door unlocked and the woman I had spoken to before stuck her head out and saw me.

"You still here?"

"Apparently so."

"Waitin' to talk to Ruthie?"

"Yes, please, if that's possible."

She shook her head. "Yeah. I don't know why, but when I told her what you said she said 'send him in.'"

"Thank you."

"Uh huh. Well, come on, then. You can talk in here. Stay in the front room. Fifteen minutes, and Ruthie doesn't leave, but you do."

"I understand. Thank you."

"Uh huh."

The front room was basically a wide hallway with a bunch of plastic chairs along the outside wall, facing a window into an office/reception area. There was another door at the far end of the room, presumably leading into the rest of the shelter. I sat in one of the chairs where the woman directed me. She went out the other door, and a few seconds later an older black woman wearing patched and mismatched clothes and a head scarf came in. The woman I had been speaking with walked into the reception area and sat down where she could watch us through the closed window.

I stood up as the older woman came over to me. I could see a gray, almost white, afro poking out under the scarf. She wore a short-sleeved purple blouse with yellow flowers on it and a pair of blue knit slacks. The clothes were well worn, patched in places, but clean. She walked with the shuffling gate of the elderly.

"Are you Ruthie?"

She nodded, with a hint of a smile. "Sure am, sweetie. And who might you be?"

"I'm William Taylor, but my friends call me 'Rip.'"

"OK, William Taylor. Why don't you sit down and tell me why you're here."

I sat in one of the hard seats, and she sat in another, with an empty one between us.

"Did the other woman..."

"Serena," she interrupted.

"Did Serena tell you what I'd said?"

"She told me something, but I want to hear it from you."

I smiled. "I can understand that. I'm here because a pair of Steller's jays named Mara and Kala told me I should come here and talk with you. And that I should tell you that they sent me, and that you were expecting me, but didn't know it."

She smiled back at me, which I found disarming. "Honey, you know that sounds completely crazy."

I nodded. "Yeah, I know. But it's the truth."

"Serena said you were psycho."

"I have schizophrenia. I'm not dangerous."

"Sweetie, when you're my age, everyone is dangerous."

"But here you are."

"Here I am. Maybe I just wanted to see the psycho. Hear him with my own ears."

"Well, am I what you expected?"

Ruthie looked at me for a long moment before answering.

"I don't know what I expected, sugar, but it sure as hell wasn't you. Or at least I didn't know I was expecting you." She laughed and shook her head. "I guess your birds were right, I was expecting you, but I didn't know it."

"Excuse me?"

"Here's the thing. Yesterday I was out hustling change. Normally, the only birds I see are the damn pigeons. But these two birds—what did you call them?"

"Steller's jays. Blue and black with a crest on their head."

"Yeah, that's them. They came down and started squawking at me to beat the band. They were all in my face and plucking at my sleeves. I tried to shoo them off when one of them stuck a piece of paper in my pocket, and then they both flew off."

I smiled. "They've done that trick before, yeah. What did it say?"

"It said 'talk to him.' Just that. Torn out of a magazine, I think."

I laughed. "That sounds like Mara and Kala."

"You trained these birds?"

"Nope. Not a bit of it. If anything, they've trained me."

"They send you notes, too, then?"

"Sometimes, but mostly they just talk to me."

Ruthie's eyes went wide.

"They talk to you? In English? Like we're doing now?"

"Pretty much. Not everyone understands them. In fact, only I seem to."

She nodded. "And you're crazy."

"I have schizophrenia. I hear voices that others don't hear. But Mara and Kala are different."

"Because they're birds?"

I smiled. "Yeah, pretty much. The other voices are just voices—no bodies to go with them. Or some things I see—eyes and mouths, typically—that others don't, but there are no sounds with them. And nobody else hears or sees anything. But everyone can see Mara and Kala. They just can't understand them."

"But you can?"

"Apparently."

"And you don't think that makes you crazy, sweetie?"

I smiled. "Well sometimes I think they drive me crazy, but no, I'm not crazy."

"You just have schizophrenia."

"Right. I'm completely functional, I'm a defense attorney—or at least I was."

"You were...?"

"I was recently let go by my firm. And I have a hearing tomorrow that might end my legal career."

"And that's not related to your schizophrenia."

"I was acting on the advice of Mara and Kala at the time."

"The jays?"

"Right."

"Who aren't part of your crazy."

I smiled. "I'll leave that for you to decide."

She laughed long and heartily. "Mr. William Taylor, I like you."

I smiled back at her. "I like you, too, Ruthie. Please call me Rip."

"So now I'm a friend?"

"I hope you will be."

"Why is that?"

"Because Mara and Kala seemed to think it important we get to know each other."

She laughed. "These birds of yours, are they often matchmakers?"

I shook my head. "No, this is the first time. Mostly they've helped me with cases."

She widened her eyes and looked at me, the laughter of a moment ago gone. "They help with the cases?"

"Yes, they seem to know a lot of what's going on around here. They've been great sources of information."

"And they told you to come find me."

"That's right."

"This is for some case?"

"No, I told you, I was let go. I have no cases pending."

"So, am I what you were expecting?"

"Honestly, I had no idea. I knew your name was Ruthie and that you lived and worked here, and that you would be somehow 'expecting me.'"

"Well, you may be crazy, but you're right, the birds gave you good information. So what are you supposed to talk to me about?"

"Honestly, I don't know. Mara and Kala didn't say. I was hoping you knew."

She laughed at that until tears came. "Honey-pie, I don't have a clue. But I like you. You come by tomorrow and I'll let you buy me lunch. Maybe we can figure something out then."

"I'm not sure how long my hearing will go—it's scheduled for 10. I can try to be here by noon, but it will probably be a bit later."

"I think my social calendar is clear." She laughed. "I'll wait for you. Will you be all dressed up, then?"

It was my turn to laugh. "I'll be wearing a suit, yes. I hope that's OK."

She smiled. "Mr. Rip, I like being seen with a fine young man. You call on me tomorrow. I'll wear my Sunday go-to-meetin' clothes and we'll have us a fancy lunch. You're buying."

"It's a date. Thank you for talking with me, Ruthie."

She laughed. "You're the best entertainment I've had in years, sweetie. Say hello to your friends for me."

"Mara and Kala?"

"The same."

"I will."

She laughed and laughed as she shuffled back to the door into the shelter while I let myself out the main door. I heard it lock behind me as I walked to my car.

So... now what?

Court Judgement

Office of the Presiding Disciplinary Judge of the Supreme Court of Colorado

The PEOPLE of the State of Colorado, Complainant, v. William R. TAYLOR, Respondent.

No. 17PDJ132

Decided: September 11, 2017

Opinion by Presiding Disciplinary Judge Peter Edgemont; Samantha Robinson, a representative of the public; and Judith Moscatello, Esq.

OPINION AND ORDER IMPOSING SANCTIONS

SANCTION IMPOSED: ONE YEAR AND ONE DAY SUSPENSION

A sanctions hearing was held on September 11, 2017 pursuant to C.R.C.P. 251.8 requesting an immediate suspension of the license to practice law. Russel White, Esq. represented the People of the State of Colorado ("the PEOPLE"). William R. Taylor, Esq. ("TAYLOR") appeared *pro se.*

On August 16, 2017 Matthew Hobart, Esq., acting for the PEOPLE, filed a Complaint in this matter citing the relevant statutes. The Complaint and Citation were served upon respondent TAYLOR by certified mail on August 21, 2017. Although TAYLOR signed for receipt of the Complaint and Citation, he failed to file a responsive pleading. Default judgment was entered against respondent by Order of this court on August 30, 2017. The factual allegations in the Complaint were deemed admitted.

The PEOPLE presented court records from People v. Marner dated August 16, 2017 as People's Exhibit 1. The PEOPLE also presented a sworn deposition by Matthew Hobart, Esq., jurist in the matter of the People v. Marner. TAYLOR testified on his own behalf. The Presiding Disciplinary Judge ("PDJ") and Hearing Board considered argument of the parties, the facts established by the entry of default, and the exhibits admitted, and made the following findings of fact which were established by clear and convincing evidence:

I. FINDINGS OF FACT

TAYLOR has taken and subscribed the oath of admission, was admitted to the bar of the Colorado Supreme Court on October 19, 2001, and is registered upon the official records of the Court as attorney registration number 13425. TAYLOR is subject to the jurisdiction of this court pursuant to C.R.C.P. 251.1(b).

TAYLOR did act in open court against the interests of his client whom he was defending. TAYLOR, without consulting with his client, called the client as a witness and questioned him about events pointing to his guilt rather than being of an exculpatory nature. TAYLOR persisted in this questioning despite objection by the witness, his client, and despite cautions from Judge Hobart. These actions resulted directly in a declaration of mistrial.

Mr. Marner was subsequently charged with additional crimes resulting from the information TAYLOR divulged in open court and is awaiting trial on those charges, as well as retrial on the previous matter.

TAYLOR offered no defense of his actions beyond "pursuit of truth and justice" despite his prescribed role as counsel for the defense.

II.   CONCLUSIONS OF LAW

TAYLOR knowingly violated the trust of his client and by his own admission acted explicitly against his client's best interests. He did so in the knowledge that these actions were improper and would likely result in a mistrial being declared. He admitted to acting on his own in this matter. These actions are clear violations of Colo. RPC 3.5(d) (conduct intended to disrupt a tribunal) and Colo. RPC 8.4(d) (conduct prejudicial to the administration of justice). Having violated Colo. RPC 3.5(d) and Colo. RPC 8.4(d) by his misconduct, TAYLOR has also violated Colo. RPC 8.4(a) (an attorney shall not violate the rules of professional conduct).

III.   SANCTIONS/IMPOSITION OF DISCIPLINE

The PDJ and Hearing Board found that TAYLOR's conduct constituted a violation of duties owed to the legal system, the profession and to the public. The ABA Standards for Imposing Lawyer Sanctions (1991 & Supp. 1992) ("ABA Standards ") is the guiding authority for selecting the appropriate sanction to impose for lawyer misconduct.

ABA Standard 6.22 provides:

Suspension is appropriate when a lawyer knowingly violates a court order or rule, and there is injury or potential injury to a client or a party or interference or potential interference with a legal proceeding.

TAYLOR's conduct meets the criteria under ABA Standard 6.22.

The PDJ and Hearing Board considered certain factors in aggravation pursuant to ABA Standards 9.22. The PEOPLE offered evidence in aggravation that TAYLOR has had prior discipline in the nature of a previous suspension in 2009 for a period of 30 days for conduct intended to disrupt a tribunal.

It was further noted from records of the previous suspension that TAYLOR was undergoing treatment at that time for schizophrenia. TAYLOR stipulates that he continues to receive ongoing medical care for this condition.

Accordingly, the PDJ and Hearing Board herein suspend TAYLOR for one year and one day, effective thirty-one (31) days from the date of this Order.

IV. ORDER

It is therefore ORDERED:

1. WILLIAM R. TAYLOR, Attorney Registration No. 13425 is hereby SUSPENDED from the practice of law for a period of ONE YEAR AND ONE DAY. The suspension SHALL become effective thirty-one (31) days from the date of this order in the absence of a stay pending appeal pursuant to C.R.C.P. 251.27(h).

2. Respondent (TAYLOR), as a condition precedent to any petition for reinstatement pursuant to C.R.C.P. 251.29(c), SHALL submit to an Independent Medical Examination ("IME") by a qualified doctor agreeable to the PEOPLE. Respondent, not the PEOPLE, shall be responsible for the cost of the IME. Once a qualified expert is chosen, it is Respondent's duty to advise the PDJ so that an appropriate order may be drafted and presented to the doctor prior to the examination as to what issues to address in a

report to the PDJ. The doctor shall have access to all records in the PEOPLE's possession, as well as this opinion, before meeting with Respondent for the scheduled IME.

3. Respondent (TAYLOR) SHALL pay the costs of these proceedings. The PEOPLE shall submit a "Statement of Costs" within fifteen (15) days from the date of this order. Respondent SHALL have ten (10) days thereafter to submit a response with payment.

Monday, September 11

Well, the hearing was short and sweet. No real surprises, and I probably got off easy with a year-and-a-day suspension. They did add a requirement that I obtain an independent medical exam if I want to get reinstated, but that's probably reasonable.

I was almost late getting to the hearing. Max was being particularly difficult, starting in as soon as I woke up:

"You might as well just slit your own throat, shithead. Your career is over. Whether you get suspended or disbarred, the effect is the same. No one will ever hire you again. You've shown you are a loose cannon, and that can't be tolerated. All those years of law school and your practice, gone to waste. You'll never work another day in your life. Sure, you've saved some money, but how long will that last? Face it, you're done. You're dead but somehow still moving. Might as well finish it."

At one point Tempest joined in. They don't normally do that; neither one likes the other much. But she agreed that everything was over for me, and she suggested I just skip the hearing and party until all the money is gone and *then* finish myself off. Max didn't argue with that. They both figure I'm doomed; it's just a matter of how quickly I finish the process.

I found myself arguing with them—something I don't usually do. For once, though, I think they might be too harsh. They're not wrong, of course. My career is done. I'll never work again as a lawyer. Not in Colorado, certainly, and probably not anywhere else, either. But that's not all I am, is it? Am I just a lawyer? Is that my only hope of survival? I'm not willing to believe that yet. Maybe Mara and Kala have infected me with optimism. They certainly seem to have something planned.

They flew down to me as I was getting into my car to go to the hearing, already running later than I intended.

Mara: We saw you last evening.

Kala: You were at the shelter.

Mara: You met with Ruthie?

Me: Yes, we met and talked for a little bit.
Kala: We told you.
Mara: She was expecting you.
Kala: Though she didn't know it.
Me: Yes, you were very clever. Look, I have to run to my hearing.
Mara: Oh, yes, do that.
Kala: But you'll see Ruthie again?
Mara: Of course he will.
Me: Yes, we'll be meeting for lunch if the hearing is done soon enough.
Kala: That's good. We'll see you then.
Mara: But you may not see us.
Kala: Or you may.
Mara: But we'll see you.
Kala: Now go.
Mara: Go to your silly hearing
Kala: Where they punish you for doing good.
Mara: But we don't.
Kala: We help you do more good.
Mara: Good for others.
Kala: And good for you.
Mara: Everybody wins.
Kala: Now go!

Fortunately traffic on I-25 was light and fast, so I made good time to Denver. I got to the hearing five minutes before the scheduled start time of ten o'clock. At least I didn't have long to sit and worry. Max had been riding me the whole way in, but he was repeating himself by then and I could mostly tune him out.

Like I said, the hearing itself was short. Judge Hobart had deposed himself, and there were the transcriptions of the trial proceedings, so there really wasn't much for either side to say. Did I engage in "conduct intended to disrupt a tribunal"? Yes, clearly that. And as for "conduct prejudicial to the administration of justice"? Well, I suppose that depends on how you define justice. Clearly their interest is in following all the rules. Mine was (and remains) in seeking actual justice. By their definition, I'm guilty.

So I suppose they are right—I'm not qualified to practice law. I believe too much in justice.

The hearing was done in less than three quarters of an hour.

* * *

After the hearing I drove back to Colorado Springs. Max was urging me to just crash my car now that my life was effectively over. Tempest was telling me to pick up every hitchhiker and just party with them. I had *Götterdämmerung* blaring the whole way—it seemed fitting to have Wagner's rousing conclusion to the ring cycle with its intrigue and deception, and ultimately the destruction of the old gods. It fit my mood. I got to the shelter just a few minutes after noon. The door was unlocked and there was no one in the waiting area. There was a person behind the glass, however. I was surprised to see it *wasn't* Serena from last night. This was a younger black woman. She looked at me nervously. I'm sure I didn't look like the usual clientele in my conservative three piece suit.

"May I help you?"

"Yes, thank you. I'm Rip Taylor, and I'm here to see Ruthie." I realized I didn't even know her last name. Fortunately it didn't seem to matter.

She smiled and looked relieved. "Oh, you're the hot lunch date. She said she had a young man calling for her today. With Ruthie, 'young man' covers a lot of territory." She covered her mouth in embarrassment, but her eyes continued to smile. "Not that you're old! I'll tell her you're here."

She got up, laughing, and stepped out of view. Less than a minute later, Ruthie came into the room. She was wearing a bright pink pantsuit that would have looked very fashionable twenty years ago. Her lined face was set off by her large silver-white afro, and her dark eyes twinkled as she smiled at me.

"Well, hello, sugar. You came after all!"

"I said I'd be here."

"Pshaw. Honey, if I had a dollar for every time a man told me he'd be somewhere and didn't show up, I wouldn't be living here, that's for damn sure!" I couldn't help but laugh. "Your meeting go alright, sugar?"

That sobered me up. "Well, it was quick, anyway."

"That's a blessing. Ain't nobody got time for long meetings. But you don't look happy about it."

"I'm not, though I'm not surprised, either. I'm no longer an attorney—my license has been suspended."

She grinned at me. "Then, honey, we have to go celebrate. This is a new beginning for you. And nothing personal, but one less lawyer in the world sounds like a good thing to me. Where you gonna take me?"

It was hard not to like Ruthie. The idea of celebrating a severe professional rebuke was not something I had even remotely considered. Nor was the location of lunch. I didn't know any places close by, and my mind was somehow blank.

"Where would you like to go?"

"Someplace fancy. Look at you, all slicked up. And I feel pretty today."

"You look lovely."

She laughed and batted her eyes at me, striking a melodramatic coy pose. "You think so? Better than last night, anyway. I still clean up good."

"That you do," I agreed. "Someplace fancy…. How about Bonefish Grill?"

"Never heard of it. But that don't mean nothin'. I haven't been to a fancy restaurant in years. Wherever you take me will be a treat. Is it close?"

"Not especially. I don't know any places near here, I'm afraid. If there's someplace else you'd rather go…."

"Honey, I said fancy. That ain't gonna be any place near here. This ain't exactly the swank part of town, if you haven't noticed. That's OK, I got my walkin' shoes on." She lifted a foot to show off a well-worn pink running shoe. I hadn't noticed the shoes before—but they did match the color of her pantsuit.

"We'll drive. It's too far to walk. My car is right outside."

Ruthie fanned herself theatrically. *"Oh la la!* I haven't had a man invite me into his car in donkey's years!"

I laughed nervously at her obvious implication.

"What's a matter, sugar? I embarrass you? Shit, you got nothin' to be embarrassed about. I'm the one admitting to being a streetwalker, and I'm not embarrassed."

My expression must have shown my surprise at that bit of news. She responded by laughing, making no attempt to hide it. It was not her customary laugh, though; this one had an edge to it, and when she spoke the ice came quickly to her voice.

"Well, what did you expect, honey? You too good to be seen with the likes of me? Yeah, I whored. So what? It's a job, and better than any other job I could find then."

"I'm sorry. No, it's not that at all. I'm happy to be seen with you, and I don't care about that. I was just surprised by the way you said it."

She relaxed a little. "Well, OK, then. At least we got that settled. You're going to lunch with an old whore, and I'm going to lunch with an ex-lawyer. I don't know which is worse."

I laughed. "I do, and I'm glad you're still willing to be seen with me."

She smiled and winked impishly. "As long as you're buying, sweetie."

"I am."

"Then let's go!"

As we left the shelter and walked to my car, Mara and Kala flew down from a nearby tree and perched on the roof rack of the car.

"Oh, are these the famous jays?" Ruthie asked.

"They are. Ruthie, meet Mara and Kala."

"We've already met, honey, remember? Tell them I said hello."

"Oh, they understand you just fine. You just can't understand them."

"Yes, we understand," Mara said.

"And she may too, someday," Kala added.

"You're going out together?"

"To lunch?"

"Someplace with food for us?"

"We're always interested in food."

"But we want to hear you, too."

"You and Ruthie."

"Not this time, my friends," I answered. Ruthie had been watching the conversation, her head moving like it was a ping pong match. "We're going to an inside restaurant. I'll tell you about it later if you don't already know."

Ruthie laughed. "Are they inviting themselves to lunch? Not this time, birdies. He's my date—all mine, and I don't feel like sharing. Now shoo!"

"We'll go," Mara answered.

"This time."

"Have fun."

"Keep telling the truth."

"She will, too."

"Bring us food!"

And with that they flew off.

"They really do talk to you, don't they? I thought that was just you being crazy, but it ain't that, is it?"

"You understood them?"

"Not a word. But you did."

"Yes. They like you."

She smiled. "Well, I like them, too, but sometimes a girl just has to insist on her own time. They can come along some other time."

"That's what they said."

"Yeah? They must be girls then."

"I never asked." Odd, I'd never even considered their gender. They were just Mara and Kala.

"They think there will be another time, then?"

"They seem certain of it."

"What about you, sugar?"

"I'm down for it. That is, if you can stand being seen with a lawyer."

She laughed. "Ex-lawyer. You done reformed. Now let's go celebrate that! This your fancy-ass car?"

I laughed. "Yeah. I've got to look the part, you know?" It was a five year old black Lexus GX. Nice, but not ostentatious—or so I thought.

"Well, then, come open the door for me, sugar. I'm hungry."

Lunch was fun and long. Max kept his mouth shut, and Tempest only said "You can do better!" once. Ruthie is a delight, completely uninhibited and genuine to a fault. We talked for hours and I think were the last of the lunch patrons to leave.

Ruthie's history is remarkable. A Denver native, she went to college at UC Boulder, graduating with an undergraduate degree in Business Administration and an MBA on top of that. Once out of school, she worked as a grants administrator, first for an environmental non-profit in Boulder and then later for the state in Denver—so she has experience on both sides of the public-sector grants game, as well as experience dealing with donors and non-governmental granting agencies and organizations. This was back in late seventies and early eighties.

She fell in with the party scene in Denver, going clubbing every weekend and, eventually, most days after work. She'd go to clubs and private parties and do lines of cocaine. When crack hit the scene in 1986, she was in her mid-thirties and it sucked her in, as it did so many others. Within two years, she'd lost her job and her home and had started turning tricks to support her habit and pay the rent on a crummy apartment.

She cleaned herself up from the drugs after a few years of that, but kept working tricks, as it was better money than she could make any other way. As she got older, the prostitution brought in less money. She lost the apartment and lived mainly in squats with the occasional short stay in a shelter.

She tried finding other jobs, but she'd picked up a few misdemeanor possession and soliciting convictions and one possession-with-intent felony. That and the long lapse in employment history meant nobody wanted to hire her, even for menial work. Certainly there was nothing that could compare with the income from prostitution.

She'd been raped and assaulted a few times while turning tricks, especially after losing the apartment. She said that was "just part of living on the street," though you could see the trauma in her face and body when she talked about it, and she dropped the subject quickly.

Her parents had died in an automobile accident not long after she got out of school, and her only sibling is a brother who is some sort of investment banker on the East Coast. He washed his hands of her when she got into drugs, and they haven't spoken in twenty years. She's not sure where he's living, or even if he's still alive. She's had some girlfriends over the years—she said she's bisexual but after years of turning tricks she's "had enough dicks for a lifetime"—but nothing serious or recent.

So now she lives at St. Andrew's. Technically she can only stay there sixty days, but they've bent the rules since she helps out with cooking and cleaning and looking after the others being sheltered there. She's been there about six months now, and every month they have to find a new way to allow her to stay on.

She also does outreach for the Colorado Springs AIDS Project, talking with the folks at the shelter and others on the streets as well as working at their office. She talks with sex workers and intravenous drug users, letting them know about programs that can give them free screenings and basic medical care, free needle exchanges and birth control, that sort of thing. Basic harm reduction work. She doesn't get paid for most of that work, but the shelter takes that into consideration with letting her stay on beyond her sixty days.

That's a lot to find out over lunch, isn't it? It's hard not to like Ruthie, and there's nothing she won't share. We stayed and talked for two and a half hours. I found myself telling her about my checkered history, and even about Max, Tempest, the mutterers, the eyes and mouths—things I wouldn't even tell my psychiatrist. She didn't bat an eye. She accepted it all without question or apparent judgement. None of it seemed to concern her in the least. Of course, it might have helped that she'd already seen Mara and Kala in action.

We set a date for another lunch—less formal this time—on Wednesday. I'll meet her again at the shelter.

Tuesday, September 12

Max had plenty to say about Ruthie. He lit into me this morning while I was still sipping my first cup of coffee.

"Well, shithead, I'll give you this, you've found someone who can teach you what you need to know: surviving on nothing. She's got plenty of nothing, that's for sure."

"And nothin's plenty for her," I sang back.

"Very funny. Get used to it, shithead. Homelessness is in your future. You're done as a lawyer and you don't have any other skills. Have you given *any* thought as to how you're going to survive?"

"Not really. I have my savings."

Max gave a short cruel laugh. "Savings. And that will last you, what? A couple years at best? What then? I have a recommendation—skip the last month and buy a gun and a bullet. You won't need more than one. Of course, if you listen to Tempest you won't last that long, but at least you'll have lived instead of just existing. Either way, your days are numbered. I suppose you think you'll support Ruthie on that same savings?"

"I haven't thought about that, either. She has her own life; she's just a new friend."

"Uh huh. Two and a half hours at lunch and another date two days later. Just a friend."

"I'm hardly looking for a relationship. When have I ever? And she's old enough to be my mother."

"You think you could do better? You're lucky to have found her. She's only interested in you for the money, you know. You're a sugar daddy, even if you are a generation younger; that's how she sees you. A paycheck to spend until it's gone, and then she'll be gone, too, and good riddance. And don't pretend you don't have long-term thoughts about her, age and history notwithstanding. You sought her out, remember."

"At Mara and Kala's behest. I don't know what they have planned."

"But whatever it is, you're game, am I wrong?"

"No, you're right. They've never steered me wrong."

That made him laugh. "Never steered you wrong? You poor dumb bastard, why do you think you're faced with homelessness now? You had that case won, and then they made you jump in and ruin your career. One, two, three, and you're out, all thanks to those fucking birds."

"I chose to do that myself."

"Like hell you did. You had no such idea until they put it in your head. Justice!" He spat that word out like it tasted bad. "That's not your job, and you know it. Your job was to defend your client. Did you sleep through your entire legal ethics class? After all this time, you still don't understand the nature of the adversarial relationship of court? You don't know your role, yet? It's the prosecution's job, not yours, to find the evidence. If they fucked up, then that's their failure and their responsibility. You didn't have to screw yourself out of the rest of your life—as I'm sure you heard from the disciplinary board."

"Yeah. I heard. But they're wrong, and so are you, this time. I did the right thing, consequences be damned."

He gave another cruel laugh. "Right, shithead. 'Consequences be damned.' Let's see if you're still saying that in two years when you're out on the street, homeless, friendless, and penniless. You'll be thinking you should have acted differently, mark my words. And you better hope your girlfriend Ruthie has shown you how to survive that way, or you'll never last a winter. She's your only hope, and that's the saddest, most disgusting thing I've ever heard."

"Shut up, Max."

"What did you say?" I'd never talked back to him like that before.

"I said shut up. I've heard enough. You're probably right, I'll grant you that, but you're not helping. If you don't have something useful to say, just shut up."

"Something useful to say? You poor dumb bastard. Yeah, I have something useful to say. Find yourself another job, fast!

Forget those fucking birds, forget that junkie whore, and find something you can do that will pay the rent. Hell, maybe she can teach you to be a prostitute. Not that you'd ever get much business. Maybe you could advise thieves and cutthroats—not to win their cases, but to get away with things without ever getting caught. Fuck, just find something. Even sweeping floors will keep you alive longer than following those birds."

"If it comes to that, I'll sweep floors. There's no shame in that. Nor in prostitution, for that matter."

"No shame! You dumb fuck, what do you know about shame? Well, keep going like you are, and you'll learn plenty. You'll be a goddamned expert in shame. You should be already, but you're too stupid and arrogant to realize it. I give you no more than a year before you're on the streets."

"No bet. You've been right too often. But for now... shut up, Max. I don't want to hear it."

"You don't want to hear it? Well, shithead, you can't hide your head in the sand forever. Let me know when you're ready to face the truth."

"Don't hold your breath."

"I won't need to. You'll be begging for me to come back."

"I doubt that."

"You doubt that? Have you forgotten what it's like when I go away? When we all go away? You were begging for us to come back just a couple weeks ago. Or have you decided you're ready to be a mindless zombie now? Take your medication like a good little robot and stumble blindly through what's left of your life?"

I couldn't suppress a shudder as he said that. "No, not that. Never that. But I don't need to listen to you."

"I'm part of the package, shithead. If you're awake enough to really experience life then you get to hear me, because I'm never going to leave you alone. Might as well get used to it."

"Maybe so, Max. And that's a price I'll pay, if it comes to that. I'll hear you. But that doesn't mean I have to listen to you."

"You don't have to believe in gravity, either, but you'll get hurt if you don't. You know I'm right, fucker. I'm always right."

I ignored that comment.

"Yeah, you can't deny it. I'm right about the whole thing, and you know it. Find a job, shithead, or wind up on the streets. You'll wind up there, anyhow, but this way it might take a little longer. And fucking have fun with your old woman, because it's the last fun you're going to have. Don't forget the gun."

* * *

Mara and Kala had more to say when they visited me while I was reading outside in the early afternoon.

Mara: You and Ruthie had a long lunch.

Kala: We sat outside and thought we'd missed you.

Mara: You took ever so long.

Kala: And you were still talking when you came out.

Mara: Together!

Me: Yes, we had a good conversation. She's quite the person.

Kala: She told you about herself?

Mara: All about herself?

Me: I don't know about that—I'm sure not all. You can't sum up an entire life in two and a half hours. But I heard a lot.

Kala: She told you about her job?

Mara: Her old job.

Kala: With grants.

Mara: Helping people.

Kala: And how she lost it?

Mara: About the drugs?

Kala: And the other job?

Mara: The sex job.

Kala: And her job now.

Mara: Helping people get more help.

Kala: But it doesn't help her.

Mara: Not enough. It's a room.

Kala: And a meal a day.

Mara: But nothing more.

Kala: And she does good.

Mara: She helps people.

Kala: She always helps people.

Mara: Every job. Just different people.

Kala: Different ways to help.

Mara: But all good.

Kala: Because she is good.

Mara: Like you.

Kala: Yes, you both help people.

Mara: And we help you.

Kala: We help you help.

Me: I hadn't thought about it that way. I suppose she has always helped people. Most folks probably wouldn't see it that way.

Mara: Most people are stupid.

Kala: They don't know what helping is.

Mara: That's why you lost your job.

Kala: You were helping.

Mara: Telling the truth.

Kala: Punishing the bad.

Mara: Speaking for the dead.

Kala: Who have no voice.

Mara: And for that, you were punished.

Kala: Because most people are stupid.

Mara: Or blind.

Kala: Yes, maybe blind. And deaf.

Mara: They don't hear us.

Kala: They hear us, but they don't understand us.

Mara: But you do. You're not blind or deaf.

Kala: Most of the time. Sometimes you are.

Mara: True. Sometimes you go away.

Kala: But you come back. Just like we came back.

Mara: And Ruthie sees and hears, too.

Kala: But not as well as you.

Mara: No, she doesn't understand us.

Kala: Not a word.

Mara: But she knows we have voices.

Kala: She knows you understand.

Mara: And she understands that.

Kala: She's not blind or deaf.
Mara: Or stupid.
Kala: And she helps people.
Mara: But she needs help, herself.
Kala: And so do you.
Mara: And so we're here.
Kala: We'll help you.
Mara: You and Ruthie.
Kala: But you have to trust us.
Mara: Yes. Trust us and we will help.
Kala: Help you both.
And with that they were gone.

I think I smell change in the wind. I don't know which way that wind will blow, but I know it's changing.

Wednesday, September 13

Max was there again this morning.

"You ready to listen yet, shithead?"

"To you? No, I don't think so. Not unless you have something actually helpful to say."

"I'm always helpful."

"No, you're always truthful. That's not the same."

"The truth is more helpful than lies."

"Usually. But sometimes silence is more helpful still."

"You want me silent, then?"

"Yes, please. For now."

"I'll be back, shithead. When you're ready to listen to sense."

"I'll be here when you have some to offer."

Yeah, I actually said that. It felt good. It shut him up, too. The eyes and mouths were both open wide in surprise at that one—though I could see laughter crinkling the corners of some of the eyes. Whether they were laughing at me or at Max, I don't know.

I stopped at the market on the way in to meet Ruthie and bought the basics of a picnic lunch. It was a warm day, projected to be in the upper eighties with afternoon storms. Lunch time, though, was sunny and beautiful. I had a bottle of wine and two glasses, a loaf of crusty French bread, some cheeses and smoked meats, pickles, grapes, a tub of store-made Waldorf salad, and two chocolate cupcakes. And cashews, of course. I figured we could eat in a park and maybe Mara and Kala would find us. If Ruthie didn't want to do that, I'd have no problem enjoying the lunch myself another day. I put it all in a big picnic basket along with a blanket we could sit on.

She was thrilled with the idea. She was dressed in well-worn jeans, a baggy sweatshirt, and the same pink running shoes, and was waiting for me in the front room when I came in. I was wearing jeans, too, though in considerably better shape, and an open collar shirt.

"Well, hello, sugar-pie. Not tired of me yet?" she said as I came in.

"Not a bit of it." I held up the basket I was carrying. "I thought we'd try a picnic today if you're game."

"A loaf of bread, a jug of wine, and thou? I love it."

"Well, it's a bottle, not a jug, but I could get more."

"Not for me, honey. One's my limit these days. Once an addict, always an addict, you know. I can handle one. No more. And don't you try and push me, either."

"I wouldn't dream of it. If you want we can pick up something else to drink and skip the wine entirely."

"Not on your life! I said I can handle one. One in the right company—someone I can trust."

"You can trust me?"

"Are you saying I can't, sugar?"

"No, I'm just surprised you feel you can."

"I saw them birds around you the other day. Animals know. They weren't just begging food. They trust you, and that's good enough for me."

"You like Mara and Kala, then?"

"Well, I don't know them like you do, sweetie, but I trust them as birds. Maybe I'll learn to trust them as something more."

"I was hoping they'd join us at lunch."

"Did you invite them, too? Are we double dating now?" she said with a laugh.

"No—I didn't invite them, but they have a way of finding me wherever I am. If we're outside long, they may well show up. They like you."

"Do they now? And what do they know about me?"

"At least as much as I do, apparently."

"Oh, did you tell them all about me and my sordid past?"

"I didn't have to, they already knew. And it's not so sordid."

That made her laugh. "Honey, I don't know what you call sordid, then. A crackhead, a whore, homeless, what more are you lookin' for?"

"You've always helped people. Mara and Kala knew that. That's not sordid."

"I don't know how I helped people doin' crack."

"Well, OK, probably not that, but the grant work helped people."

"Well, yeah. And sex work?"

"Isn't that helpful?"

She graced me with a broad smile "Well of course it is, honey, but most folks don't see it that way."

"Most people are stupid—or blind and deaf." I realized as I said it that I was quoting Mara and Kala.

She laughed. "And you're not."

I could feel myself blushing. "I'll leave that for you to decide."

We walked a few blocks to the park. It was already quite warm, and Ruthie took off her sweatshirt and tied it around her waist. She was wearing an old AC/DC t-shirt underneath. I hadn't seen one like that in years.

"You lookin' at my shirt or my girls, honey?"

"Your shirt!" I answered, quickly. I could feel heat rising into my face. "I was just thinking I had one just like that once. Haven't seen it or one like it in years though."

"Uh huh. Well, you could say you were lookin' at my titties and make me feel pretty, you know? And for all I know, this shirt is yours. A thrift store special. Think I paid a whole fifty cents for it."

"I paid considerably more for mine, even back then. Maybe it is the same one—I have no idea what I did with it."

She gave me a skeptical look. "You don't strike me as the hard rock type, sugar."

"Well, opera is more my thing, it's true. But I saw them in a concert in Denver with a bunch of college buddies—it must have been 30 years ago now. I bought a shirt at the show, one just like that one. It looks better on you, I must say."

"Nice save, sweetie. I'll let you off this time." We both laughed at that.

"Opera, huh?" she continued. "I don't know the first thing about it. You gonna teach me?"

"Maybe. Would you like that? Do you like classical music?"

"I don't know enough to know if I like it or not. My mama made me take piano as a girl. I learned some Bach and some Chopin—badly. That's about all I know. Now blues and funk, that's something I can get into."

"Well, then, if I teach you opera, you'll have to teach me blues and funk."

"That's a deal, sugar."

We got to the park and I spread out the blanket. We'd barely sat down on it before Mara and Kala landed at the far corner of the blanket.

"These your friends?" Ruthie asked.

"Yes, that's Mara and Kala."

"Well, it didn't take them long! You weren't kidding about them finding you."

"No, they usually seem to know where I am."

Mara: It's true, we see you.

Kala: You're different from everyone else.

Mara: We can find you from a long way away.

Kala: But you weren't far.

Me: No, not far at all. Look, Mara and Kala, how is this going to work? If you talk like that, I can't possibly keep Ruthie caught up. Why don't you just listen?

Ruthie: Now don't you go shutting them up on my behalf, sugar. They got voices, too; let them use them. You fill me in when you think you should, and I'll just enjoy the sun and the company.

Me: I'm here to spend time with you, Ruthie. I'll see Mara and Kala other times.

Ruthie: You'll see me, too—or are you trying to get rid of me?

Me: No, not at all!

Mara: You'll see her.

Kala: That's why we're here.

Mara: You and Ruthie have things to do.

Kala: Places to go.
Mara: Not today, though.
Kala: No, not today. We don't know when.
Mara: No, no particular day. But soon.
Kala: When you're ready.
Mara: And you're not yet.
Kala: But you will be.
Mara: We'll help.
Me: OK, hush now.

Ruthie laughed. "Well they certainly seem to be saying some-thing."

"They said you and I have things to do and places to go."

"What, together?"

"Apparently."

"Sugar, that's the strangest pick-up line I've ever heard, and I've heard them all."

"No, Ruthie, I'm not trying to pick you up."

"What did I tell you about making me feel pretty?"

"Not like that. I mean, I'm not using them as a pick-up."

"It sure sounds like it. What is it we're supposed to do?"

"I don't know yet—they haven't said. They said we're not ready yet—or maybe just I'm not. But they said they'd help."

"I bet they will." She laughed. "Honey, I'll give you points for originality. But a blow job is still fifty bucks."

"Ruthie!" I could feel myself blushing again.

"What, you thought you'd get it free? You such a charmer? Or I'm too old?"

"No, neither. Ruthie, I'm not interested in sex. Not with you, not with anyone. I'm happy just to have a friend." It was true—I couldn't remember when I'd last had a friend like Ruthie.

"For now. OK, Mr. Rip, we'll go with friends. You're not my type either, sweetie. I like boys and girls, but I've had enough D for a lifetime. You want a BJ, it's fifty bucks."

"I don't, thanks. And it's not the money, either."

"You're not making me feel pretty, sweetie." She sounded deadly serious, but I could see her eyes twinkling.

"No, it's not you. Ruthie, please. Let's start over. I don't know what Mara and Kala have planned. I don't think it's romance or sex—that's never been their thing—but I don't know what it is. They said something yesterday about helping other people."

"Yeah? Helping how?"

"I don't know. They haven't told me yet."

"You could ask—they're right here."

I looked at the jays. "Well, do you have anything to add?"

Mara: No, you told us to hush.

Kala: So we hush.

Mara: Don't speak.

Kala: Just listen.

Me: But what do you have planned? What are we going to do, where are we going to go? Does it have something to do with Lake Powell?

Ruthie chimed in at that. "Lake Powell? Who said anything about Lake Powell?"

"They did. Now let them answer, please."

Mara: Not Lake Powell. You won't go there.

Kala: You might go by there.

Mara: True, it's on the way.

Kala: But not far enough.

Mara: No, you'll need to go further.

Me: Both of us?

Kala: Yes, of course.

Mara: But not now. Later.

Kala: Later, but soon.

I told Ruthie what they'd said.

"You think you're gonna haul me off to Lake Powell and beyond? You takin' me to Vegas? Maybe Hollywood? I thought those days were behind me."

"You've been there?"

"Vegas, yeah. Not LA, though I dreamed of it. Years ago."

"Well, apparently they think we're going to go there, or at least somewhere beyond Lake Powell. Together."

"Well, I won't say it can't happen, but you better treat me right."

"Ruthie, I don't even know what that means with you."

She laughed hard at that, nearly spilling the wine I had poured for us. "You'll learn, honey. Stick with Ruthie and I'll teach you. Now, helping people—in Vegas or LA? Well, there's plenty of folks there who need help, that's for damn sure."

"No doubt. But I don't know what they have in mind. Who we'd help, or how."

"But they do?"

"So they say."

"And you believe them?"

"They've never steered me wrong yet in twenty years."

"Twenty years? Well, that's quite the long-term relationship, sugar. Longer than any I've had including my mama. If you trust them, then I guess that's good enough for me. For now. But a blow-job is *still* fifty bucks."

"Ruthie, you're incorrigible."

"You better believe it, sweetie. Now break out that food. This old girl is hungry."

We talked and ate and fed Mara and Kala and just enjoyed the warm weather. The jays came and went, doing whatever it is they do during the day. They didn't speak much, but they enjoyed having Ruthie feed them, eating grapes and cashews right from her fingers. It was almost four o'clock and starting to look like it could storm when we packed the few leftovers into the basket and folded the blanket. We might have stayed longer, but Ruthie had to get back to the shelter for supper duty.

"Should I call for you tomorrow?" I asked her as we walked back to the car.

"Sugar, I'd love to, but I need to make a little money."

"Surely you don't have many expenses at the shelter."

"No, my room and supper come with the work I do there, but I still need clothes, and medicine, and books, and any other food I want. Bus fare to get those. Supplies for the harm reduction work."

"So you'll be working tomorrow, then?"

She laughed. "You could call it that, I guess. I'll be handing out needles and condoms in the morning, and in the afternoon I'll be hustling folks for change."

"Panhandling?"

"Uh huh. You have a problem with that, Mr. Rip? Used to be I could make more in less time by offering my professional services, but nobody much seems interested in that from me anymore."

"I have no problem with that. We all do whatever we do for money. I don't think lawyers have any particular ethical high ground."

"Well, there you go, then."

"And 'a blow-job is fifty dollars,' after all."

She laughed again. "Nah, sugar, that's just your price. On the corner I charge twenty-five. Used to be more, but I can't even get that now."

"Oh, so you charge me more? Why is that?"

"All the market will bear, sugar. That's a discount, really, if you think about it. Twenty-five bucks to most of my customers—back when I had customers—was more like a couple hundred to you, I suspect. But I like you."

"And I like you..."

And in chorus, "...but a blow-job is still fifty dollars."

Thursday, September 14

Another unseasonably warm day. I tried to avoid the worst of it, heading up to the Catamount trail near Woodland Park in the morning before it got too hot. It was still warm there, near 80, but it was a pleasant enough five-mile hike with about 1,500 feet of elevation gain. It felt good to be outside and alone with my thoughts. That was the plan, anyway. Max joined me on the trail.

"So, shithead, you still think you've got a future?"

"Hello, Max. I don't remember inviting you back."

"Since when do I need an invitation? I live here, remember? And you miss me when I stay away too long."

That last bit was true enough. I didn't respond.

"And you're still planning on letting a pair of fucking Steller's jays tell you how to live your life."

"I'm open to what they have to suggest. As you have pointed out, I don't have a lot of options."

"Look, shithead, if your best option is doing what a couple of birds tell you, you might as well just kill yourself now."

"It may come to that, but I don't need to be in a hurry."

"You like to prolong the agony?"

"I'd hardly describe this as agony, Max. Uncertainty, yes, but I'm surprisingly not anxious about it."

"Because the birds tell you it will all be OK?"

"That's part of it, yes. But also because whatever may be coming, I'm enjoying the present."

"Oh, please! Hanging out with a junkie turned whore who is old enough to be your mother? Are you shitting me?"

"Ruthie is a good person, Max."

"According to who?"

"According to me."

"The rest of society disagrees with you, you know. Associating with her just shows how far you've fallen and how impossible it will be to ever get up again."

"Then fuck society! If this is having fallen, then I'm glad to be down here on the ground."

"That'll go away pretty quick when she takes all your money. Or are you going to find some sense and get a job? Not that you'll ever be able to do much, but at least it might stave off the inevitable for a little while."

"I'll worry about that later."

"When the birds tell you."

"Well, yes. And when things settle down a bit more."

"Oh, they're settling, shithead. Settling like a collapsed building. Like a sinkhole that just keeps sinking. It'll be too deep to get out of soon, if it's not already."

"You're so comforting, Max."

"Fuck you, shithead."

"Well, I can't say it's been nice talking to you, Max, but it's time for you to go."

"Like hell. Somebody has to talk some sense into you."

He continued on for some time while I hiked. I tried to focus on my breathing and on the path. Eventually he quieted down. As always, he wasn't wrong. Everything he said was true. But I found I didn't really care. I can't explain it, but my future doesn't seem so concerning. It should, I know. I can't live like this without income. My needs are simple enough, and I have quite a bit of savings, but I'm not ready to retire. Not yet, and with my current prospects, maybe not ever. But that's OK, somehow. I don't understand it. After the hike, I stopped in Manitou Springs for a late lunch or early supper and then headed home.

Mara and Kala were waiting for me in the back when I went out with some cashews.

Mara: Things are coming together.

Kala: It will soon be time.

Me: What are you talking about? Time for what?

Mara: Time to go!

Kala: Yes, soon.

Me: Go where?

Mara: You'll know soon.

Kala: Yes, we'll tell you.
Mara: Then you can go.
Kala: Not before.
Mara: You can't before, because you don't know where.
Kala: That's why we're not telling you.
Mara: So you don't leave too soon.
Me: It's somewhere far from here?
Kala: Yes, very far.
Mara: Farther than we've been.
Kala: Ever.
Mara: But we'll follow.
Kala: Not as fast as you.
Mara: No, you will get there first.
Kala: Unless you go very slowly.
Mara: Which you must not.
Me: And how long will I be gone?
Kala: Forever.
Mara: You don't know that.
Kala: True, you might come back.
Mara: To visit.
Kala: Or maybe stay.
Mara: But not soon.
Kala: No, you will be gone.
Me: You're saying I'm supposed to leave Colorado Springs and
move somewhere else?
Mara: Yes! You and Ruthie.
Kala: Nothing to stay for here.
Mara: No more work.
Me: What about my apartment? What about Ruthie's work?
Kala: Your apartment will stay.
Mara: Only you will go.
Kala: Others will help out with Ruthie's work.
Mara: The shelter will stay.
Kala: But you and Ruthie will be gone.
Me: We're traveling together?
Mara: Yes, of course.

Kala: She can't get there without you.
Mara: She could.
Kala: It would be dangerous.
Mara: And take a long time.
Kala: Much better she goes with you.
Me: When are we supposed to leave?
Mara: Soon.
Kala: Not long.
Me: Can you be more specific? It will take time to end the lease here, to do something with my stuff. And that's just me. I'm sure Ruthie has things she has to do to get ready to go, as well—if she even decides to go. Why should she?
Mara: You'll convince her.
Kala: She can help others.
Mara: She can have a stable life.
Kala: Because you will help her.
Mara: It's what she wants.
Kala: It's what you want.
Mara: It's good for you both.
Kala: The best, really.
Me: I'm not even convinced of that. How am I supposed to convince Ruthie?
Mara: You'll find a way.
Kala: That's your job.
Mara: We set it up.
Kala: You make it happen.
Me: And when are we leaving?
Mara: Soon.
Kala: Not long.
Me: Is that days? Weeks? Months?
Mara: Not tomorrow.
Kala: Or the next day.
Mara: Maybe next week.
Kala: Probably not.
Mara: But soon.
Kala: Before the weather gets cold.

Mara: Before the first snow.

Kala: Unless it snows early.

Mara: But probably before.

They didn't provide me with any more information. So it looks like I need to look into storing my stuff until I figure out where I'm going to end up—and to figure out what to take on a road trip with another person to an unknown destination. And then settle up my lease, which isn't due for renewal until January. Maybe I can sublet it out to some snowbirds who waited too long to get reservations at the ski resorts. And what about my medications? I'll worry about all that tomorrow.

This is insane—which coming from me, may be saying something. Am I really considering packing up and moving to points unknown because Mara and Kala have a secret plan? And bringing a delightful but destitute old woman I just met with me? Max is right. This can only end badly. But I don't care.

Friday, September 15

I met Ruthie again for lunch today. She'd spent the morning at the Colorado Springs AIDS Project, volunteering with their mobile testing service. She does outreach for them, particularly with the sex worker and homeless communities. Her history gives her credibility there that others lack. It's solid harm reduction work and something she's very dedicated to.

She's not HIV positive, but she knows plenty of sex workers and intravenous drug users who are, many of them old friends. And while there are good treatment options available now, they are expensive, and most of the people she knows have no insurance of any kind. AIDS is still a potent killer for them, sadly.

Too many old friends have died, so she does what she can. Today two of her friends came in for testing and learned they were both HIV positive. They gave Ruthie the sad news on the way out. She gave them information beyond what the doctors had offered and, more importantly, talked with them and cried with them, helping them come to terms with the diagnosis.

It was a depressing start to the day, and it took its toll on her. But she took action, and that action supports her, too, spiritually if not financially. I had known in a detached, intellectual way that there was an HIV problem here, but I have been isolated from it for the most part. My privilege has let me be blind to the magnitude and personal cost of the problem. A privilege not shared by Ruthie.

The gravitas of the morning weighed on Ruthie. I wanted to lighten things and tell her what Mara and Kala had planned for us, but I couldn't think of any way to bring it up. How do you tell someone that you are planning to drive across the country with them and relocate there for an unknown purpose, solely on the advice of a pair of talking jays? Fortunately, Ruthie gave me the opening I needed.

"Rip, sugar," she said as we were shopping for picnic sup-plies—it was another beautiful day. "I don't know what I'm going to do."

"What do you mean, Ruthie?"

"I'm not going to be able to keep staying at the shelter. Even with the volunteer work there, I've exceeded all the limits for how long someone can stay. They've been looking the other way and fudging the paperwork to help me out, but I'm going to have to leave soon."

"How soon?"

"I don't know. They're still trying to figure something out that will give me more time, but probably in just a couple weeks. Another month at the outside."

"What will you do?"

"Nothin' I can do. I'll be back on the streets. Maybe I can find a squat for the winter, but probably just a camp. I've done it before, but I'm getting old. I don't tolerate winter like I once did. I'm afraid another one would be the death of me. It might be time to move on to someplace warmer. But this is my home, you know? I've lived here pretty much all my life. I know how this town works. Anyplace else I'd be having to learn the ropes all over again. I'm getting too old for any of that shit, you know?"

This defeatist attitude was out of character for Ruthie, clearly a reflection of how deeply the morning had affected her. She was not the bright bubbly woman I had known previously. She needed some spark of hope to rekindle her joy of life.

"It's funny you should mention that today, Ruthie."

"Ain't nothin' funny about it, sugar."

"I've told you my situation—with the loss of my license, not only is my job gone, but any ability to find another like it."

She shook her head. "It ain't the same thing, Rip. Look, I know you feel bad about it, and all, but you're still livin' in your apartment, you're still buyin' this fancy food. You ain't gonna go hungry, and you ain't gotta worry about freezin' to death in a couple months.

"Look, Rip, I like you, I really do, but you don't know my world. It ain't your fault—no way you could know it—but you and I, we don't live in the same world. Your worst is a thousand times better than the best I could hope for."

"What if I have another option—one that involves both of us?"

"Yeah? I'm listenin'. But a blow job is *still* fifty bucks."

"I'm surprised it's not a hundred now."

"Don't tempt me."

"I've told you how Mara and Kala have given me counsel."

"Yeah. They talk to you and gave you information about cases and shit. And now they're talkin' about some crazy-ass trip to Vegas or LA. Only no one else can hear them talk."

"Right. And they are the ones that told me to talk to you."

"Great, I'm being pimped by a couple of birds." It sounded bitter, but she laughed after she said it.

"No, it's not like that. They have a plan for both of us moving forward."

"I'm listenin'."

"They aren't very forthcoming with it. It's hard getting a straight answer from them at the best of times, and they are being very cryptic about this."

"But they told you something. Something about this trip?"

"Yeah. They still haven't said where, but from what little they've said I'm thinking it's probably Los Angeles."

"And that's gonna last through the winter?"

"Longer. They're not talking about just a trip, they're talking about moving there."

"Both of us?"

"Yeah."

She gave a derisive snort. "So I'm supposed to just shack up with you and let you drive me wherever because your birds said so?"

Maybe bringing this up today wasn't such a good idea. "At least consider it, Ruthie. What other options do you have? I'm going, regardless. But Mara and Kala say you have to go, too. They say what they have planned needs us both."

"And what do they have planned?"

"I wish I knew. Something related to helping other people is all I know."

"'Helping people.' What the hell does that mean?"

"Your guess is as good as mine."

She shook her head. "Honey, you must think I'm dumb, crazy, or desperate."

"Not dumb. And crazy is my job." That made her chuckle, though she sobered up quickly.

"OK, so you think I'm desperate. Maybe I am. But I ain't that desperate."

"You said yourself that maybe you needed to leave Colorado Springs—go somewhere that doesn't have winters."

"And I said that wasn't possible, too."

"Only because of the expense and the time it would take to learn your way around a new town."

"Yeah. 'Only' that."

"Well, I can help with that. I'll drive us there, wherever there is. And I can support us both for a while, while we both learn our way around."

"Support us how?"

"I've got money saved up."

"Uh huh. And you're offering me this why? I ain't lookin' for a sugar daddy. I ain't got nothin' to pay with, and you ain't even bought one fifty-dollar blow job. Rip, you ain't makin' any sense at all today. Are you off your meds?"

"No, Ruthie, look, this is real. My head is clear. Max—he's the voice that torments me most—he thinks this is crazy, too. He doesn't trust Mara and Kala. But I do. You've seen them. They aren't my imagination, they aren't part of my schizophrenia."

"I've seen them. They look and act like they're talking to you, I'll give you that, but they're just birds. They clearly trust you, and that counts for something, but they're still just birds. Look, sugar, I want to believe, really I do. I heard you talking to them, but Rip, they just squawk back at you. I don't know what you think you hear, but they aren't speaking words, they're just god-damn jays."

"You just don't understand them, Ruthie. No one else does, either."

"Just you."

"That's right."

"And you don't think that's connected to your mental illness? Seriously? You're not the first schizophrenic I've run into, you know. There's lots of people on the streets that hear all sorts of things talking to them."

"It's not, Ruthie. I can't tell you how I know. I just do. Max and Tempest, yes, they're from the schizophrenia. And the eyes and mouths and mutterers—all of that. But not Mara and Kala. They know things I couldn't possibly know. I don't know what Mara and Kala are, but they aren't inside my head."

She shook her head. "I hear the words you sayin', but they don't make sense. You seriously going to drive across the country because these birds told you that you should?"

"Yes."

"What about your home? Your stuff?"

"The stuff will go into storage, except what can fit in the car. I rent an apartment here, I can let that go. I have no real ties here anymore."

"And you want me to go with you."

"Mara and Kala said you need to. That's enough for me."

"So it ain't your idea."

"No, they've had something planned for a while. This is why they connected us in the first place."

"What if I told you blow jobs were ten bucks?"

"Ruthie, this isn't about blow jobs. I like you—I enjoy your company—but not that way."

"Good, because they're still fifty bucks. Or more. You gay?"

"No."

"Into kids, then?"

"No, nothing like that. I've never really had much interest in sex at all, honestly. The schizophrenia doesn't make stable romantic relationships easy, you know. What interest I have is for women my own age, though."

"You think I'm sexy?"

I laughed. "Are you coming on to me now, Ruthie?"

She didn't laugh back. "Answer the damn question. Do you think I'm sexy?"

I sobered up and looked at her. "I think you are an attractive older woman, Ruthie, but no, I don't think you're sexy."

"'Cause I'm black?"

"No, I don't care about that. I find plenty of black women sexy."

"Like who?"

"What?"

"Like who? Name one black woman you think is sexy."

"Halle Berry. I think Halle Berry is sexy, OK?"

"You know Halle Berry?"

"What? No, of course not."

"But you'd fuck her."

"I doubt I'd ever have the opportunity."

"But you'd take it if you did."

"I suppose so. If she were interested in me, which I seriously doubt."

"No sex without romance, is that your thing?"

"No sex without consent, anyway. I wouldn't know anything about romance."

"Uh huh. What about white women. You think they sexy?"

"Some, sure. And Asian women, some of them. What does that have to do with anything?"

"You ever paid for sex?"

"Not lately."

"That's no answer."

"OK, yes. Years ago, not long after my diagnosis. A few times. And just recently I hired a prostitute but we didn't have sex."

"Why not?"

"I found I didn't want it. It was something Tempest talked me into—I've told you how she is."

"Did you pay her?"

"The prostitute? Yeah, and gave her a good tip. She gave me what I needed, it was just companionship and an ear, not sex."

"So no sex in years?"

"No. Not with another person, anyway."

"Seriously? Why'd you stop?"

"I started to get attached. For me it was a relationship, for her it was a job."

"Uh huh. So you wanted it for free."

"No, it wasn't that. I just wanted the attraction to be mutual. It wasn't."

"Since then? You have any girlfriends?"

"A couple short-term relationships, nothing serious, nothing beyond a few dates, and nothing at all recently. What's with all the questions, Ruthie?"

"Just answer them. When's the last time you got laid?"

I was beginning to wonder if this was really what Mara and Kala had meant when they told me to be honest with Ruthie. I'd never told anyone any of this.

"I don't know. It's probably been ten years... twelve, I guess."

"Twelve years with no sex?"

"I masturbate. But no sex with anyone else, no."

"Porn?"

"Sometimes. Stuff I can find free on the internet."

"Kinky stuff? Violent?"

"Not by choice."

"So by now you're ready to bust out with anyone at all, even me who you don't find sexy?"

"What? No. Ruthie, this isn't about sex."

"Then what is it?"

"Just what I told you. Mara and Kala say this is something we need to do. That it will be good for both of us, and that we'll be helping other people."

"But you have no idea what it is?"

"No."

"Nor where?"

"Not beyond what I told you. South and west, past Lake Powell for sure. I'm guessing Los Angeles."

"Nor how long?"

"Not really. Mara and Kala said it would be permanent. They're planning on joining us there eventually, but I'm guessing it will take them a month or longer to fly that distance. I know they've flown as far as Lake Powell, so the mountains aren't a barrier, but I don't know how they'll cross the desert. Following the Colorado River, I guess."

"So they'll just send you off there, alone."

"Yes, I think so. Well, not alone, if you'll come with me."

"And we do what when we get there? Wait for them if they decide to show up?"

"I don't know. They haven't told me that yet."

"And when is this all supposed to happen?"

"I don't know that, either. 'Soon,' they said. Before the first snowfall."

"And you're going?"

"Yes."

"With or without me?"

"Yes, though I really hope with."

"Why?"

"Because Mara and Kala are clear that we both are needed."

"That's all?"

"I like your company."

"I like your company, too, sugar, but..."

I interrupted her "Let me guess. Blow jobs are still fifty dollars."

She laughed. "Nah, honey. For you, a hundred."

"So you'll go?"

"I didn't say that. But like you said, I don't have a lot of options. I can starve and freeze in a camp this winter or I can go with a sex-starved crazy person driving across the country on a fool's errand. Which would you choose?"

"The food is better with me. And the car's heater works."

"We ain't sleepin' in the car."

"No, we'll stay at hotels on the way. Separate rooms."

"Well, you don't have to go all formal on me. I've shared plenty of rooms, you know. You ain't ugly, sugar."

"Uh, thanks?"

"Don't get your hopes up. You pay for it all, and blow jobs are still a hundred bucks."

"So you'll go?"

"Unless and until somethin' better comes along. I guess you got yourself a travelin' companion, sugar. I hope I don't live to regret this." She shook her head, but her eyes betrayed the beginning of a smile.

We spent the rest of the picnic talking about plans and wondering what would be waiting for us wherever we ended up. She was almost late getting back to the shelter for her dinner shift.

Saturday, September 16

I woke up early this morning, not long after sunrise. It wasn't my choice. Max was yelling at me—which normally doesn't happen until after the medication fog burns off. Today, though, he was riled up and ready to have a go at me.

"Jesus fucking Christ, shithead, you are out of your ever-loving mind? What the hell do you think you're doing? Not only are you going to abandon everything you know, everything you own, and traipse across the country on a wild *jay* chase, but you're going to drag an ancient black whore and drug addict with you? I suppose it figures, nobody else could possibly be desperate enough to say yes to such a ridiculous stunt. And you know she's only in it because you're her meal ticket, the only way to keep warm this winter because her life is complete shit. She'll abandon you as soon as she sees an opportunity, count on that. Because almost any opportunity would be better than what you're offering.

"I mean, what the hell *are* you offering? Seriously. You have only the vaguest notion where you are heading, and no earthly clue what the fuck you'll do once you get there. You can't even pretend the fucking jays will be there to advise you once you land wherever, because they said they wouldn't. You're going to be on your own, in a place you don't know, responsible for not only you but this crazy old woman, with no prospects of anything for either of you. And if you go to LA like you think, you're going to be in one of the most expensive places in the world to live. How the fuck is *that* going to work?

"At least most of the people who go there have a dream—albeit a lousy one—of being in the movies. At best, they end up waiting tables or becoming porn stars. You're not either of you attractive or young enough for either of those possibilities. You'll both be starving and homeless inside of a year—two tops—no matter what you do. Better get that gun and a bullet before you go. You don't want to go broke so fast you can't get one. Maybe you better get two bullets. Maybe *she* will have the balls to pull the trigger when the time comes. It's a cinch that you won't. What a fucking jackass."

There was more. Lots more. It took him most of an hour to wind down. I didn't try and stop him—what could I say? He was right. He always is. I showered and made coffee and was on my second cup when he finally spluttered to a stop, reduced to muttering imprecations under his breath.

"Are you through, Max?"

"Not hardly, shithead. Not unless you're finally listening to reason."

"No. I mean, yes, you are right."

"Of course I'm right."

"But it doesn't matter. I'm going. And if Ruthie will go with me, I'll take her."

"Motherfucker."

"Swearing at me isn't going to change my mind, Max. Nothing is."

"You're an idiot."

"No doubt. Nevertheless, I'm going."

"You're a fucking idiot. A goddamned mother fucking shit-for-brains idiot."

"I don't disagree."

"You're proud of it."

"No, Max, I'm not proud of it. But I'm resigned to it. I don't really have any choice."

"The hell you don't. You have a million other choices, all of them better. Nobody is making you go."

"Nobody is forcing me, that's true. But I got where I am by throwing in with Mara and Kala. They made me—gave me all my successes."

"And your failures."

"No, that was my own doing in their absence. By the time they came back, the die had been cast. There was no way out."

"Fucking idiot. Of course there was a way out. You could have done your job. Remember that job? Defense attorney? Looking out for the welfare of your client? That was your fucking job."

"That was my assignment, but at what cost? Could I let a murderer go free—free to maybe murder again?"

"That was not your responsibility. Not your decision to make."

"If not me, then who, Max? Only I knew the truth—well, me and Marner."

"You didn't know fucking anything. You had no evidence."

"I had no evidence. But I knew it, as clearly as I know anything. And I was right, wasn't I? Mara and Kala have never let me down."

"Bullshit. They let you down big time. That's why you're sitting here without a job, about to go off on this harebrained trip."

"No, they were right. They've always been right, Max. Just like you."

"Well at least you acknowledge that I'm right."

"I never argued it."

"We've argued plenty lately."

"Not about the truthfulness of what you say. I never doubted that, and I still don't. I just don't care."

"You don't care about starving to death homeless in some unknown location?"

"It won't be unknown then, and I don't know that I'll starve or be homeless."

"You don't know that you won't. And you don't have any prospects to ward that inevitable outcome off."

"That's true."

"So?"

"So. Neither you nor I know the future, Max. You are telling me the most likely outcome of my decisions. I don't disagree. But it's not known. If anyone knows the future, it's Mara and Kala, but I don't think even they know that. They see things neither you nor I do. They have more information than us. That's enough."

"You're fucking crazy."

"I don't deny it. Especially not to you."

"I can't change your mind."

"Not this time, Max. You're right, but that doesn't matter."

"Well, shithead. I'll give you this. You've got moxie. It'll be the death of you, but at least you're going out with some character. I'll give you credit for that."

"Thank you, Max."

"Shithead."

"Now, go away."

"I'll be back."

"I don't doubt it. I don't even mind it. I rely on you, Max, in your own way. But right now, I rely on something else more."

"Your fucking birds."

"Yes."

"OK, I'll leave you alone with your folly for now. Not for long."

"That's enough." I finished my coffee in peace.

The eyes were there, but not too many. They looked a little alarmed, but surprisingly not judgmental. The mouths mostly hung open, though some were clearly saying things—I don't know what. The mutterers kept up their chorus, too, but didn't seem too upset. Could it be that Max was the only one fighting me in this? Well, Max and my own sense of reason. A sense of reason that suddenly didn't seem to matter.

I think that once I took the step to pick morality over duty, the good of the world over my own personal gain, something fundamentally shifted. I committed to Mara and Kala in a way I never had before. They went beyond being my counselors to being my voice of... of what? Truth, maybe?

It wasn't that they changed. I've changed. It's almost a religious conversion. That may describe it better than anything. I've found my god, and it has manifested as two talkative Steller's jays. So be it. One could do worse, I suppose. And it's not like I'm going to worship them, build idols and churches to them, convert others to the One True Path. Except for Ruthie, I guess. But that's her choice, and only at the direct behest of Mara and Kala. Nobody else. Perhaps my faith has limits after all.

This line of reasoning was far too philosophical for a Saturday morning. It was a few hours yet until the Metropolitan Opera broadcast, so I put on *Porgy and Bess*—somehow that felt right. It Ain't Necessarily So after all, and before long I'll be able to say I've Got Plenty of Nothin'. And the finale of Oh Lawd, I'm On My Way felt altogether poignant.

The broadcast—a repeat, since the new season doesn't start until December—was *Tristan und Isolde*. Somehow that felt a little less apropos, or at least I hoped it was. A tragic love story is not what I had in mind. Still, it's beautiful music, and Wagner provided a fitting contrast to Gershwin's familiar tunes. Nevertheless, as I was fixing a salad for myself between the second and third acts, it was "Bess, You Is My Woman Now" that I was whistling.

After the broadcast, I went outside. Mara and Kala soon found me.

Mara: So you told her.

Kala: And she's going.

Mara: We knew she would.

Kala: We knew you'd find a way.

Was there anything these two didn't know?

Mara: Now you're ready to go.

Me: Not quite. I still need to deal with my stuff. I don't have a lot, but I'll have to get what I do have into storage and then deal with the apartment. I'll need to arrange for mail somehow—it would help if I knew where I was going—and I'll want to get the car serviced before the trip. I need to figure out what to take and how to arrange to get the rest of the stuff to me. And medications—good Lord, I'll need to come up with something to have enough until I get situated. And Ruthie will have to finish up her work, too.

Kala: Yes, much to do.

Mara: Not ready yet, then.

Kala: But soon.

Mara: Soon.

Me: When will we leave, do you know that? I'll need a date to get things set up.

Kala: After the days get shorter.

Mara: When the aspen drop their leaves.

Me: Could you be more specific? A date would be nice.

Kala: You and your dates.

Mara: As if one day is different from another.

Kala: What is a week? What is a month?

Mara: We don't know months.

Kala: We know moons.

Mara: We do! Yes. You can leave on the next full moon.

Kala: Yes. Not before then.

Mara: But definitely before the new moon after that.

Kala: Well before.

Mara: Yes. When the moon is getting smaller, but still big.

Kala: Bigger than it is now.

Mara: Yes, much bigger.

Kala: Full.

Mara: Or past full.

Kala: Not long past.

Mara: But not before.

I didn't know when that was, but I knew I could find out. The moon was a fat, waning crescent now, so I had something like three weeks. Not much time for such a big change.

Me: I'll try and be ready then. Hopefully Ruthie can be ready, too.

Kala: Ruthie is no problem.

Mara: She could leave tomorrow.

Kala: She will need to leave before you do.

Mara: Maybe, but you can't leave that soon.

Kala: No, not that soon.

Me: She said she was not going to be able to stay at the shelter much longer.

Mara: Not much, no. She will have to stay with you.

Kala: Before you go.

Mara: But that's OK.

Kala: You'll be staying together after you go.

Mara: So start sooner.

Kala: Staying together, not going.

Mara: Right. Don't go until after the full moon.

Kala: Then things will be ready.

Mara: Well, not quite.

Kala: But soon enough.

Mara: Before you arrive.

Kala: Yes. Before you arrive.

Me: Arrive where? Are you going to tell me where we're going?

Mara: You already guessed.

Kala: You're clever.

Mara: For a human.

Me: Los Angeles?

Kala: Yes. City of Angels.

Mara: That's what they call it.

Kala: There aren't any angels.

Mara: Or at least, none we can see.

Kala: But there aren't any here either.

Mara: That we can see.

Me: What will we do when we get there?

Kala: Too soon.

Mara: Yes, get there first.

Me: But you won't be going with us.

Kala: No. We will go.

Mara: Stay with you.

Kala: But slower.

Mara: We can't fly that fast.

Kala: Not that far.

Me: So how will we know what to do?

Mara: You'll know.

Kala: When it's time.

Mara: Not now.

Kala: Too soon.

And with that, they flew off.

So.... We are LA-bound. In something like three weeks. That's more than I knew before. Still less than I'd like, but it's better than nothing. Nothing—that I've got plenty of.

Sunday, September 17

I had agreed to meet Ruthie for church. I'm not a churchgoer normally, but she told me if she was going to travel with me that she had to know I wouldn't burst into flames if I walked into a church. I felt reasonably confident that we were safe from that, though it had been many years since I last tested it. We went to the Resurrection African Methodist Episcopal Church. I'd never been to a predominantly black church before—I wasn't the *only* white person there, but close. I'm not used to people shouting "Amen" and the like during the sermon, but otherwise it felt comfortable and welcoming very quickly.

I surprised Ruthie by actually knowing a couple of the hymns—I surprised myself, actually. The service ended, as it apparently always does there, with the whole congregation singing Lift Every Voice and Sing. I've known that song for years but never realized it was something of a black anthem. I did lift my voice—a passable baritone—and swayed along with the rest of the congregation. I got lots of smiles and hugs after the service. I could maybe get used to this, as long as I didn't have to actually believe. In any case, Ruthie seemed to approve.

After the service we went to lunch and I told her about yesterday's conversation with Mara and Kala. It still felt so odd discussing this with someone. I've lived in fear of someone finding out about them for so long that it feels incredibly dangerous to talk about it. I know she doesn't trust and believe in them like I do, but she accepts that I do, and I'm grateful for that.

I'd looked up some dates. The next full moon is on Thursday the fifth of October, with the third quarter a week later. We'll have to leave somewhere in that week. Ruthie didn't feel that would be a problem—in fact, sooner would be better. She indicated that despite all their efforts, the shelter wasn't going to be able to let her stay past the end of the month. She'd be out on the streets after that.

I told her that she wouldn't be on the street, that I could pay for a hotel room for her, or she could sleep on my couch for the week before we left.

"Well, sugar, we're gonna be spending a lot of time closer than that driving to LA. Might as well start it early. Save your money, I'll take the couch."

"I'm sorry I don't have a spare bed. If you'd like you can take the bed and I'll sleep on the couch."

"I'm not puttin' you on the couch in your own apartment, sugar. I've slept on worse than couches, believe me. But let me ask you this. How big is your bed?"

"What? It's a queen."

"Well, honey, if you behave yourself, we could share the bed. If not, I'll take the couch—that's not a problem. But we're going to be sleeping in the same hotel room on the road, so again, we might as well get used to it."

I opened my eyes wide in mock outrage. "Ruthie! Are you coming on to me?"

She laughed. "No way, sugar. I said you have to behave yourself. A blowjob is still a hundred bucks. And more is more, as they say. I'm talkin' about sleepin'. Just sleepin'. You OK with that?"

"That's fine, Ruthie," I laughed. "I should warn you, though. I snore."

"How do you know?"

"I've been told."

She elbowed me in the ribs playfully. "So you don't always sleep alone! Glad to hear that. Is she cute?"

"Is who cute? I was told by my roommate in college. A guy. Who didn't share my bed but did sleep in the same room. The few who've shared my bed since then haven't said one way or the other, but I doubt they would, anyway. It's not part of the contract."

"OK, honey-pie, don't get your feathers ruffled. I can put up with snoring. I may snore myself. Delicately and lady-like, of course." We both laughed at that.

"Then it's settled. We'll move you in on the 30th. Sound good?"

"Sounds wonderful. When will we leave?"

"That depends on what I can get arranged in the next week. I've got to put my stuff in storage—someplace that will accommodate it being shipped to me later. And sign off on the apartment, and do something about medications. And mail! All sorts of things, really. Mara and Kala said we need to leave before the first quarter moon, which is on the 12th, so it will need to be somewhere in that week."

"They're pretty demanding for a couple of birds, aren't they?"

"I assume they have their reasons. They haven't shared everything with me, but then, they don't."

"But they know things you don't?"

"Yes, clearly. They've been the key to most of the cases I've had as a lawyer. They are my 'undercover network' that has made all my peers jealous." I laughed. "When they'd ask, I'd just say 'I heard it from the birds.' They never knew how literally I meant it."

She laughed, too. "That's probably a good thing, honey. Most people wouldn't believe you've got birds that talk to you. Especially with your schizo stuff."

"Yes. The voices—Max for instance—I know they are part of the schizophrenia. They're still real, and he's always right, but it's my particular sensitivity to them—what some call my 'illness'. I know that. Mara and Kala are... different."

"So you've said. Well, you sure seem to believe that, anyway."

"And you don't? Yet you're still going along with me?"

"Sweetie, we've been down this road. If I didn't go with you, what exactly do you think I'd do? Besides starve and freeze to death, that is. Nah, I don't believe they're real—not the voices, anyway. The birds are real enough, I've seen them. But what they tell you? Nope. Sorry to bust your bubble, sugar, but I don't believe it. But I ain't sure I disbelieve it either, you know? If it works, it works, and I don't have to understand it. There's lots I don't understand and it still works. As long as it keeps working, then I'm fine. You believe it. That's good enough for me."

"Ruthie, you ever consider becoming a psychologist?"

She laughed so hard she nearly spilled her iced tea. "A shrink? Honey, ain't nobody got time for that. Who'd pay to talk to me?"

"Plenty of people. They've paid for... other therapy, right?"

She smiled. "True, true. And some do want to talk—and if they're payin', I'm listenin'.'"

"It all comes down to empathy, and you've got that in spades. If I ever had a psych say what you just said, I'd feel like I'd finally found one who got me. That hasn't happened. I don't trust any of them—not like I trust you."

She thought about that for a moment—I didn't interrupt. "Well, honey, maybe you're right. Maybe it's not so different from the 'therapy', as you put it, that I've given others. I never thought of it as therapy, just what it takes to make the client happy so they tip well and come back. But I guess it amounts to the same thing."

"Of course it does."

"So maybe I should be chargin' you for this, sugar."

"Besides room and board, you mean?" I said with a wink.

She laughed. "Fair enough." She thought quietly for a moment. "Doing the needle exchange work, the IDUs talk to me all the time."

"IDUs?"

"Intravenous drug users. The ones who shoot up. The smart ones use fresh needles and get tested for AIDS and Hep C regularly. We see a lot of regulars, and they all stop and chat to me. Not to the docs, or employees, but to me. I always figured that was just because I'm on their level."

"That's part of it, probably. They can trust you—you're not in a position to judge them."

"Nah, honey, don't think that. The most judgmental people I know are other whores and junkies. But also the most generous and caring people. Poverty and marginalization doesn't make you a saint—it just makes you more of what you already are, whether that's kind and generous or mean and spiteful. You can't afford to play games, don't have the time or energy for it."

I nodded, listening without comment.

"Some of them, all they can do is complain and blame everyone else for their problems. Sure, they've caught some bad breaks. Awful ones. Most of them have been abused, whether sexually or physically or emotionally. Usually multiple times. But it doesn't help to blame someone else—a grudge is just pain you take on for someone else's benefit. Better to just deal with what you've got. Be thankful for the good things that come your way, and let the rest roll off your back. And that's what I try to do. If they come in and want to complain, I let them. I listen and sympathize and take that pain from them, but I don't hold onto it. I let it go. And I share what I'm thankful for and what gifts I have, even if it's just a smile and touch."

"No doubt about it, Ruthie. You're a therapist. Better than the shrinks who get two hundred dollars an hour."

"Two hundred an hour? That's a high-dollar whore. I haven't seen that kind of money in years."

It was my turn to spit my drink. "High-dollar whore. I'll have to remember that, next time I see Dr. Filtner."

"Now don't you go tellin' on me."

"Oh, don't worry, Ruthie. You're safe. I wouldn't tell her about you any more than I'd tell her about Mara and Kala. Either one might get me put away again."

"You don't talk about your psych stuff, then?"

"Not those details. I tell her I'm fine. I might mention the mutterers once in a while, but even that might get my dose raised."

"That's a bad thing?"

"That's a terrible thing. Ruthie, those meds steal my soul. They rob me of me. I don't hear voices—not even Mara and Kala—but I don't hear much of anything else, either, and I feel nothing."

"Then why do you take them?"

"Because without them, the voices take over. I lose myself in a different way, then."

"So it's like a balancing act?"

"Yes, exactly. And one I have to work out on my own because the psychiatrist's goals are always to medicate until I'm incapable of feeling anything. That's what they call 'normal'. If that's normal, I don't want it."

"Normal ain't nothin' but a setting on the clothes dryer. Fuck normal."

"Amen, Ruthie. Amen."

Psychiatric Progress Notes

Patient Name: William "Rip" Taylor

Date: September 19, 2017

Diagnoses:
   Schizophrenia (Paranoid) *F20.0*
   Tardive Dyskinesia (subacute, drug-induced) *G24.01*

Medication List:
   Risperidone 4 mg PO SID (QHS)
   Ingrezza 80 mg PO SID (QHS)

Physical Findings and Mental Status:
   Vitals: Unremarkable.
   Mental Status: Alert and oriented to person, place, and time.
   Comportment: Well-groomed, alert posture, unremarkable.
   Mood and affect: Cooperative and situationally appropriate.
   Ability to concentrate: Unremarkable.
   Tone and rate of speech: Appropriate and unhurried.
   Danger to self/others: None.

Symptoms:
   Mr. Taylor reports no significant symptoms and normal sleep.

Interventions:
   Upon arrival, Mr. Taylor reported that because of the change in his employment status, he intends to travel on an extended basis. I countered that that might be inappropriate given his recent hospitalization.

   Mr. Taylor indicated that he would be traveling alone by car, heading west, probably to California. I asked about his departure date and how long he would be away.

   We discussed medications during his trip including not only the Risperidone and Ingrezza but also Alprazolam (Xanax) as an anxiolytic to avoid travel stress precipitating another psychotic break. We also discussed the use of an SSRI antidepressant.

Patient Response to Interventions:

Mr. Taylor insisted that he was fully recovered from his recent psychotic break and that he intended to travel despite any objections I might raise.

When pressed about the length of the trip, his response was, "I don't know. At least a few weeks, maybe permanent. I have nothing keeping me here." He indicated that he was looking forward to the trip, and his manner confirmed this. He became quite animated, but not rushed, talking about the planned travels. When I assured him that we would continue his therapy upon his return, he smiled and replied, "If I come back."

Mr. Taylor has made it quite clear that he is leaving regardless of anything I might do or say short of another involuntary commitment, and I have no justification for hospitalization at this time.

Mr. Taylor requested a 90 day prescription of both the Ingrezza and Risperidone so that he would have enough for any travel and possible relocation.

Clinical Impressions:

Mr. Taylor's apparent mental state is as good as I have seen, despite his recent psychotic break. Nevertheless, I remain concerned about his planned course of action. An extended time without psychiatric evaluation this soon after hospitalization is not advised.

His apparent quick decision to leave, even putting his possessions into storage and allowing his apartment to be re-let, gives every impression of physical and possibly mental fugue if not outright mania. This is likely a result of the trauma of his recent hospitalization, his involuntary separation from his employment, and the subsequent suspension of his law license. His spirits remained high throughout the appointment, especially when discussing travel plans, so perhaps this may be a (short-term) boon.

I am deeply concerned that his symptoms are highly volatile in light of all these changes, and that he may suffer another psychotic break while distant from any care. Mr. Taylor appears to be discounting any stress associated with travel, contrary to all past experience.

While my concerns about his future are substantial, my assessment of his present state is acceptably good.

Plan:

I am opposed to dispensing a 90-day quantity of psychotropic medication in principle, but can see no particular reason to deny it given the circumstances and his obvious need. Certainly his running out of medication would be far more problematic. I will prescribe the medication at his next appointment, prior to his departure. This will ensure at least one more opportunity to evaluate him.

I also intend to prescribe Alprazolam as an anxiolytic, as I anticipate that stress and reality will catch up with Mr. Taylor while he is traveling. I can only hope that it relieves the stress to an extent that he is able to return here or locate suitable psychiatric care before he lapses into a dangerous state of mind.

Next appointment in two weeks.

Rx:

None.

Signed:

JoAnne Filtner, M.D., Ph.D.

Friday, September 22

The new moon was two days ago, and now there's a thin crescent in the west this evening. That tells me we'll be leaving in a couple weeks. It's been busy. I had my appointment with Dr. Filtner and let her know I'd be leaving. She agreed to give me a 90 day supply of both medications, so that should hopefully hold me until I get settled. I'll pick those up at my last session right before we go. She is insisting on giving me a scrip for Xanax, too. I don't want it, and won't fill it, but if it keeps her from messing with the other meds, that's fine. It's a "take as needed" thing, so I can just not need it. She was really pushing to put me on Zoloft or Prozac or the like, too, but I said no. I don't want that on my prescription history, or I'll have to fight the next doc over it, too. I'm sure she wrote something down about it anyway, but at least I won't have it in my actual medication history.

Max has been surprisingly quiet lately. He lets me know that what I'm doing is ridiculous ("fucking nuts," actually), but that's fine. I agree. I'm doing it anyway. He seems resigned to my travels at this point. Whatever; I'll take it. Tempest has been after me a bit, too—trying to convince me to make it a final epic journey of destruction. Shades of Leaving Las Vegas. She thinks I should dump Ruthie, though, so that's easy to shut down. The eyes and mouths are there, but fewer, and they just watch. The mutterers, too—they mutter about their own business—or maybe about mine, I don't know. But they're easy to ignore these days.

It helps that I've been busy getting everything arranged before we leave. It turns out the manager of the storage place where Marner hid all his loot remembers me fondly. He thinks I brought them business with the publicity from the trial. He gave me a good deal on a storage shed large enough to hold all my furniture and possessions. It's temperature and humidity controlled, too, so my vinyl collection and CDs should fare OK until I land somewhere. I've already started moving things into it. He said that when I get settled and ready to move stuff out to LA that I can just let him know. I'll give him the name of the moving company and he'll give them access to load the stuff to send it out to me. That's a big relief—I thought that might be the hard part.

I've been starting to introduce Ruthie to opera. She was pretty dubious at first, but I started with the fun and easy stuff. Mozart, Gershwin, that sort. Wagner and Puccini will come later. In return she's been introducing me to Rhythm and Blues, Funk, and Motown. Some great stuff there—I'm as surprised by it as she is by opera. We should have no shortage of music to listen to as we drive across the west.

Mara and Kala are still being cryptic, promising to tell me more before we go, but not before the full moon. I got my final paycheck from Mike, so my business affairs here are pretty well wrapped up. I still need to sort things out with the apartment management company. They are insisting that I have to pay rent through the end of the lease—and if that's the way it ends up, it won't break me. But I bet I can convince them that they'd be better off finding another renter and letting me out early. We'll see. I'll keep my bank account here for the time being—I can move it once I'm settled. That will let me continue the auto-pay bills and keep the credit cards active.

There's still plenty to do, but I'm beginning to believe it can all get done in time. I'm actually excited about this new start— the biggest change I've seen in decades, maybe ever. That should scare me. I've always hated change. I'm not sure why I'm excited rather than in a panic, but I'm not going to argue with success. Ruthie says it's because I'm discovering the real me. Maybe she's right. She knows more about me than any shrink, that's certain.

She likes Mara and Kala, too, and it's mutual. She doesn't understand them, of course, but she's learned to recognize them when they come, and she can even tell them apart now. She talks to them and listens when I tell her what they said in response. I suppose she doesn't really believe that they talk, but that doesn't seem to bother her or get in the way. If she can deal with that, than I guess I can, too. It's nice to at least have someone I can be open with about my friends.

I feel better than I have in months. I'm sure Ruthie is a big part of that. Being able to talk honestly about everything going on in my head without any fear of judgment or repercussions is a real gift. The medication seems to be at a good balance, too. I can still think and function and use all my talents, but I'm not overwhelmed by Max and the others.

The Ingrezza has been a godsend. I still have the occasional grimace and that damned blink, but it's so much improved over what it used to be. I at least don't feel like an obvious freak when I'm out in public now. I'm no stranger than most of the other weirdos out there. That's a good thing.

I still don't know what's waiting for us in Los Angeles. But to my surprise, that's OK. I'm excited to find out. Counting down the days, now!

Psychiatric Progress Notes

Patient Name: William "Rip" Taylor

Date: October 3, 2017

Diagnoses:
   Schizophrenia (Paranoid) *F20.0*
   Tardive Dyskinesia (subacute, drug-induced) *G24.01*

Medication List:
   Risperidone 4 mg PO SID (QHS)
   Ingrezza 80 mg PO SID (QHS)

Physical Findings and Mental Status:
   Vitals: Unremarkable.
   Mental Status: Alert and oriented to person, place, and
   time.
   Comportment: Well-groomed, alert posture, unremarkable.
   Mood and affect: Cooperative and situationally appropriate.
   Ability to concentrate: Unremarkable.
   Tone and rate of speech: Appropriate and unhurried.
   Danger to self/others: None.

Symptoms:
   Mr. Taylor reports that all symptoms of schizophrenia—positive, negative, and cognitive—are in remission.

Interventions:
   We discussed Mr. Taylor's planned travels and ongoing medical concerns. No challenges to his delusional thoughts were
made at this time given the inability to follow up for an unknown
period.

   We discussed medications during this travel break, including
maintaining the Ingrezza and Risperidone, introducing Alprazolam (Xanax), and introducing an SSRI antidepressant.

   I assured Mr. Taylor that, should he not return, I would immediately forward his records to a new therapist upon his
request and that of the provider. I made sure that he has my

business card with all my contact information and advised him to call if he encounters problems while away.

Patient Response to Interventions:

Mr. Taylor appears in genuinely good spirits and seems excited about beginning his trip west. His travel dates are still uncertain—he expects to leave in the next several days and is uncertain when or even if he will return. He has made careful plans for his affairs in his absence, and has taken the time and effort required to execute them.

Mr. Taylor continued to request a prescription for a 90-day supply of both of his current medications, which I am reluctantly willing to provide. He was less accepting of the Xanax but acknowledged that it could be useful if things "get crazy." He indicated that he would take that prescription but would probably not fill it right away. I cautioned him not to wait until it was too late and to definitely fill it before traveling out of the country if his journeys should take him there.

Mr. Taylor remains completely opposed to the idea of introducing an SSRI, and I declined to pursue it given the inability to follow up on it in his absence. The risks of unmonitored response to new medication outweighs the potential benefits. Given his present apparent good regulation, this does not overly concern me.

Clinical Impressions:

Mr. Taylor appears in better mental health than at any previous visit. His focus is good and undistracted; his answers to questions are clear and complete. He initiates conversation appropriately and has appropriate and active mannerisms coincident with speech. Without knowledge of his history, I would see no reason to suspect any mental illness based on today's visit. I can only hope that this will continue while he travels. Whatever he is doing, it seems to be working. Even the tardive dyskinesia symptoms are much abated, with only occasional grimaces or chewing and the remaining pronounced eye-blink.

Plan:

As discussed previously, I am issuing a prescription for a 90-day supply of both the 80 mg Ingrezza and 4 mg Risperidone, as well as a prescription for Alprazolam (Xanax) 0.5 mg Q 90 to be taken as needed for anxiety. I have cautioned Mr. Taylor as to the use of the Alprazolam and he understands the risks as well as the benefits of benzodiazepines in general and Alprazolam in particular.

Next appointment open upon his return.

Rx:

Risperidone 4 mg PO SID (QHS), Q 90
Ingrezza 80 mg PO SID (QHS), Q 90
Alprazolam 0.5 mg PO Q4H PRN, Q 90

Signed:

JoAnne Filtner, M.D., Ph.D.

Thursday, October 5

Sing it with me: "Shine on, shine on Harvest Moon...." That's today. I had my last visit with Dr. Filtner on Tuesday, and, as promised, she gave me 90-day scrips for both the Ingrezza and the Risperidone at the present doses. She also gave me a scrip for Xanax, but I don't intend to fill that. She commented that I appeared in better mental health than any time she had seen me, and in better mental health than most of the people she knows. I think she may be right, though we define it differently.

Max has been haranguing me most days. He starts first thing in the morning and doesn't let up until late, but I can tell his heart isn't in it. He seems resigned to the future, somehow. He even complimented me this morning on having the balls to stick with a plan, even if it was a bad one. From him, that counts as high praise.

Tempest, too, seems resigned to my plan. She doesn't bother me much, and when she does, it's very half-hearted. Ruthie clearly isn't what she has in mind for me, but I think she senses that it's what is good for me. She'd love for me to have some sort of torrid affair, but she knows that's not going to happen. She's always known and that never stopped her before, but I don't think I've ever been this content. I suppose that matters, even to her.

Ruthie has been staying here since the 30th, sharing my bed. She does snore, but not enough to keep me awake. She says I don't keep her up, either, so I guess that works. We had some issues with bathroom stuff: how we squeeze the toothpaste, leaving the toilet seat up, that sort of thing. I always thought those were just jokes, but apparently they are real. Whatever. We've worked things out without fighting.

Most of my stuff is in storage now. All that's left is the bed, the table and two chairs, the stereo, and a few kitchen implements that we won't be taking with us. I've arranged to rent a small truck on Saturday morning to take those to the storage unit, and then we'll be on our way. The apartment will sit empty for the rest of this month. If someone can be found to rent it, I'll be let out of the lease early; otherwise, I'll be paying rent for an empty apartment through the end of the year. Not ideal, but workable. I've made arrangements for all the outstanding bills to be auto-paid, so I think I should be covered that way.

Ruthie and I were talking about music in the yard this afternoon when Mara and Kala came. They've been making brief visits lately, enjoying Ruthie's attention and not saying much of consequence. Today was different.

Mara: Today is the day.

Kala: Every day is a day.

Mara: But today the moon is big.

Kala: Yes, big and round. That's right.

Mara: So you can go.

Kala: Yes, any time.

Me: Well, we're set to leave on Saturday, the day after tomorrow. But we can't leave yet.

Mara: You could.

Kala: You could leave right now.

Me: And go where? I still don't know where I'm going or what I'll do once I get there.

Mara: You're going to Angel City.

Kala: We already told you that.

Me: Yes, Los Angeles. But that's a big city. Where do we go once we get there? And what are we supposed to do there?

Mara: Yes, a very big city.

Kala: That's what we're told.

Mara: We've never been there.

Kala: But we will be.

Mara: Not long.

Kala: But after you.

Mara: And we'll find you.

Kala: Yes, you're easy to find now.

Mara: But you can't find what you need.

Kala: Not without us.

Mara: Or others.
Kala: Yes, others could help.
Mara: But they don't know you.
Kala: Not like we do.
Mara: But we can tell you some.
Kala: What we've been told.
Mara: You want to be in an orange.
Kala: Is that what they told us?
Mara: It was like that.
Kala: I don't remember that.
Mara: It was an orange for sure.
Kala: Yes, that's true.
Me: Orange County maybe? Is that what you're saying? There's an Orange County near Los Angeles.
Mara: Yes, that's it. Orange County.
Kala: Yes! I remember that.
Kala: Go there.
Mara: And look for... what was it Kala?
Kala: Nuevo Comienzo.
Mara: You say that so well.
Kala: I memorized the sounds.
Me: Nuevo Comienzo? Spanish?
Ruthie (overhearing me): Fresh start. *Nuevo comienzo* means fresh start in Spanish.
Mara: Yes, that's it. That's it. Ruthie knows.
Kala: She knows so much.
Me: (to Ruthie) You speak Spanish?
Ruthie: Un poquito. You pick it up on the streets.
Mara: She knows.
Kala: Fresh start, *Nuevo comienzo,* yes!
Me: So I'm looking for a fresh start? In Spanish?
Mara: Nu...
Kala: Nuevo Comienzo. Yes.
Mara: Find that. Tell them who you are.
Kala: Tell them what you do.
Mara: What you've done.

Kala: All of it.

Mara: Both of you.

Kala: Be truthful.

Mara: Always truthful.

Kala: Just like Ruthie.

Mara: Yes, it worked with her.

Kala: It will work here, too.

Mara: Very important!

Kala: Tell everything.

Mara: All the truth.

Me: Tell them about the lawyering and the schizophrenia? Tell them about Ruthie's work, and, uh, other work? And the drugs? Homelessness?

Kala: Yes, all of that.

Mara: They will understand.

Kala: And they need you.

Mara: Like you need them.

Me: Need us, like giving us jobs?

Kala: Give you work to do, yes.

Mara: Lots of work.

Kala: Good work.

Mara: Helping people.

Kala: People who need help.

Mara: Like what you did.

Kala: And Ruthie.

Mara: Only different.

Kala: Different people.

Mara: Different help, too.

Kala: But work for you.

Mara: And work for Ruthie.

Me: Work that pays? Orange County is not a cheap place to live. No place near Los Angeles is.

Kala: We don't understand money.

Mara: Not much, anyway.

Kala: They don't have money.

Mara: Nu....

Kala: *Nuevo comienzo.* No money.
Mara: That's not what it means.
Kala: No, it's what they have.
Mara: Or don't have.
Kala: Not much money.
Mara: What money they have they use.
Kala: For good. To help.
Mara: But that is your work.
Kala: You'll help them find money.
Mara: You'll bring in the money.
Kala: They'll use it to help others.
Mara: But bring in enough…
Kala: …and they'll help you, too.
Mara: Enough to live.
Kala: Enough.
Mara: Live better than Ruthie has.
Kala: But not as well as you have.
Mara: But not bad.
Kala: Walls.
Mara: Food.
Kala: And lots of work.
Mara: Good work.
Me: So, we find this Fresh Start…
Ruthie: Nuevo Comienzo.
Me: Right, *Nuevo Comienzo,* tell them our complete histories.
Ruthie: What?
Me: And that will inspire them to give us jobs.
Ruthie: What sort of jobs?
Me: Jobs helping people, only jobs that don't really pay. But our jobs will be to bring money in so they can provide more help, and that will cover our own pay as well.
Kala: Yes, that's it.
Ruthie: Oh! So grant work? Like I used to do? I can tell them about that. I hope I remember how.
Mara: Yes, but tell it all.
Kala: That's important. Tell everything.

Mara: Always true.

Kala: All of it.

Me: They say you need to tell the whole story. Not just the grant work, but the drugs, the prostitution, the homelessness, everything. And I have to tell about the schizophrenia, and losing my license, too.

Ruthie: That's insane.

Me: It worked with you.

Ruthie: What?

Me: They told me I had to be completely honest with you, too. Tell you everything. Ruthie, I've never told anyone half of what you know about me. And that worked out OK.

Ruthie: But I'm a special case.

Mara: Not special.

Kala: Not unique.

Mara: Same thing here.

Kala: Tell it all.

Mara: You must.

Me: They're very insistent. 'Tell it all.' We'll see what we find when we get there. They say we can bring in enough to live. Not well, maybe, but live. Better than a shelter, anyway.

Ruthie: I don't know....

Me: Getting cold feet, Ruthie? Gonna back out on me now?

Ruthie: And do what, sugar? No, I'm in it for the duration. But dear lord, tell everything?

Me: Trust them. I do.

Ruthie: I can't trust them, honey, I can't even understand them. I'll just have to trust you, instead.

Me: That will do.

Kala: Yes, that will do.

Mara: Perfect.

Kala: Now you can go.

Mara: Soon.

Me: The day after tomorrow.

Kala: Yes, soon.

And with that they flew off. *Nuevo Comienzo.* A fresh start. Well, that seems fitting, I guess.

Friday, October 6

Last night here—tomorrow we set off for LA. Max knows it and has gone all out today.

"So, shithead, you're still going through with this?"

I ignored him. Ruthie doesn't like it when I talk back to Max. She doesn't say anything, but you can tell it makes her uncomfortable.

"This is your last chance to back out and find something better. Face it, shithead, *anything* would be better. Go back to school, find another profession. Find any sort of job—you're young and fit enough. Schlep baggage at an airport—no wait, you'd never pass the screening. Teach school—no, you wouldn't be allowed to work with kids, either. OK, face it, you're well and truly fucked. But still, anything would be a better choice than this.

"You're leaving everything you own in some cut-rate storage facility and driving halfway across the country with an old junkie whore who would rob you blind in a heartbeat. Only reason she hasn't run off is she thinks you're already playing into her hand. She's right, by the way. Why don't you just make her the beneficiary on your life insurance and kill yourself? It would be quicker and have the same net effect for both of you. Better for her, really. You're going to wind up dead, and she's going to wind up with whatever is left. Might as well leave her the whole thing.

"You don't know where you're going. Orange County is a big place. You're looking for something called *Nuevo Comienzo*—and you could hardly find that on the web. A Facebook page pointing to a nearly empty website. No contact information, no address, just a donate button. What a scam! This is what the birds are sending you to? Really? And you trust them? What do you think will happen? You think they are going to welcome a washed up, disgraced lawyer and an old woman with a prison record and a drug history, who makes what little money she can by begging and taking advantage of people with a fetish for old black women? Seriously? You are out of your mind!"

This went on more or less all day. I know Ruthie could tell. She was down herself—no doubt having her own second thoughts. She reacted badly to Mara and Kala's instructions that we tell all when we get there. It goes against her every instinct—and against all common sense, I admit. I should be helping her through that, but it's hard with Max continually haranguing me. We spent the day avoiding each other as much as possible in this small apartment. What will we do when we're shut in a smaller car together for hours?

I hoped Mara and Kala would be back this afternoon—I need their encouragement, and I think it would help Ruthie, too, even if she can't understand them. But the hawks were circling all afternoon. I pointed them out to Ruthie, but she wasn't impressed and didn't even notice when they'd cry. I told her they hunt jays, but she insisted they catch more mice than birds, and rarely anything as big as Mara and Kala. As if she knows anything about raptors. I fear for Mara and Kala. I fear for us. Hunters hunt, and I am prey.

We loaded up the last of the boxes tonight—everything except the sheets on the bed, which we'll put in the last box (dirty!) tomorrow morning as soon as we rise. I picked up the rental truck this evening, so we'll run things over as soon as the storage place opens, return the truck and be on our way. We went out to a sandwich shop for dinner tonight since all the plates and kitchen utensils were cleaned and packed. Sitting across from each other waiting for our food, we couldn't manage to avoid and ignore each other.

"So, sugar, tomorrow we're doin' this crazy thing?" Ruthie asked.

"Yep. Heading west looking for a fresh start."

"*Nuevo comienzo, sí. Es un plan loco.*"

"I don't speak Spanish, but I know what *loco* means. You think we're crazy."

"No, I *know* we're crazy—you have the diagnosis to prove it, honey—but I said that what we're doing is crazy."

"It probably is. Max thinks so, certainly."

"Max, the voice in your head?"

I nodded. She laughed.

"That's a kick. Even the crazy voices in your head think this is crazy. Too crazy for crazy!"

I smiled. She doesn't understand that Max is always right. He's mean, and he always brings out the worst aspects of anything, but ultimately, he's right every time.

"You don't have to come, Ruthie. I'm not going to hold you hostage."

She smiled at me. "What makes you think you could, sugar? I've fought off worse than you. Nah, I'm going. Nothing that makes sense is working, I better try crazy. I can't do any worse."

"You'll do what Mara and Kala say, then? Tell the truth about everything when we get there?"

She shook her head. "I don't know about that, honey. That's the craziest part of all. And I didn't hear Mara and Kala say that— only you. And I know you're crazy, sugar."

"They said, it, Ruthie, trust me. I think it's a risky thing to do, too. But I've learned to take the risks that they recommend. Without risk there is no gain, and they've never steered me wrong."

"Uh huh. That's why you ain't got a job, or even a license anymore."

"That wasn't their fault."

"Then whose fault was it, sugar? The way you tell it, you had that case won."

"I did. Marner would have walked free, I'm a hundred percent sure of it."

"Then why didn't you let him?"

"Let a murderer just walk?"

"Why the hell not? It happens every day. You're not an idiot, sugar. You know it's true. He'd walk like all the others, and then maybe he'd get caught later. Or not, and who cares? What's one more bad guy? There's thousands more like him. But no, you had to step in and open your mouth because of what the damn birds told you. And look what that got you—no job, no license, and stuck with me and a crazy-ass scheme. Don't tell me it's not the birds' fault."

"It's not, Ruthie. It was because I lost them. I should never have taken the case—they wouldn't have let me. That's what caused it."

"That, and going off the rails. Why the fuck did you bring it up in court, anyway?"

"If not, he'd have gone free. And once acquitted of the theft charges, he couldn't be tried for them again."

"So forget the theft. Wait until he's not your client, and then show that he's a murderer."

"I couldn't show it, Ruthie. I had no evidence. Nothing that a court or even a cop would accept. I only had the information Mara and Kala gave me."

"So tip the police off. An anonymous tip. Simple."

"Most anonymous tips are ignored, Ruthie. On the off-chance I could convince someone to take a look and maybe find the body like they did, it would have been days, and there'd be nothing to tie it to Marner. Oh, he'd be a suspect, but he'd have been long gone before that. I had to act then."

"Why? What if he did get off?"

"Ruthie! You can't mean that. Don't you have any sense of justice?"

"Honey, from my view, justice is just some lily-ass bourgie fiction. There ain't justice on the streets, not unless you make your own. Not to put you down, but the shit you do doesn't mean squat on the street. Yeah, sure, if we get charged we hope we get someone like you. But that's the last resort when we're caught up in the prison industrial complex. Justice means don't get caught. Justice means screw the other guy if it gives you what you need. Your ivory tower philosophy doesn't mean shit when it comes to survival. On the street, you do what you need to.

Kindness, sure, if it doesn't cost you. But justice? Fuck that shit. Ain't no such thing."

"Then why are you going with me?"

"Cause what the fuck else am I gonna do? Seriously. You're gonna give me a roof and food, and I don't even have to blow you? I'd be stupid not to take that."

"That's it?"

"What else is there? Sorry to burst your bubble, sugar."

"What about helping people?"

"What about it? That's great. And if it keeps us fed and housed, then so much the better. But I'll believe it when I see it."

"What do you mean? Mara and Kala said that's what this is all about."

"Uh huh. So you say. We'll see. I ain't holdin' my breath."

"I trust them. You'll see."

"Well, you'll have to trust them for the both of us."

We were mostly silent for the rest of the meal. After we got back to the apartment, we sat reading books we'd picked out for the road. The stereo was all packed, so there was no chance to listen to music. After a bit, Ruthie spoke up again.

"Hey sugar."

"Hmm?"

"I ain't mad. I'm just scared. Don't take it wrong. This is a big change for me."

"For me, too, Ruthie. Don't worry about it."

"We're good?"

"We're good, Ruthie. We'll get through it. Together."

"OK. But a blow job is still a hundred bucks."

Sunday, October 8, Las Vegas

Yesterday was a mess. It took forever to get the last items loaded into the truck, and then the truck broke down before we got to the storage facility. It was two in the afternoon before we got started heading west, which made it seven o'clock before we got into Grand Junction. We were tired and hungry, and had been bickering the whole way—not over anything serious, just our mutual fear and frustration. Max took every opportunity to point out that it was just the beginning of the problems with the plan, and being in the car with Ruthie, I just had to listen to him. We decided to stop there for the night rather than trying to press on.

We let ourselves sleep in, and so we didn't get started this morning until almost ten. Max was quiet today—sulking, maybe. Ruthie was quiet, too, lost in her own thoughts, I guess. We listened to music and she watched the scenery. Our conversation on the road was mostly limited to the next music selection. We took turns picking tracks—which made for a very eclectic playlist. The late start put us into Las Vegas around supper-time.

We could have pressed on and made Orange County by late tonight, but landing in an unknown city late on a Sunday night didn't sound like fun. Besides, it had been years since Ruthie had last seen Las Vegas. We drove down the strip, and Ruthie goggled at all the casinos and lights. I told her to pick where she wanted to stay; we deserved something good after two trying days. She picked the Bellagio—I should have known—and I stopped and checked. They had rooms available and I got a room with two queen beds. The room was about the size of my old apartment and set me back nearly three hundred dollars, but it was worth it.

We had a fabulous dinner which, along with the fabulous people in the restaurant, gave us enough to talk about while we ate. After dinner we watched the fountains out front, dropped a few bucks in the slot machines, and then crashed for the night. We didn't talk much—I think we both felt we'd said too much yesterday. But we stood close in the desert coolness watching the fountains, and when I put my arm around her, she leaned in and put her old gray head on my shoulder. We must have looked like quite the sight. Any place else, people would have probably stared at us, but in Las Vegas we were relatively normal. It felt good.

Tomorrow we'll sleep in again, maybe enjoy the town a little, and then drive the last four hours or so. If we get an early start, I might look at trying to find a cheap apartment, but most likely we'll be in a hotel for the first few days while we get our bearings. Who knows, maybe we'll find something to talk about. Today's quiet felt good, though. It was what we needed.

Thursday, October 12, California

It's been a busy four days. Ruthie and I are still in a hotel, but with luck, tonight will be the last night. I found a little two bedroom apartment in Fullerton, just 1200 square feet total for $1400 per month. That's a bit more than I was paying back in Colorado Springs for decidedly less room and shabbier accommodations, but it's a good deal for the location. I'll sign the lease tomorrow and we'll get keys right away. With utilities, food, and normal living expenses, I figure we're good for maybe two years before I'm flat broke. We'll have to find some money before then.

Ruthie loves the place. It's more space than she's had in a long time, and she'll have her own bedroom, though we'll be sharing a bath. In a way, it will be nice to have a bed to myself again, but after just a couple weeks, I think I'm going to miss the company. I've gotten used to waking to a body next to mine, gently snoring.

I tried to track down Nuevo Comienzo using all the conventional means, and I wasn't coming up with much. It was Ruthie who struck gold. It's well known on the street—that's their clientele. I guess they don't see any reason to advertise—just time and money that won't reach the people they care about anyway. Everything is word of mouth, and all the local street life—homeless, streetwalkers, intravenous drug users, and the deinstitutionalized mentally ill—know "NC." And they all know 'Llita (pronounced YEE-tah): Estrella Moreno, also called Estrallita, 'Llita, Mama Moreno, or just Mama.

Mama Moreno pretty much *is* Nuevo Comienzo. She started it and runs it out of her home, a little bungalow not far from our apartment. She works a full time job to cover expenses and handles Nuevo Comienzo nights and weekends. There are a handful of other volunteers, but mostly it's just Mama. At any given time there are two or three women staying with her, whether for a few days or a few months. She works with all the marginalized women of the area, regardless of their history, legal status, or anything else. Any woman looking to make a break—a fresh start—from her present situation is Mama's concern. She'll counsel them, get them to a safe place, provide what support she's able, get them connected with the various local agencies and organizations that can help them—whatever it takes. The volunteers are all women who've felt Mama 'Llita's loving touch.

Nuevo Comienzo is apparently primarily (if not entirely) for women. Most of the women they help have been abused in one way or another, almost always by men. All are poor, most are black or Hispanic, and many have criminal records. They may be gay, straight, trans... it doesn't matter to Mama Moreno. It's an organization built entirely on trust, and being white and male presents a high barrier to that trust. Ruthie is helping me understand that—she thinks it's obvious.

Ruthie is in love with 'Llita already, even though they haven't actually met yet. She's heard stories from many women who have been helped by Nuevo Comienzo. Not all of them have succeeded in making their fresh start, but without exception they all appreciate the love and support they received. Ruthie says if there'd been someone like 'Llita back in Colorado Springs she might not have ended up where she did.

We don't have a phone number yet—all the street people know how to get hold of 'Llita, but they don't share it unless someone can vouch for you. Too many cops, too many for-profit "rescue" operations, too many bureaucrats—they've learned to protect their own. Ruthie thinks that's completely sensible, but it seems like a hell of a way to run an organization. I can tell I'm going to be learning a lot more from Ruthie than the other way around. Ruthie did manage to convince some of the women to let 'Llita know we're interested in meeting her. Hopefully she won't be surprised when we show up at the needle exchange on Saturday.

I say "we," but it will be Ruthie who shows up. She'll tell 'Llita about us, and then, maybe, I'll be invited to the conversation. I cautioned her that she needs to be totally honest and thorough about us—all our history, all our conditions, just like Mara and Kala have instructed. Ruthie still wonders about that, but she's more willing to open up to Mama Moreno than she was to a hypothetical employer. I did tell her that if I get to talk, I'm going to be completely honest, so at least she'd better not create any surprises. We'll see how it goes.

Max has been relatively quiet since we've been here. He still lets me have it, and he had plenty to say about the apartment hunting. To listen to him, we'll be out on the street in two years, both of us, broke and without a job. As always, he's right, but I guess I just don't care. I'm excited by my own fresh start and anxious to give it a fair chance. If it fails, we'll figure something else out. We've got the time.

Tempest has been the bigger problem—between Las Vegas and here, she's been finding all sorts of things to needle me about. So many opportunities to abandon everything and just cut loose. Sex, drugs, whatever—a short but fun ride leading to an early death. Thanks, Tempest, I'll pass. Your suggestions are less attractive than ever, and I feel almost optimistic.

I was going to start trying to find a psychiatrist tomorrow, but Ruthie convinced me to wait until after we talk to 'Llita. I'm not in any hurry—I've got plenty of meds for now. I guess we'll just get ourselves moved in and wait for Saturday.

I wish Mara and Kala were here.

Saturday, October 14

We met 'Llita today! Ruthie went to the needle exchange when it opened at one o'clock. It just runs for two hours, so she wanted to have time to talk. She met 'Llita right away; apparently our inquiries had already reached her ears. She was dubious at first, but she welcomed the volunteer help. Ruthie handed out the clean needles after 'Llita checked in and disposed of the dirties. They also handed out male and female condoms and dental dams to any who wanted them and literature on various places to get services or treatment.

'Llita quickly warmed up to Ruthie, who did as Mara and Kala instructed. She told her whole story and the basics of mine while she helped out with the needle exchange. 'Llita just let her tell it, and if she was surprised by anything, she didn't show it. The questions came after Ruthie had finished her tale.

"So what brings you here?" 'Llita asked. "Looking to escape the winter or what?"

"That's part of it for sure, for me. I didn't have any shelter options and can't earn enough for rent any more. It was this or starve."

"So you used Rip to get you out here? Smart. Do you need help getting away from him now?"

Ruthie laughed. "No, mama, he's OK. He's got us an apartment—separate bedrooms. He pays the rent and buys all the food."

"Sugar daddy? They can start nice, then get ugly. What does he expect in return?"

"That's just it. Nothin' He never does anything. Hell, we slept in the same bed for almost two weeks, and he never laid a hand on me."

"Is he gay?"

"Nah, I don't think so. Just not interested."

"You said he has schizophrenia."

"Uh huh. Think that's it?"

"Maybe, or maybe the meds he takes. That might explain what he doesn't do, but it doesn't explain what he *is* doing. What's up with that, Ruthie?"

"Mama, you'll have to ask him. I told you all my story, the whole thing. I ain't told hardly a soul any of it, and you've heard it all. But for the why, you'll have to ask Rip."

"Ruthie, look at me."

She did.

"Are you trying to scam me?"

"No, ma'am. Honestly, I don't know what this is all about, but if it's a scam, I don't know nothin' about it. And I know scams—shit, you've heard my story, you know I know scams. I've pulled plenty of them myself. This is... I don't know. It's different."

'Llita nodded. "OK. You're telling the truth as you know it, I can see that. Alright. I'll talk to him. Not here. Not now. After I pack up. Can you and he meet me at the fountain over there at four? Tell Rip I'll talk to him, but it will cost him dinner."

Ruthie smiled. "You bet."

* * *

Ruthie called me and filled me in on what happened. I met her and 'Llita at four. Mama 'Llita is a small compact woman, probably close to my age—mid-forties, give or take. She's completely bilingual: Spanish is her native tongue, but she speaks English with only a slight trace of an accent. She gives off an aura of motherhood, instantly making anyone around her both comfortable and on their best behavior. It's an odd mix of feelings.

I'd thought about how to introduce myself, but once I got in her presence, all I could do was stand there like a shy child. She looked me over thoroughly, head to toe and back, before she said anything. Finally, looking me square in the eye, she said, "You're Rip."

"Yes, ma'am." See what I mean? "William Taylor, but folks call me Rip. I'm very pleased to meet you."

"Estrella Moreno, if we're being formal, but only lawyers and cops call me that."

"I'm a lawyer—or used to be."

"So I heard."

"How would you prefer I address you, then, Ms. Moreno?"

She looked hard at me and thought about it. "Let's leave that alone for now. Why don't you tell me why you're looking for me?"

I swallowed. Here it was. "I was instructed to do so by my most trusted counselors. They indicated that Ruthie and I should find you, and that we could help you and eventually find a position with Nuevo Comienzo."

"A position? That seems unlikely. Who are these counselors? How do they know about me."

"I don't know how they know about you, ma'am, but they are a pair of Steller's jays."

"Excuse me?"

"Steller's jays. The birds. Blue, with a crest."

"I know what a jay looks like. Your counselors are birds."

"Yes, ma'am."

"They talk to you?"

"Yes, ma'am."

She nodded. "You have schizophrenia." It wasn't a question.

"Yes, ma'am."

"You hear other voices, too?"

"I hear voices, yes, ma'am, and some visual hallucinations, too. I know those are part of the condition. But Mara and Kala are different."

"Mara and Kala? The jays?"

"Yes, ma'am. They aren't hallucinations; they're real birds."

Bless her heart, Ruthie jumped in. "They are real birds, Mama. I've seen them."

I smiled, not so much at the confirmation as the incongruity of my nearly seventy year old companion calling this woman "Mama."

'Llita looked at her. "They talk to you, too?"

"Not that I can understand. They sound just like other birds. But Rip can understand them, he says."

"You believe him?"

"I don't know what I believe, Mama. They told us to come here and find you."

'Llita raised her eyebrows. "*They* told you?"

Ruthie looked down. "Well, that's what Rip said. He seemed as confused as me. I don't know that I believe the birds do all this, but I don't know that I believe they don't. We're here, ain't we?"

'Llita turned back to me. "Perhaps you should tell me your whole story. Over dinner. You're buying."

"Yes, ma'am. Where would you like to eat? We're new in town and don't know many places."

'Llita directed us to a homey little Mexican restaurant where she was apparently well known. We didn't get menus, but 'Llita ordered for all of us in Spanish. Once we'd received our iced teas, I started to tell her my story—the whole thing from the onset of the schizophrenia in law school through my short career as a prosecutor before my first suspension, and then my longer career on the defense side, including the events leading to my present suspension. I didn't downplay Mara and Kala at all.

'Llita didn't ask any questions, but Ruthie did a couple times when I told things she hadn't heard before. I brought the tale up to the present time, including the odd directions that got us here and the details of our trip. I ended by saying that Mara and Kala should be joining us here at some point, but that it would take them a while.

'Llita looked at me intently for maybe a full minute when I finished. It was hard not to say anything more in response to that scrutiny, but I resisted. I think I was afraid to speak. Fortunately, Max and company had been quiet, and the walls were covered with enough pictures and tchotchkes that there were few places for any eyes or mouths. Finally, she nodded her head.

"That is quite a tale. You've told me why you're here. It's not very believable, but I see that you believe it. But tell me this: what is it you think you can do for me? You say that the jays said you can help—and Lord knows I need help—but what kind of help in particular are you offering?"

"I don't know, ma'am. They didn't say. I guess I hoped you might know."

Again the silent intent stare. Then she turned to face Ruthie.

"You used to write grant proposals?"

"Yes, Mama. Write them and review them. But that was a long time ago."

"I doubt they've changed much. What little income I get for my work comes mainly from grants. But I don't have the time to work on them, and even when I do, I'm not very good at it."

"It helps to know the system, Mama. The code words and dog whistles."

"No doubt. You think you know that lingo, Ruthie?"

"Probably not—not what's needed here. But I could learn it fast, I remember that much. These grantors—they provide copies of the proposals they have funded?"

"Yes, some of them do."

"I could look at them and get a pretty good idea."

'Llita nodded. "That I could use. I can't pay you for it, mind you, but I could use it." She turned and faced me. "And you were a defense attorney?"

"Yes, ma'am."

"Ever try any cases in California?"

"No, ma'am, just Colorado."

"What's your stance on prostitution?"

"It's a job. Not a particularly safe one—but often the best paying alternative for those who practice it. It's dangerous, but that's mostly because it's illegal."

"You think it should be legalized?"

"Yes. Decriminalized, actually."

She nodded. "Good. You know the difference. What about drug use?"

"What about it?"

"You use?"

"No, ma'am. Just the medications for my schizophrenia, and for the TD—the grimaces—and I have a drink now and then."

"What about people who do?"

"What about them? They're people, same as you or me. They have the same rights and deserve the same respect and care."

"You ever defend possession charges?"

"Sure, plenty of times."

"You win?"

"Almost always. Though with Mara and Kala's help I was pretty selective about the cases I took."

"They told you which ones to take."

"They told me what the person did or didn't do. I used that to make my decisions."

"So you were the *de facto* judge for them."

"Not really—they all were defended by someone, just maybe not me."

"So if they did the crime, you didn't take the case."

"No, not always. If what they did was only nominally a crime—like prostitution—or if they were facing a ridiculously severe penalty—like mandatory drug sentencing—then I'd defend them. I believe in justice, not necessarily the law. That, after all, is why I lost my license."

"Who decides?"

"Excuse me?"

"Who decides what's justice? You?"

I thought for a few seconds before answering. "I think ultimately we all decide for ourselves. My concept of justice has evolved over the years, and I trust it will continue to. I find that for the most part I've gotten more liberal. Certainly more compassionate, more concerned with the individual."

She continued to look hard at me. Her stare was as uncomfortable as any lecture from Max. It was worse than any law school exam. I felt like a little boy standing in front of my mother after doing something bad. Finally she smiled, and I found I had been holding my breath. It felt good to let it out and take another.

"OK, Rip. There's hope for you. To answer your first question, you can call me 'Llita, or Mama if you'd rather. And maybe I can use you, too. How quick can you learn California law?

"To pass the bar? I'd want to study for six months at least. It'll be a year before I could sit for it anyway—after my suspension. I'd have to reapply for the Colorado bar, and then use that standing to sit for the California bar. It'd probably be fifteen to eighteen months before I could practice law, even assuming I pass on the first try. From what I've heard, that's hard to do here. California has one of the hardest bar exams in the country."

She nodded. "OK, so you couldn't go to court. But you could advise my clients?"

"Not as a lawyer, no. There are strict rules about practicing law without a license, and that includes legal advice."

"What about as a person, not as a lawyer?"

"I would have to be very explicit that I am not a lawyer and that my opinions and advice are not legal advice. I would have to recommend that they consult with an actual attorney."

"They can't afford a real attorney."

"I know that, 'Llita. I still have to say it, though."

"But you could do that? You could help as long as you say those things?"

I hesitated. "Yes. I'll have to figure out exactly what the limits are, but I'm sure I could talk to them on an informal basis, anyway. I'd have to study the relevant laws—I'm familiar with Colorado and federal statutes, but not California."

"How long would that take?"

"I don't know. Days or weeks for any given topic. Less, really, since I'm not giving legal advice. The principles are the same, even if the actual statutes vary. It wouldn't take long to learn the basics."

"And you'd be studying for the bar." Again, not a question.

"I'd need to study more than just those statutes, but yes. I intend to study for and take the California bar exam if it looks like we'll be staying here."

"How are you gonna afford all that?"

"I have savings—I live pretty frugally. I can support Ruthie and myself for a while."

"How long's a while?"

"A year. Maybe two at the outside."

"Ruthie, what sort of grants you think you can find?"

"I don't know Mama. I'd have to see what's out there. I don't have any idea what's available now—I haven't looked at any of that stuff since before you were born."

'Llita smiled. "I'm not as young as you seem to think. I have some connections that would get you started."

"Mama, you know I'm sixty-eight years old, right?"

"Is that a problem, Ruthie?"

"Not to me. I want to work again. But I don't know how long I'll be any good. I don't even know if I can do it, let alone work all day."

"We'll worry about that as it comes. OK, here's the deal." She took a deep breath and composed her thoughts. "Ruthie, you come by my house tomorrow morning, and I'll get you the grant materials to look over. You do all that there; don't take anything with you for now. I only have one copy of things, and I'm not giving it up. So evenings and Sundays, mostly."

"Yes, Mama."

"You'll be looking for grants that mostly help the girls but that also that cover administrative costs. I can't do a tenth of what I want to do, even if I could do it full-time. But having to earn a living another way and do this on the side is the best I've got. Your job is to change that. Help me help the girls—but do that by paying me—and you—enough to live on. Maybe even Rip, especially if he can start being a *pro bono* attorney for the girls later."

"Yes, Mama."

She turned to face me. "And you, Rip. You start studying that California law. Focus on prostitution, trafficking, drug possession and sale, vagrancy, shoplifting, that sort of thing. I may call you from time to time to meet with someone. You'll meet them with me in a public place. You're only contact with them will be through me, and you won't know their real name. Can you handle that?"

"Yes, 'Llita. That sounds best to me, too."

"OK. That's settled, then. Thank you for dinner, Rip."

"My pleasure, 'Llita. Any time."

She chuckled. "Careful, Rip, you may regret that offer. Ruthie, I'll see you tomorrow. You know where I live?"

Ruthie repeated the address we'd been given.

'Llita smiled. "Well, that's in the neighborhood. That's the address I tell the girls to give out. It's an abandoned building. I don't know what I'll do if someone buys it." She told Ruthie the real address, a couple blocks away. "I'll see you in the morning. Nine o'clock? I'll have coffee."

"I'll be there then, Mama."

"Good. Until then!"

Nuevo Comienzo. A fresh start.

Wednesday, November 8

It's been almost a month since I've written here—I've been busy! A lot has happened, good and bad. Ruthie and I are still here in LA. Ruthie is working hard for Nuevo Comienzo—she has her own key to Mama 'Llita's house now, and she spends hours there every day researching grants, writing applications and proposals, and networking with other non-profits, government agencies, philanthropic organizations, lobbyists and the like. It has kept her busy and hasn't brought in a dime yet, but she's optimistic that this work will materialize into an actual grant within a few months. Regardless of whether it does, she is delighted to have a purpose again. She literally looks and acts ten years younger.

I've been busy studying. I spend most of my days at the Loyola or UCLA law libraries getting caught up on the finer points of California law. I can see why this is considered the hardest bar exam in the country—there's more peculiarities and special cases here than I have ever dreamed of. Like Ruthie, I'm not bringing in a dime, but I'm enjoying learning again and looking forward to being able to do something useful (and lucrative). We're existing on my savings, for the time being. This is an expensive place to live, but we've found ways to be frugal. We don't eat out often, and never any place fancy. It turns out Ruthie is a good cook, and she's introduced me to all sorts of new food—"soul food," she calls it. Good food, full of flavor and made from inexpensive ingredients. If we're careful, we might make it until we have an actual income—whenever that might be.

Ruthie has also been helping out Mama 'Llita with day-to-day activities. She counsels some of the women, helping them see alternatives and find hope again. She helps out every Saturday at the needle exchange, and lately I've been helping there, too—mostly moving boxes and other physical stuff. I think slowly 'Llita is beginning to trust me a little, but that will take time. She has had a couple of women talk with me when they were facing legal issues. I can't advise them on specifics—both for ethical reasons and because I just don't know the local laws well enough yet—but I can talk about their options in general terms and help them understand the process and what the long-term implications may be.

I hope it's helpful. The laws are often repressive and unfair, and there are few good options available to these women. California is more progressive than many states, but it's still basically illegal to be poor, especially if you're a woman, a person of color, or a member of any other marginalized community. There's lots of work to be done.

I've found a new psychiatrist—one Mama 'Llita recommended. A lovely African-American woman about my age named Dr. Porter. She's actually helpful—she listens to me. She understands that there is a balance between untenable chaos of life without medication and the unbearable dullness of life with too much. She's willing to maintain my dose at whatever level strikes that balance best for me, and doesn't treat any mention of voices or hallucinations as grounds to immediately raise my dose. I've told her about Max and Tempest, the mutterers and the eyes and mouths—things I didn't dare tell Dr. Filtner. Her reaction has been that if I think they are manageable, and if the problems they cause are less than the problems of too much medication, then she's happy with that.

Max has been a little quieter lately. He's still around, and I'm still "shithead," but it almost seems friendly now. I can tell that he approves of the changes in my life, not that he would ever admit that. He still finds plenty to criticize me about, and he's still always right. Maybe that's a good thing.

Tempest, on the other hand, has been more active. She keeps trying to get me to be more sexually active, but really, I think she just wants me to be more social, and sex is the way she sees to do that. I have to say she's starting to persuade me. I haven't followed any of her recommendations exactly, but I'm at least trying to be a bit more friendly. Ruthie approves of that and keeps trying to encourage me to branch out more. We'll see. I don't think I'm quite ready for that yet, but I can feel my arguments weakening.

Mia has been absent through all of this, which I think is a positive thing. She was never much help, anyway, just a pathetic self-centered vestige of motherhood. Maybe this means I'm finally growing up.

Dr. Porter is in favor of all of this. She's also interested in trying some other medications that might work better for me, but not until we have a good baseline on the Risperidone, and only when I'm ready. I'm her first patient taking Ingrezza, but she's reading up on it and is happy to continue my prescription. It's such a relief to find a psychiatrist like this—I didn't know they existed.

All of these changes have taken place without Mara and Kala—my trusted counsels. I've been expecting them to show up any day, and lately I'm growing alarmed that they haven't yet appeared. Today I learned why. Mara found me while I was walking to the Loyola law library. Just Mara.

I let out a whoop of joy when Mara landed on a street sign just in front of me.

Mara: I told you I'd find you.

Me: You did—but where is Kala?

Mara: Kala is gone.

Me: What? What do you mean gone?

Mara: A golden eagle attacked us.

Me: Oh no!

Mara: I got away. Kala did not. It's just me.

Me: You're alone now?

Mara: Yes, alone. Just me. But that is enough. Our work is done.

Me: What do you mean?

Mara: You're where you need to be. This is what we wanted. This is why we existed. You don't need us.

Me: But I do! There's so much work to be done here.

Mara: And you will do it.

Me: But you could do so much to help. Help like you did with my other cases.

Mara: You don't need help now. You have Ruthie. You have 'Llita. They are enough.

Me: But they don't know things like you do. All that information you gave—finding the truth.

Mara: You will find truth. You know how. You have help. Believe the women. Look for power and assume lies. Look for weakness and assume truth. That will suffice.

Me: Will you at least stay and keep me company?

Mara: No. I came to say goodbye. My time is done. My purpose fulfilled.

Me: I can't persuade you? Where will you go?

Mara: I will join Kala. We are a pair. We always have been. I am nothing alone.

Me: You'll die?

Mara: We served a purpose. It is done. Without that there is nothing. Not death. Not life. We are complete.

Me: So I won't ever see you again?

Mara: Not me. Others may come. If there is a need. But I think not. Not now.

I could feel hot tears rolling down my cheeks, but I didn't feel sad—not exactly.

Me: Thank you, Mara. For everything. I owe you my life.

Mara: You owe nothing. You gave us purpose. You gave us existence. Without you, we would not exist. Now that purpose is done. We are done. It is enough. Complete.

Mara took wing. I wept openly as I watched my old friend climb high in the sky and fly east; staring long after I could no longer pretend to see any trace. I don't know how long I walked after that, nor where. I never made it to the library.

I told Ruthie about it when we were both back in the apartment. She cried with me, even though she never really knew Mara and Kala. But they were tears of celebration as well as grief. Ruthie had taught me that trick back in Colorado Springs when I lost my license. Even losses can be blessings.

I was blessed with uncommon counsel, and that brought me to where I am. I am still blessed. Ruthie and 'Llita are no less a blessing, even if they are a bit more ordinary. No, that's not the word. They are extraordinary, no less than Mara and Kala; they are just human.

Nuevo Comienzo. A fresh start.

About the Author

Art Smith lives in central Missouri with his wife Amanda. Having lived nearly sixty years, Art is still trying to figure out what he wants to be when he grows up. Working with computers has best supported his various habits so far, but that hardly counts, right? In addition to writing, for eleven months out of the year, Art also enjoys studio photography, playing tuba with the ShowMe Brass, listening to live music, reading, and playing various tabletop and role-playing games. November, though, is devoted to NaNoWriMo (National Novel Writing Month, from which this novel was born—more at www.nanowrimo.org). Uncommon Counsel is Art's first published novel.

www.ingramcontent.com/pod-product-compliance
Lightning Source LLC
Chambersburg PA
CBHW071453110726
47908CB00003B/596